Rough and Ready

PROGRAM AUTHORS
Richard L. Allington
Ronald L. Cramer
Patricia M. Cunningham
G. Yvonne Pérez
Constance Frazier Robinson
Robert J. Tierney

PROGRAM CONSULTANTS
Bernadine J. Bolden
Ann Hall
Sylvia M. Lee
Dolores Perez
Jo Ann Wong

CRITIC READERS
Jeanne Guthrie
Julia Johnson
Patricia Lacey
Bonnie Middleton
Brenda Sykes

John C. Manning, *Instructional Consultant*

SCOTT, FORESMAN AND COMPANY
Editorial Offices: Glenview, Illinois

Regional Offices: Sunnyvale, California •
Tucker, Georgia • Glenview, Illinois •
Oakland, New Jersey • Dallas, Texas

ACKNOWLEDGMENTS

Text

Pages 20–24: Adapted from "The Camp Out" by Darlene Davies, *Canadian Children's Annual* 1976. Copyright © 1975 by Potlatch Publications. Reprinted by permission.

Pages 30–32: "Chipper the Chopper" by Eleanor Bartel. Adapted from *Ranger Rick's Nature Magazine,* © November 1981, by permission of the publisher, the National Wildlife Federation.

Pages 33–36: *From an Otter's Story* by Emil E. Liers, illustrated by Tony Palazzo. Text Copyright 1953 by Emil E. Liers. Copyright renewed 1981 by Patricia Liers McMurry. Reprinted by permission of Viking Penguin Inc.

Pages 42–43: From *Children's Digest* magazine, copyright © 1981 by The Benjamin Franklin Literary & Medical Society, Inc., Indianapolis, Indiana. Adapted by permission of the publisher.

Pages 44–50: From "911" by James M. Summers, Jr. Text copyright © 1980 by Johnson Publishing Company, Inc. Reprinted by permission of Johnson Publishing Company, Inc. All rights reserved.

Pages 98–103: Adapted from *Dragon Stew* by Tom McGowen. Copyright © 1969 by Tom McGowen. Reprinted by permission of the author.

Page 105: From *A Pack of Riddles,* compiled by William R. Gerler. Text copyright © 1975 by William R. Gerler. Reprinted by permission of the publisher, E. P. Dutton, Inc.

Pages 110–117: Adapted from "The Woman Who Flummoxed the Fairies" from *Heather and Broom* by Sorche Nic Leodhas. Copyright © 1960 by LeClaire G. Alger. Reprinted by permission of Holt, Rinehart and Winston, Publishers, and McIntosh and Otis, Inc.

Pages 118–126: *From McBroom Tells the Truth* by Sid Fleischman. Copyright © 1966 by Sid Fleischman. Reprinted by permission of Little, Brown and Company in association with the Atlantic Monthly Press and Bill Berger Associates, Inc.

Acknowledgments continued on page 511.

ISBN 0-673-72658-4

1991 printing
Copyright © 1988, 1985

Scott, Foresman and Company, A Division of Harper Collins *Publishers*. Glenview, Illinois. All Rights Reserved. Printed in the United States of America.

This publication is protected by Copyright and permission should be obtained from the publisher prior to any prohibited reproduction, storage in a retrieval system, or transmission in any form or by any means, electronic, mechanical, photocopying, recording, or otherwise. For information regarding permission, write to: Scott, Foresman, 1900 East Lake Avenue, Glenview, Illinois 60025.

45678-RRC-9594

Contents

mow

Section One

FIGHTING FOR SURVIVAL

CAMPING

Imagine what it might be like to camp in the woods near a river with your friends. While a few of you set up a tent, someone else gathers firewood. Then you fish and swim in the river. Later you take a long hike in the woods.

After cooking your dinner over the campfire, you sing songs and tell stories. Finally, you get into your sleeping bag carefully, making sure there are no creepy, crawling things inside with you. You close your eyes and float off to sleep.

Suddenly you hear a loud, long sigh. It might be the wind—or a visitor in camp. How would you find out?

An Important Discovery

Kim's mom parked the car at the family's camping spot near the highway. After Kim and her cousin Marie got out of the car, they went for a hike in the woods.

Secretly, Kim wished that her cousin had not come along. Marie knew all about the city, but she didn't know much about the woods. Kim loved the forest. Watching the animals was what she enjoyed most.

After walking for half an hour, Marie said, "Let's rest, Kim." Marie flopped down on a rock. She rubbed the places where twigs had scratched her legs.

Kim could have sat there all day and listened to the forest sounds. But a soft rain began to fall, and Marie wanted to leave. They stood up to find their path. Then Kim began to frown. Their path was hidden by thick bushes. Kim bit her lip.

Marie looked at Kim. "Don't tell me you're afraid of being lost!" she said. "Listen!"

Kim listened. She heard rain on the leaves of the trees above her head. She heard thunder. And she heard cars. Then Kim began to understand. They had walked in a circle. They were back near the highway and their car.

Kim had been so busy watching the animals that she hadn't been listening. Marie was the one who knew where they were. Who would have thought that would happen?

"I sure am glad you came along today," Kim told Marie.

Sharpen Your Skills

Characters in a story have thoughts, feelings, and desires that usually explain why they act as they do.

1. At first Kim wished Marie was not with her. Why do you think she felt that way?
2. Does Kim change her mind about Marie by the end of the story? What does she do or say to make you think so?

In "The Camp Out," read to figure out what Jim and Pete are like.

The Camp Out

by Darlene Davies

Jim Chen and Pete Clark were camping ten miles from town in the woods of northern Alberta, Canada. They had spent a long day, hiking and setting up camp. Now they were trying to sleep in their tent.

"This sleeping bag is getting too short, or I'm getting too tall," said Jim. He pulled the bag tighter around his body.

"Just go to sleep," Pete said. "Tom will be arriving at seven. After teasing him about meeting us on time, you sure don't want to get caught sleeping in."

Pete watched Jim fiddle with the radio until he thought he would go crazy. "Will you shut that thing off? I thought I heard a noise!" Pete was sitting up straight. He held his head close to the door.

"What do you think it is?" whispered Jim.

"I don't know. Could be a bear." Pete tried to sound brave. He didn't want to scare Jim. Jim

was a city boy. He wouldn't know how dangerous bears were in the spring.

"Oh, it's just the fire." Pete pulled his bag up around his neck. "Better get some sleep now. We have a big day tomorrow."

Soon both boys were asleep. All was quiet except for the wind blowing through the trees.

At the edge of the clearing, a bear paced back and forth. It came up to the camp several times. Each time it came close to the fire, it backed away. Finally, it lumbered to the safety of a bush and lay down. The bear looked at some food hanging from a tree next to the tent. After a while the bear fell asleep.

At dawn the bear woke up. There was no sound from the tent. The fire was out, so the bear started toward the tree.

Inside the tent, Pete and Jim were sleeping. A sudden crash woke Pete up. He pulled the sleeping bag away from his head. Then he saw a furry foot right at the opening of the tent. A bear's huge, brown paw was ten inches from his head!

"Pete, wake up," Jim whispered in a shaking voice.

"I know," Pete mouthed. He moved away from the opening, closer to his frightened friend.

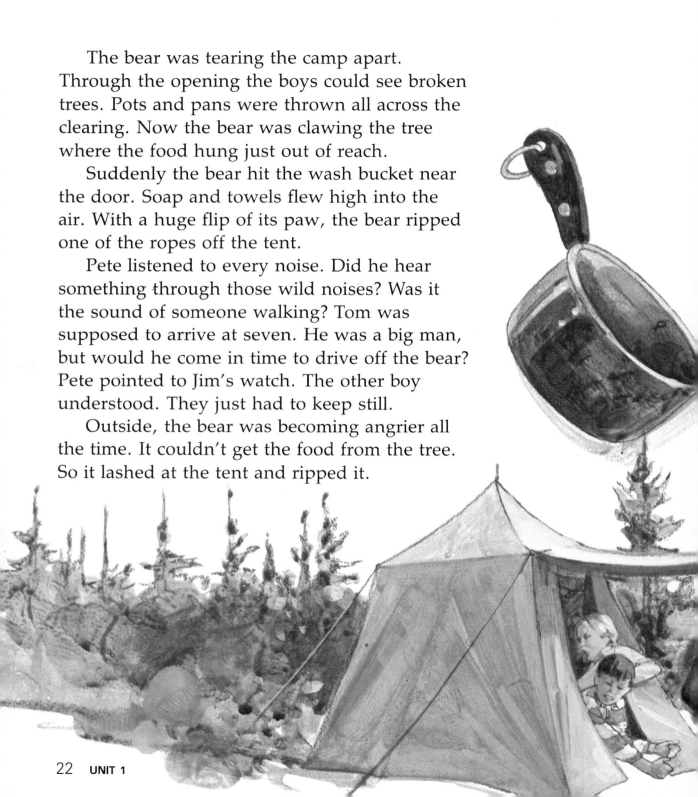

The bear was tearing the camp apart. Through the opening the boys could see broken trees. Pots and pans were thrown all across the clearing. Now the bear was clawing the tree where the food hung just out of reach.

Suddenly the bear hit the wash bucket near the door. Soap and towels flew high into the air. With a huge flip of its paw, the bear ripped one of the ropes off the tent.

Pete listened to every noise. Did he hear something through those wild noises? Was it the sound of someone walking? Tom was supposed to arrive at seven. He was a big man, but would he come in time to drive off the bear? Pete pointed to Jim's watch. The other boy understood. They just had to keep still.

Outside, the bear was becoming angrier all the time. It couldn't get the food from the tree. So it lashed at the tent and ripped it.

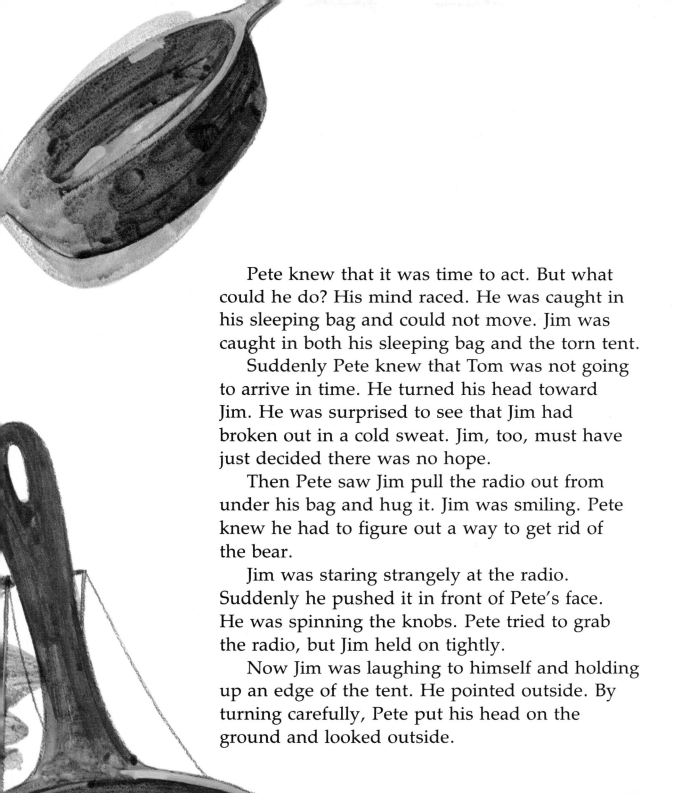

Pete knew that it was time to act. But what could he do? His mind raced. He was caught in his sleeping bag and could not move. Jim was caught in both his sleeping bag and the torn tent.

Suddenly Pete knew that Tom was not going to arrive in time. He turned his head toward Jim. He was surprised to see that Jim had broken out in a cold sweat. Jim, too, must have just decided there was no hope.

Then Pete saw Jim pull the radio out from under his bag and hug it. Jim was smiling. Pete knew he had to figure out a way to get rid of the bear.

Jim was staring strangely at the radio. Suddenly he pushed it in front of Pete's face. He was spinning the knobs. Pete tried to grab the radio, but Jim held on tightly.

Now Jim was laughing to himself and holding up an edge of the tent. He pointed outside. By turning carefully, Pete put his head on the ground and looked outside.

Pete could see the bear just about to tear into the tent once more. Then he heard a loud blast of rock music. The bear pulled back as if it had been shot. It cried out in anger and fear. Then it turned and ran.

The woods were quiet again. Pete wondered if the bear had really gone. Wait! He heard something—the faint sound of whistling and footsteps. Then silence.

Pete lay back and listened. Finally, he heard a loud voice.

"It's Tom!" Pete yelled. The boys poked their heads out of the tent. They smiled at a man standing outside. He looked at them for a moment. Then he said slowly, "Looks like you two had a bit of trouble."

Jim and Pete looked at each other. "Oh, nothing we couldn't handle," Pete said proudly. "What's the matter, Tom? Don't look at us like that. It's not our fault the camp's a mess. You *are* five minutes early!"

Checking Comprehension and Skills

1. Where does "The Camp Out" take place? (20)
2. In the beginning of the story, how did Pete feel about telling Jim that a bear could be in their camp? (20 and 21)
3. Why did the bear knock over pots and pans and claw the tree? (22)
- 4. How do you think the boys felt once they knew the bear was in camp? (21)
- 5. Which boy showed his feelings more openly? Give an example. (21 and 23)
- 6. Do you think it was wise of Pete to try to remain calm? Why or why not?
7. How did Jim scare off the bear? (24)
8. Did Tom arrive before or after the bear left? (24)
- 9. After Tom arrived, how did Pete show that he had a sense of humor? (24)
10. What do you think you would have done if you were Jim or Pete?

Choose the word that fits each sentence.
○11. Pete heard a loud bl_st of music from the radio.

    sound   black   blast
○12. Pete thought he heard the f__nt sound of footsteps.

    faint   found   soft

- Story Elements: Character   ○ Context and Consonants

Animal Survival

Sometimes life in the wild can be hard for animals. Can you think of some reasons why?

The biggest problem animals face is finding enough food to keep them alive. In places where winter is cold and snowy, most animals have to store food in the fall so that they can survive the winter.

Some animals eat other animals as their food. If they don't hunt and kill other animals, they will not have enough food to live.

All animals have some way to protect themselves from their enemies. Some are strong and can fight their enemies. Others are fast and can run away. Can you think of other ways animals can protect themselves?

Trapped

Stars filled the summer sky. A hungry young raccoon crept slowly out of the dark woods. The animal looked all around for something to eat. Finally, it noticed a tent.

A tall pine tree stood behind the tent. Under the tree was a big, open, metal garbage can. Lovely smells came from it. The little animal walked past the tent. It climbed up the tree and out onto a branch that spread over the can. The animal jumped down lightly into the garbage.

"What a wonderful place!" it thought. All about it were bits of pleasing food.

The raccoon ate until it was sleepy. A newspaper in the can made a fine bed. Proud of itself for finding a good dinner and a soft bed, the animal fell asleep.

Morning sunlight woke the animal up. After eating breakfast, the little raccoon tried to climb out of the can. But the sides were too slippery. It was trapped!

The animal was very frightened. It began to jump against the sides of the can.

The can began to rock from side to side. Suddenly, the can fell over. The little raccoon rolled out of the can. Fast as lightning, it ran off to the safety of the woods.

Sharpen Your Skills

It is often easier to understand what happens in a story if you know the **setting**—where and when the story takes place. Sometimes the time or the place affects how characters act.

1. Where does the raccoon go to look for its food? Why is this a dangerous place for the animal?
2. Where was the raccoon trapped? Why couldn't it get out?

As you read the next selections, "Chipper the Chopper" and "An Otter's Story," notice how the settings affect what happens in the stories.

CHIPPER THE CHOPPER

by Eleanor Bartel

A cold wind blew across the lake as Chipper, the beaver, waddled toward the water. He slipped into the lake. Only his head peeked above the surface. Chipper glided along. He was slow on land. But he was fast in the water.

Chipper kicked smoothly with his powerful hind feet. They were webbed just like a duck's. His broad, flat tail served as a rudder for steering. He held his front paws like tiny fists. Chipper used them to push away things in his path.

Chipper swam in the water close to the shore. Now and then he smelled the air for danger. Just a few minutes earlier, while he was chopping down a willow tree for food, Chipper had smelled a mountain lion. He quickly swam away even though the tree was ready to fall. Chipper didn't want to meet an enemy face to face!

After a while, Chipper caught no more signs of the big cat. So he climbed out of the water.

Fall was Chipper's busiest time of the year. With winter on its way, food would be harder to find. Chipper had to chop down lots of trees. This food he would store under the water near his home for the cold months ahead.

It didn't take Chipper long to chop down a tree. When it was about to crash, he ran into the water. He knew it would be dangerous to stay on land. Chipper's enemies knew the sound of a falling tree meant a tasty beaver was nearby.

Chipper waited a long time before he came back for his tree. But he didn't wait long enough. As Chipper towed the tree into the lake, a mountain lion crept close to the shore. Suddenly the big cat saw a thick branch hanging over Chipper's head. It climbed to the branch without a sound. It got ready to attack.

Chipper smelled the mountain lion just before it leaped toward his back. He smacked his tail on the surface of the water and dived just in time. The mountain lion got nothing but a bath!

Chipper quickly swam straight to his home. Safe and cozy inside, he curled up for a nap.

AN OTTER'S STORY

by Emil E. Liers

Ottiga[1] the otter was still very young when he first learned that life held danger as well as games.

It was one of those cloudy, foggy days that are common in the spring on Michigan's Keweenaw Peninsula. The cubs could hear the sad sounds of the foghorn as they played. They were interested in their game. The cubs ran through the tunnels of their home. But they forgot Mother Otter's orders to stay in the pine stump while she was away feeding. Ottiga ran outside. He was closely followed by his sister Tetawish[2], who was trying to tag him. In the gray spring light Ottiga made a half-turn about the stump. He planned to duck inside a hollow log and hide.

Ottiga was about two feet from the log. He heard a frightened hiss and scream from Tetawish. He glanced over his shoulder just in time to see a great horned owl diving straight

1. Ottiga (o tē′ gə) 2. Tetawish (te tä′ wish)

at him. Ottiga was frightened. He reared back to fight off the owl's attack, screaming as he did so. For a moment the owl was fooled. It stopped. The owl wasn't sure whether this baby otter was safe prey after all. Before the owl could rise for a second attack, Ottiga ran into the hollow log. He crawled to the farther end. Ottiga hid under one of the shelves.

Ottiga was shaking with fear. How he wished that he had obeyed his mother and stayed safe at home in the stump. For a time he kept very quiet. Tetawish, who had run back under the stump, thought the big owl had caught her brother and carried him off to feed to its owlets. Ottiga hid in silence. He strained his ears for any sound. It was hard for him to be quiet when he was so frightened. He had never been so all alone before. Soon he began to call for help.

Ottiga's sisters heard him and peeked out of their den. There was the owl, big and angry. It was sitting on top of a tree branch between the stump and the log. The owl was waiting for Ottiga to come out. The sisters hissed in fright, trying to warn their brother. They ducked back under the safety of the stump. For a time Ottiga kept quiet again. He

crept forward carefully. Ottiga looked out from under a shelf at the log's opening. He did not see the owl until it was almost too late. He noticed a movement just as the owl started a dive to grab him by the head.

Just in time, Ottiga rushed back into the log. He screamed in fright. Ottiga was afraid the terrible owl would come into the log and catch him. The owl clicked and snapped its beak. Its great round eyes and feathery horns appeared in the opening. Suddenly, before the

owl could move into the log, a dark, furry
streak of lightning rushed up. It knocked the
big bird off its feet. Ottiga's mother had
returned from her feeding trip. She was just
in time to hear her cub's frightened scream.
Running like the wind on her broad webbed
feet, she charged the owl in anger. She grabbed
a big mouthful of its feathers. The owl seemed
to be all feathers. Now that it was tumbled in
a heap at the mother otter's feet, it no longer
looked so frightening. Ottiga's mother did not
stop to take another bite but ran into the log
to see if her son was safe, spitting feathers out
of her mouth on the way.

Ottiga was never happier to see his
mother. Finally he was safe.

Checking Comprehension and Skills

- 1. Where and during what part of the year does "Chipper the Chopper" take place? (30–31)
  2. Why did Chipper get out of the water from time to time? (31)
  3. How was Chipper's problem like Ottiga's in "An Otter's Story"?
  4. Why do you think beaver homes are located in the water?
- 5. Where did Ottiga hide from the owl? (34)
  6. How was Ottiga saved from the owl? (36)
  7. Why do you think Chipper was better able to take care of himself than Ottiga was?
  8. Did the authors of these two stories seem to know about the ways of beavers and otters? What makes you say so?
  9. What wild animal do you know most about? How is that animal able to protect itself?

  Choose the word that fits each sentence.
- ○10. Cloudy, foggy days were c_mm_n in spring.
  coming   common   expected
- ○11. He planned to duck inside a h_ll_w log.
  hanging   hollow   hello

- Story Elements: Setting   ○ Context and Consonants

EMERGENCY!

Sometimes being safe means staying away from danger. You've heard it all before: "Don't skate on thin ice. Don't play in the street. Don't get into a stranger's car."

But once in a while an emergency comes up no matter how careful you are. An emergency, such as a fire or an accident, occurs suddenly. There isn't much time to decide what to do or how to get help. So it is important to be prepared for emergencies before they happen.

Some towns and cities have a telephone number you can dial in an emergency. The number is *911*.

Using Context and Consonants

With the bridge washed out,
our car was **tr_pp_d.**

What word belongs at the end of the
sentence above? Can you think of a word that
makes sense? Try one of these words:
stuck   tripped   trapped

Sharpen Your Skills

Both *stuck* and *trapped* make sense in the
sentence. *Tripped* has the same consonants as
tr_pp_d, but it doesn't make sense. Only

trapped has the right consonants and makes sense in the sentence.

- When you come to a word you don't know, use the context—the words around the new word—and the consonants in the word to help you.
- First think of a word that makes sense in the sentence.
- Then see if the consonants in your word are the same as the consonants in the new word.
- Remember that all the consonants must match. Also, they must come in the same order as in the new word.

What words belong in these sentences?
1. If the road flooded, we would be in d_ng_r.
   danger   trouble   dagger
2. Mom told us to be as quiet as a wh_sp_r.
   mouse   whisper   whisker
   Did you pick *danger* and *whisper?* Now read the words in these sentences.
3. Dad took the <u>flare</u> out of the trunk and lit it.
4. The bright, <u>dazzling</u> light would show other people that the bridge was out.
5. Then we drove to a <u>motel</u> to spend the night.

Use context and consonants to help you read new words in "911."

The Night It All Paid Off

by Victoria Smith Peters

Mom used to worry a lot. She was afraid that we were not prepared for emergencies in our house. But then she decided to do something about the problem.

She started by filling our two-story house with first-aid kits. After that, she put in all kinds of alarms. And then we began having monthly fire and storm drills.

We used to think it was silly business. We ribbed Mom all the time—until one cold, frightening night last October.

I was asleep in my bed, having a wild dream. In my dream, the school bell kept ringing, and I knew I was going to be late.

The ringing finally woke me up. It wasn't the school bell. It was the smoke alarm.

I tumbled out of bed. The smell of smoke was strong. I could hear popping sounds coming from the door. I got scared.

"Fire drill! Fire drill!" I said out loud. Out of habit, I reached under the bed and pulled out my rope ladder. I crawled to the window and threw it open. Quickly, I attached the ladder and climbed down.

As I reached the ground, I heard Dad say, "Everyone is out now." If it hadn't been for Mom's alarms and drills, we might not have gotten out.

Sharpen Your Skills

A character in a story usually has a **goal**—something he or she wants. The story often describes what the character does to reach the goal. The **outcome** of the story tells if the character reaches the goal.

1. Mom's goal was to make sure her family was prepared for emergencies. How did she do that?
2. When a fire actually broke out, what was the outcome of Mom's preparations?

Mary finds herself with an urgent goal in the next story, "911." Read to see if she achieves it.

911

by James M. Summers, Jr.

Ice crunching under the tires and a rumbling noise from the old car were the only sounds in the alley that night. A strong wind blew snow outside the frosted windows of the car. Mary Jordan watched with sleepy eyes. Curled up on the back seat, she felt warm and safe from the cold.

It had not been a wonderful day. Mary had skated on the frozen pond near Aunt Grace's house. She had fallen on some rough ice and broken her arm. Now Mary and her mother were returning home from the hospital. Mary's left arm was in a cast.

As Mary's mother opened the car door, cold air rushed in. The big garage door made a strange groaning sound when Mrs. Jordan lifted it up. She turned on the garage light.

With a slam of the car door, Mrs. Jordan was back in the car. She brought more of the cold and snow with her. She backed the car into the garage. The wheels slipped until they were on the dry floor. When she shut the motor off and opened the car door, a strange silence was all around.

Mary looked over the front seat. Slowly she got herself up. She could see her mother through the windshield, hurrying to close the garage door.

The garage light was dim and made strange, long shadows. The big garage door began to roll down with loud noises. Then there was a squeaking sound. The door got stuck.

As her mother pushed against it, Mary watched. The giant door groaned as it began to move. Suddenly there was a rumbling sound and the light dimmed. Mrs. Jordan looked up with fear on her face. "Mary!" she screamed.

The rumbling grew louder and the car shook. Beams of wood were suddenly everywhere. The windshield broke as a big beam of wood crashed through. Mary saw the garage roof cave in. Snow fell all around. The light went out. Mary slid down to the car floor.

The crashing sounds, the flying glass, and the sweeping snow all ended suddenly. Then there was nothing—no garage light, no sound, no noise.

Mary pulled herself up from the floor. The giant garage door was a pile of snow and wood. There were parts of the roof mixed in. She couldn't see her mother. Mary screamed!

Then Mary grabbed the handle of the car door, but couldn't turn it. She tried the door on the other side. But it wouldn't move either. Now she felt trapped. The cold was creeping in. The silence was all around her.

An orange glow from the alley light made everything look frightening. It was in that glow that Mary thought she could see her mother's hand. It was just a shadowy shape, but she knew it at once. She could tell that her mother was half-buried under parts of the fallen garage door. Mary knew that her mother needed her. Even though Mary was afraid, she had to get to her mother.

Mary rolled the back window down and crawled through it. She dropped down beside the car. Then she began to move along the floor. But pieces of the roof blocked her way.

Mary knew she would have to crawl under the car. She crept along the floor, over broken glass and splintered wood. She moved toward the orange glow near the garage door.

Finally, Mary was out from under the car. There before her, half-buried by the snow, lay her mother. Mrs. Jordan had a cut on her head, and her eyes were closed.

"Mother!" Mary cried, tears filling her eyes. The snow blurred as she stared at the sight. Mrs. Jordan did not move. She was cold, and her hand was limp. "Mother, answer me," Mary screamed again and again. Both pain and fear were in Mary's voice.

The sound carried down the empty alley. No one came out to help.

"Help! Help!" Mary yelled. No one answered her call. "Where are all the kids on the block?"

"I've got to get help," Mary decided. She stood for a moment. She wanted to run for help. But she wanted to stay with her mother too. "Help!" she yelled again.

Suddenly Mary knew what she had to do. She turned back to the pile that was once their garage. She felt around in the wreck for a few minutes. Then Mary found what she needed. She grabbed the keys that were lying inches from her mother's hand.

The walls that were still standing groaned in the cold wind. Mary ran to the house. She slipped and fell in the knee-deep snow and tripped up the icy steps. She searched for the right key. The top lock clicked easily. But the bottom lock had to be wiggled.

Mary ran into the kitchen. She grabbed the phone on the wall and dialed 911 quickly.

Sirens brought the sleeping alley to life. The strange orange glow was mixed with flashes of blue from the police-car lights. A fire engine rumbled into the alley, waking the neighbors. Two men rushed out of an ambulance. After getting the snow and pieces of the door off Mary's mother, they lifted her onto a stretcher.

"She's going to be all right," the ambulance driver said to Mary. "Thanks to you."

"You're a very brave young girl," the police officer said as he rode with Mary to the hospital. "Your smart thinking saved your mother's life."

Checking Comprehension and Skills

1. The story "911" takes place in winter. What clues on page 44 tell you this? (44)
2. How had Mary and her mother spent the day before arriving home? (44 and 45)
3. What were Mary and her mother each doing when the garage roof caved in? (45)
4. Why did the garage roof cave in? (44–46)
• 5. Once Mary reached her mother, what was the thing she needed to do? (49)
• 6. Was she able to do it? If so, how? (49–50)
7. Was Mary able to think clearly and quickly during this emergency? Provide evidence to support your answer.
8. In what other ways could Mary have solved her problem?
9. What lesson could you learn from this story about what to do in an emergency?

Choose the word that fits each sentence.
○10. Two men took a str_tch_r out of the ambulance.
   radio   scratcher   stretcher
○11. Mary grabbed the phone and started to d__l 911.
   dial   deal   call

• Story Elements: Goal and Outcome
○ Context and Consonants

Be Smart, Stay Safe

Every day there are people who are hurt in accidents in and around their homes. Many of those accidents could be prevented if people were a little more careful. Below are some posters showing ways people could keep from having accidents. Try to think of other ways people could keep from getting hurt around their homes, and draw your own poster.

Keep out of reach.

Use a potholder.

Use a stepladder.

Picture This!

Look around your classroom. What do you see? How are the desks arranged? How many lights are there? Where is your teacher? Is anyone in your class wearing something red? Now close your eyes. Try to picture as many things in the room as you can.

As you read, try to picture the people and places described. Forming a picture helps you understand a story and makes the story seem real. Read the following part of the story "Trapped." Try to picture the place described.

Stars filled the summer sky. A hungry young raccoon crept slowly out of the dark woods. The animal looked all around for something to eat.

A tall pine tree stood behind a tent. Under the tree was a big, open, metal garbage can. Lovely smells came from it. The little animal walked past the tent. It climbed up the tree and out onto a branch that spread over the can. The animal jumped lightly into the garbage.

What kind of place does the story describe? Look for words that tell you about it: *stars; summer sky; dark woods; tall pine tree; tent; open, metal garbage can.* These words describe a camping place on a summer night. Close your eyes and try to picture it. Now think about the raccoon. Look for words that describe the animal: *hungry, young, little, jumped lightly.* Can you picture this raccoon?

Now that you have pictured the story yourself, look at the two pictures here. Which one shows the story as you had pictured it? What details make it like the picture you had formed?

As you read, remember to make a picture in your mind. Picture the place you're reading about as well as the characters in the story.

Section Two

THE GREAT OUTDOORS

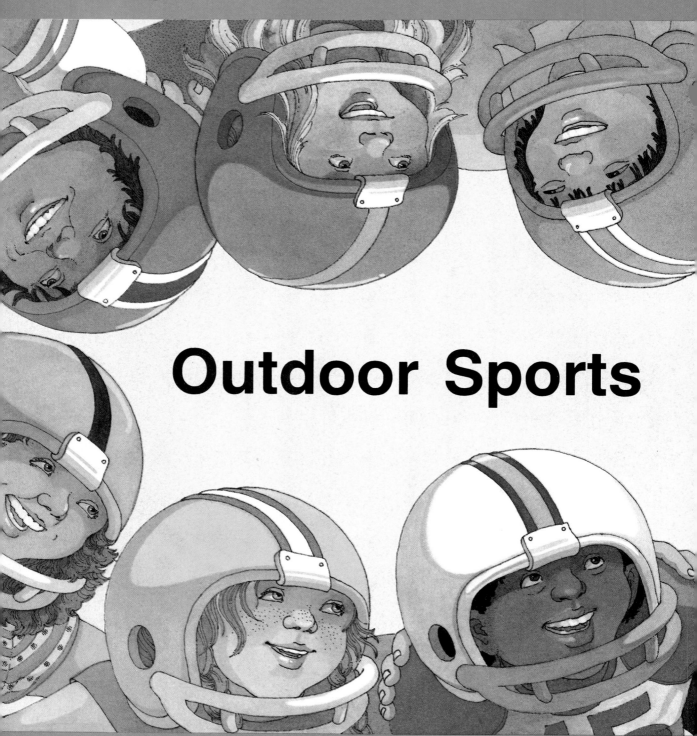

Outdoor Sports

Throwing a baseball on a sunny summer day or kicking a football into the cool fall air can be fun. Any outdoor sport can give us pleasure. An important part of enjoying sports is getting along with the other people who are playing. Sometimes we need to learn how to do that.

A NEW GAME FOR MARIA

When Maria Le Thi first came to the United States, everything seemed new and confusing to her. She did not know many words in English. She had not played many of the games that the children in her school liked to play.

Maria's new friend, Brenda, invited her to play baseball one morning. "Try on my extra glove," Brenda said.

Maria looked puzzled. Why should she wear that thick, brown leather glove on such a warm day? Maria did as Brenda asked. The glove felt heavy and stiff and much too big.

Next Brenda handed Maria the baseball. Maria held the ball in both hands. She was surprised at how hard the ball was. It was old and dirty. The red stitches on the ball were wearing thin. Brenda walked several yards away from Maria. Finally she stopped.

"Throw me the ball," Brenda said.

Maria tossed the ball to her friend. Brenda caught the ball easily and then threw it back. The ball made a popping sound as it landed in Maria's glove.

"Good catch," Brenda said. "You're going to be a fine ball player!"

Sharpen Your Skills

Certain words and phrases in a story can help you imagine how things look, sound, feel, or taste. These small pieces of information are called **details.**

1. What details in the story tell how the glove felt?
2. What details help you picture how the baseball looked?

As you read the next story, "Shooting Star," look for the details that help you imagine how things look, sound, and feel.

Shooting Star

by David Milton

"Clay, would you come and watch my soccer game tomorrow?" Donna asked. She tried to sound happy. Donna didn't want her brother to know she was worried about him.

Clay shrugged his shoulders. "I suppose I can," he said. He didn't seem very interested, though. Clay had always been a good soccer player. But a bicycle accident had left him with a broken arm. Clay couldn't play the game again until his arm healed. Now he didn't seem to be interested in anything.

"Remember, you taught me about soccer in the first place," Donna said. "Maybe you

could give me some tips on shooting. Please, Clay." Clay nodded, but he did not say anything.

The next day was sunny and warm. Donna woke up early. She put on her bright blue team shirt. It had the name *Hawks* printed on the shirt in big white letters. Today the Hawks were playing the Raiders. The Raiders were in first place. With Clay coming to watch, Donna really wanted the Hawks to win.

On the way to the field, Donna became more and more excited. "Know what?" she asked. "The coach is letting me try a new spot on the team. I'm a forward now. That's a very important job. I can shoot that old ball right into the net for a goal. I could be a shooting star."

"A shooting star, like the ones we see on summer nights?" laughed Clay. "Shooting stars are bright, but they don't last long."

"You'll see," she said. "I'm going to be great. I might even be the star of the team."

"Soccer is a team sport. It isn't a game for one or two great players," Clay said. "You all have to work together. That's the best way to get the ball past the other team and into their goal. If you don't play as a team, you're not going to win many games."

When Donna and Clay got to the field, the Hawks were warming up. Donna joined them. Jan was passing the ball to Ruth. Carol was running a lap around the field. Tracy was dribbling the ball toward the goal. She moved quickly. With each step, she kicked the ball a short way ahead of her.

"Good work, Tracy!" Clay shouted. Tracy was good at moving the ball down the field. She was not good at shooting, though. Donna wanted Clay to praise *her*. So she ran toward Tracy. Tracy was just about to shoot the ball.

"Pass the ball to me, Tracy!" Donna called. Tracy kicked the ball to Donna. With a fast, powerful smack, Donna sent the ball on a long, smooth curve right into the net. It was a great kick. As the coach came toward her, Donna expected praise. But the coach was angry.

"Donna, you should have let Tracy shoot the ball!" she yelled. "I want everyone on the team to get a chance to shoot. We don't need stars on this team. We need teamwork."

Suddenly Donna remembered Clay's words. "You all have to work together," he had said. Maybe Clay was right.

Finally, the game was about to begin. Donna walked over to the bench. She poured herself a cup of ice water. Slowly she slid a piece of ice over her hot, dusty face. Donna thought some more about what Clay and her coach had said. She shook her hair out of her eyes and threw the ice on the ground. Then Donna ran out on the field, ready to play.

Both teams played hard during the first half of the game. But neither team scored. Then, just after the second half began, Donna got the ball away from a Raiders' player. She moved it down the field near the Raiders' goal. Donna was just about to shoot when she saw the goalie move in her direction. The goalie was getting ready to block Donna's shot.

Donna had to decide quickly what to do. Then, out of the corner of her eye, she saw Tracy. Donna turned and passed the ball to Tracy. Sharp and ready, Tracy shot the ball. It whistled through the Raiders' defense and into their goal.

The Hawks' players went wild. They cheered loudly for Tracy and Donna. From that moment on, the game went to the Hawks. They scored two more goals quickly. Just before the game ended, Donna kicked the ball into the goal for the last score of the game. The Hawks beat the Raiders easily.

Tired, hot, and dusty, Donna walked home with her brother. Clay was excited and happy.

"You were great, Donna!" he said. "Will you come and watch me next season, when I get back into soccer again?"

"You bet," she said smiling.

Checking Comprehension and Skills

- 1. What did Clay do that made it seem as if he were not very interested in going to Donna's soccer game? (60)
- 2. Why was Donna excited as she walked to the soccer field on the day of the game? (61)
  3. Did Clay support Donna's desire to become a star? How do you know? (61)
  4. Why did Donna ask Tracy to pass the ball during practice? (62)
  5. Do you think the coach was right to criticize Donna? Why or why not?
  6. Did Donna change her mind about being a star? Explain your answer.
- 7. How did Clay feel after the soccer game ended? How do you know? (64)
  8. Do you think the Hawks would have won if Donna hadn't changed her mind? Explain your answer.
  9. What are two other games in which cooperation among players is important?

   Choose the word that fits each sentence.
   smack   curve   team
  ○10. Donna hit the ball with a loud ____.
  ○11. Donna sent the ball on a long, smooth ____.

- Details   ○ Phonics: Vowels

An Outdoor Favorite

Kite flying has been a favorite outdoor activity for hundreds of years. Most of the time kites have been flown by people who just wanted to have fun outdoors. But kites have also been flown for other reasons. Sometimes they have been flown to test new ideas or to answer questions about the weather.

Vowels in Words

draw
because

join
boys

The kites in the picture are flying high. These kites are special. The two words on each kite have the same vowel sound. Can you read the words on each kite? Try it! Remember that different vowel letters can stand for the same vowel sound.

Sharpen Your Skills

draw
because

Look at the words in the first box. They are words from page 68. Here's a rule to help you read words like these:

- The letters *aw* and *au* can stand for the same vowel sound.

join
boys

Read the two words in the next box. Here's a rule to help you figure out words like these:

- The letters *oi* and *oy* can stand for the same vowel sound.

As you read the following sentences, don't forget that different vowel letters can stand for the same vowel sound. Use the rules on this page to help you read the underlined words.

1. There was a little <u>soil</u> on my kite. I got a cloth to wipe it off.
2. After I <u>paused</u> for a minute to clean the kite, I was ready to fly it.
3. Then my kitten came along. It scratched its <u>claw</u> on my kite and tore it.
4. Why do so many things happen to <u>annoy</u> me? I just want to have fun with my kite!

Try using the vowel rules on this page when you need to figure out a word.

HAPPY KITE FLYING!

Airplanes and kites are alike in some ways. They are both heavier than air and yet they can fly. Both airplanes and kites need to be built in special ways to be able to fly. Both airplanes and kites need to move forward to lift off the ground.

Of course, the airplane and the kite move forward in different ways. An airplane needs its engines to move forward. A kite does not have engines. A kite needs the wind and the person flying it to move forward.

You must follow a few rules to fly a kite. First, find a large open field. There should be

no tall buildings, trees, or power lines nearby. Make sure there is a good breeze. The wind should be blowing at least strong enough so that leaves and small twigs are blowing around. Then, stand the kite up or have a friend hold it up. Hold the kite string. Walk about fifty feet[1] into the wind. Give the kite a good tug. Get it into the air by pulling on the string. Happy kite flying!

---

1. 15 meters

Sharpen Your Skills

The **main idea** of a paragraph is the most important idea given about the topic of the paragraph. Knowing how to find the main idea of a paragraph in an article helps you understand the entire article. Look at the first paragraph of "Happy Kite Flying."

1. In a word or two, what is the topic of this paragraph?
2. What is the most important idea given abou the topic in this paragraph?
3. What details support, or tell more about, the main idea?

As you read the next two selections, look for the main ideas in the selections.

More About Kites

by Martha Weintraub

What was the first kite like? Different people have different ideas about what it was like. One person thinks the first kite was made from a Chinese farmer's hat on a string. Someone else thinks it was made from a flag. Still another person thinks the first kite was made from an arrow with a string on it.

Most people do agree, however, that the first kites were made in the Far East.[1] Kites have been known there for over three thousand years. Old stories tell of people flying kites in Malaysia. The kites were made of leaves and vine. People in China also flew kites. Some Chinese thought kites could carry away bad luck and sickness. People in Korea believed this too. Kites did not come to the Western World[2] until around 1600.

1. China, Japan, and other parts of eastern Asia.
2. The countries in Europe and America.

Kite flying in Japan in the early 1900s.

Long ago, kites were even used in wars and battles. In 206 B.C. a Chinese general wanted to get inside an enemy palace. The only way was to dig a tunnel. First, the general had to figure out how long to make the tunnel. So he flew a kite over the palace. When the kite got over the palace, the general figured out how much string he had used. The length of the kite string told him how long to make the tunnel.

Some people used kites to do experiments. In 1749 two Scots used kites to record the temperature of clouds. They fastened a group of kites together. The first kite had a thermometer on it that fell to the ground when the kite reached a certain height. This made it possible for the Scots to record the temperature of the clouds.

Ben Franklin used a kite to show that electricity and lightning are the same.

Benjamin Franklin believed that electricity and lightning were the same. He set out to prove it in 1752. One stormy day he flew a kite that had a long, pointed wire fastened to it. Near his hand he tied a key to the kite string. When lightning struck the pointed wire, electricity flowed through the wire and hit the key. He felt the electric shock come through the key. Benjamin Franklin saw and proved that lightning was electricity.

Today kite flying is enjoyed by people all over the world. Kite days are held in many countries. In early spring, people fly kites at fairs all over the United States, in Thailand, and in Australia. On May 5th in Japan, children fly kites that look like fish. People there also try to fly huge kites. The kites sometimes weigh as much as a small car. In India kite days are held in January and in July. The people there fly fighter kites. These kites have string that is covered with ground glass. The people who are flying the kites use their kites to try to cut the string of other kites.

Kites have been flown for many different reasons. But today people fly kites mostly just for fun.

KITES
Come in All Shapes and Sizes

by Mars Traub

If your teacher asked everyone in class to draw a picture of a kite, some pupils would draw a diamond shape. This is the kind of kite you often see in toy stores and at the park. It is an easy kite to make. The diamond-shaped kite is a well-known kind of kite.

However, kites come in many different sizes and shapes. A kite can be as little as a scrap of paper. Or it can be very, very big. People have made kites that are as big as airplanes. Kites can be made in the shape of a bird, a dragon, or a fish. In fact, they can be made in just about any shape or form.

One kind of kite is the *flat kite*. It is made with two or more crossed sticks. Flat kites can be made in different shapes. The diamond and the square are two of the shapes.

Flat kites are easy to make. They can be made on a table or desk. They can be made small or large. Some flat kites can be made in an hour or less.

The *bow kite* is another kind of kite. It is made by tightly pulling the string on one of the sticks used to make the kite. This causes the stick to curve. A kite made like this is easy to fly. Bow kites often do not need tails. When the wind is strong, it is easier to fly a kite without a tail than one with a tail.

Bow kites can be made in different shapes. They can be in the shape of a diamond. Or they can be made in the shape of a square. They can even have six sides.

Another kind of kite is the *box kite*. It is not easy to build. It isn't easy to fly either. But box kites can go very high. They have gone as high as five miles[1] above the earth! And the box kite is very strong. It can be made strong enough to carry a person. The Wright Brothers' plane was really like a box kite with an engine.

Box Kite

---

1. about eight kilometers

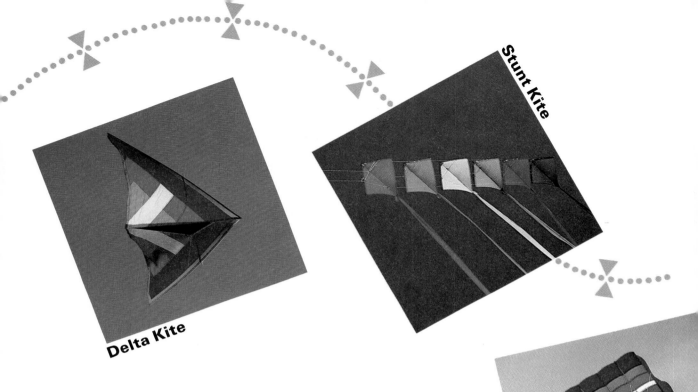

Stunt Kite

Delta Kite

Sled Kite

Delta kites are made in the shape of a triangle. They are easy to fly. These kites are often made to look like birds.

Stunt kites use two lines, or strings. By pulling on the two lines, a person flying one of these kites can make it do tricks.

Some kites don't have sticks. They are often hard to fly. The *sled kite* is a kite that uses no cross stick. The wind fills it and makes it fly. If the wind drops, the sled kite will fold up and float to the earth.

You can buy some kinds of kites in stores. However, many people who fly kites think it is more fun to build and fly their own kites.

Checking Comprehension and Skills

- 1. In "More About Kites," what is the topic of the second paragraph? (72)
- 2. Which sentence in that paragraph tells the main idea? (72)
- 3. What are three details that support that main idea? (72)
  4. How did a Chinese general use a kite? (73)
  5. Do you think the experiment performed by Benjamin Franklin was dangerous? Why or why not? (74)
  6. What are four kinds of kites described in "Kites Come in All Shapes and Sizes"? (76 and 77)
- 7. What sentence gives the main idea of the last paragraph on page 76? (76)
- 8. What are some details that support the main idea of that paragraph? (76)
  9. What did you learn about kites that you didn't know before?

Choose the word that fits each sentence.
causes   toy   enjoyed

○10. The kite most often seen in ___ stores is the diamond-shaped kite.
○11. Pulling tightly on one string ___ the bow kite to curve.

• Main Idea and Supporting Details   ○ Phonics: Vowels

Let's Make a Flat Kite

Materials: two thin sticks (36 inches long and 30 inches long), paper, string, glue, crayon, strips of cloth for tail.

1. Make a crayon mark in the center of the 30-inch stick. Lay the center of that stick on the 36-inch stick, about 9 inches down from the top, so the two sticks cross. Glue and tie the sticks together.

2. Notch the ends of the sticks crosswise. Run string around from tip to tip and tie where it meets.

3. Cut the paper covering in the same shape as shown in the drawing. Use the frame with the string as a guide. Leave at least a 2-inch margin all the way around. Lay the frame on the covering. Fold the margins of the covering over strings and glue down.

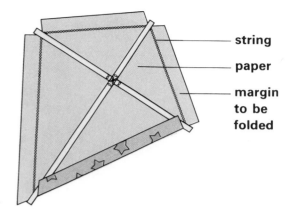

string

paper

margin to be folded

4. Lay your kite down flat on its sticks. Tie a 34-inch string to the ends of the crosswise stick. Tie a 40-inch string to the ends of the lengthwise stick. Attach a flying cord, as shown, where the two strings cross. Attach a tail.

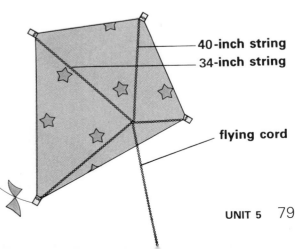

40-inch string

34-inch string

flying cord

Working Outdoors

People who plow snow, grow crops, deliver the mail, and build houses are alike in at least one way. They all work outdoors. Can you think of other jobs that people do outdoors? Why do you think some people like to work outdoors?

The Inside Story
of Outside Jobs

What makes people choose a job? Why do some people choose to work indoors while others would rather work outdoors?

One woman got interested in rocks through family camping trips when she was a child. When she grew up, she became a geologist. Her job was studying rocks. One man explained, "I grew up on a farm. I always wanted to learn more about how plants grow. So I went to school to learn about plants. Now I live in the city and help people plan their gardens."

"I like working outdoors," another worker said. "But I started working indoors, learning how buildings are put together. It was interesting at first. Then I found I didn't like working indoors. So now I work outdoors. I use the training that I got from my indoor job. My new job is knocking old buildings down safely."

Working outdoors means being out on sunny, warm days. It also means being out on cold, snowy, and rainy ones. But many workers don't seem to mind as long as they are outdoors.

Sharpen Your Skills

Knowing how to find the main idea of paragraphs in an article will help you understand the entire article. Sometimes the main idea isn't stated. Then you have to figure it out yourself.

1. In a word or two, what is the topic of the third paragraph?
2. What is the main idea of the third paragraph?
   a. Some people like to work outdoors.
   b. Some people train to work indoors and end up working outdoors.
3. What details support, or tell more about, the main idea in the third paragraph?

See if you can figure out what the main ideas are in "They Really Like Their Jobs" and "The Window Cleaner."

They *Really* Like Their Jobs

by Kate Holland

Charlie Suggs and Alfreda Franco don't do the same job. They don't even know each other. But they are alike in one way. They love to work outdoors.

Mr. Suggs works for the telephone company. He puts in and fixes telephone wires. Sometimes Mr. Suggs works above ground. Sometimes he works below ground.

Mr. Suggs must follow safety rules whenever he works near electric power lines or in manholes. Mr. Suggs always wears a hard hat and safety glasses when he is working.

"When I first started this job, I didn't know much about it," Mr. Suggs said. "But I learned while I worked. The telephone company taught me how to put in and fix telephone wires. I also learned how to work safely around electricity. The telephone company even taught me how to climb telephone poles."

Mr. Suggs works with a partner. The telephone company may send them to work at an office building or a factory. The two workers may make many stops in one day. Or they may work at one big job for many days.

"I enjoy my job," Mr. Suggs said. "I like to know that I am helping to get telephone calls from one place to another. And I like the freedom I have to move around on my job. It's nice to be able to work outside."

Alfreda Franco is in charge of the gardens at Lincoln Park in Chicago, Illinois. She plants and takes care of the flowers there. "In the summer I plant and water the flowers. I edge the lawn and mow it. And I weed and cut back flowers that are too big," Ms. Franco said.

"Summer is my favorite time," she said. "I spend most of the day outside in the gardens. In the winter I'm busy with the plants inside the greenhouse. After working outside all summer, it is hard to work inside during the winter."

Ms. Franco has learned most of what she knows by working in the gardens. She had no training in gardening before she started working at Lincoln Park. "I started out cleaning benches and pulling weeds," she said. "But I worked hard. Now I'm in charge of the large garden. I have two workers helping me.

"There is a lot of hard work in this job. But there are only a few things I don't like about it. Sometimes insects can be trouble. And sometimes we have trouble with people who visit the park. They like our flowers so much that they try to take them home with them. It makes us feel good that people like our gardens. But we feel even better when they take good care of the flowers too."

The Window Cleaner

by Jackson Harper

"In the summer, it's a great job," Bob Rogers said. "You're out on the side of a building. You're high above the street. You're doing a job that few people want to do or can do."

For seven years Bob Rogers rode to the tops of some of the world's tallest buildings. He made the trips on a narrow board that hung from the outside of the buildings. On his way up, Bob's ears would pop. His job was to scrub the dirt off the windows of high-rise apartment and office buildings. Bob worked all through the year. Only freezing temperatures and very strong winds kept him from cleaning dirty windows.

Bob doesn't clean windows any more. But he likes to talk about his window-cleaning days.

"Window cleaners don't like to be called window washers," Bob said. "A window washer stands on the floor or on the ground and wipes dirt from the glass with a towel. Window cleaners must work at heights from which a fall would be deadly."

Window cleaners must also figure out how to reach windows in buildings of a thousand different shapes. Sometimes window cleaners are afraid, but they learn to hide their fears. Years later the fear might catch up with them. Then they have to quit their jobs. Some window cleaners work alone. They just don't trust other people at that height. They are afraid another person will make a mistake that could cause a bad fall.

Window cleaners are often asked the same question. People want to know if the window cleaners get paid more for high windows than for low windows. Workers are paid by the hour. They earn the same for a window a thousand feet up as for a window thirty feet up.

Sometimes window cleaners get stuck up in the air on their narrow boards. This happens when the electric power fails. Then the motors that move the boards up and down won't work. It does no good to scream at people in the street. They can't hear sounds from up there. "When it happened to me," Bob said, "I wrote the word 'help' backwards on a soapy window. Finally the building engineer came over to see what was

wrong. We shouted at each other through the glass until he understood I was stuck."

"The best time for a window cleaner," Bob said, "is when he can lean back against his safety belt, thirty stories up, on a warm spring day. He is alone in the air with the wind blowing down the wall and the sun shining on his face. It's a moment of pure peace."

Checking Comprehension and Skills

1. How did Alfreda Franco and Charlie Suggs learn their jobs? (84 and 86)
2. Do you think either Alfreda or Charlie would like to work indoors? Why or why not?
3. What is the topic of the story "The Window Cleaner"?
•4. Sometimes the main idea of a paragraph isn't stated directly. Which of these sentences best states the main idea of paragraph one, page 88? (88)
   a. Window cleaning can be difficult and dangerous.
   b. Some window cleaners want to work alone.
•5. What are two sentences that supply details supporting this main idea? (88)
6. Which of these words describes Bob Rogers' behavior in paragraph three, page 88: calm, panicky, foolish. Why? (88)
7. What outdoor job would you like to do?

Choose the word that fits each sentence.
ground   peace   fear   snow
∘8. Window cleaners learn to hide their ___ .
∘9. Standing alone with the sun shining on my face was a moment of pure ___ .

• Main Idea and Supporting Details
∘ Phonics: Vowels

A Quick Look Ahead

Sometimes it pays to look ahead. Which boy in the picture below is looking ahead? Which boy is headed for trouble?

It's a good idea to look ahead when you read too. Before you read a book, look it over. Flip through the pages. Glance at titles, headings, and other print. Look at the pictures. Get an idea of what is coming. That way, you can see what the pages are about. You can see what's important and what you most want to read. This quick kind of looking ahead is called **previewing.** You can preview anything you read.

Let's take a quick look at this book. Turn to the Table of Contents on pages 3 to 14. How is this book divided up? How many sections are there? How many units? Find some titles that look interesting to you. Turn to those selections. Look at the pictures. See what you would most like to read.

Turn to page 135. What is under the heading "Sharpen Your Skills"? Have you seen that same heading anywhere else in this book? Now turn to page 165. What does "Just for You" tell you about this page? What kinds of things do you think you will find on other "Just for You" pages?

Next, preview one of the other books you are using this year. Try your math, science, or social studies book. Check these things:

- **Contents pages.** How many parts does the book have?
- **Titles and headings.** What are some of the important things you will be studying?
- **Pictures.** What kinds of pictures are there? How can they help you understand what some parts of the book are about?

Remember—previewing is looking ahead to see what's important and what you want to read.

Section Three
Quick and Clever

WHO'S CLEVER?

People who are quick to see ways of doing things are clever. If one idea doesn't work, they think of another way to do the same thing. Clever people figure out ways to make something better or ways to make a job easier. They often invent new things.

Can you think of other ways a person might show cleverness?

The Perfect Shopping Cart

Mike and Lynn stared at the shopping list their father had left for them. Mike said, "Maybe Dad can carry all this food, but we can't. We need a shopping cart."

The two children hunted through the garage. At last Lynn shouted, "Come here. I've got it!"

Mike ran to his sister. "Look over there," Lynn said. She pointed at an old baby buggy sitting in the corner. "That will make a perfect shopping cart!" she said proudly.

"I'm not so sure," answered Mike. "What if our friends see us pushing it around? They'll think we look silly."

"Don't worry," Lynn said. "We won't see any of our friends at the store."

Later, Lynn and Mike were on their way home from the store. No one had seen them shopping. Suddenly Mrs. Mullen and her son, Teddy, rounded the corner by the bank.

"Look! There's Teddy!" Mike groaned.

"Just cover up the groceries with this blanket," Lynn said. "Maybe he'll think we're baby-sitting."

They all met in front of the bank. "It's so nice of you two to baby-sit," Mrs. Mullen said. "Say hello to the baby, Teddy."

Before Teddy could get a good look inside the buggy, Lynn and Mike started to leave.

"We'd like to stay here and talk, but the baby needs a nap. Good-bye!" Mike yelled.

Sharpen Your Skills

Sentences often have words like *they* or *here* that refer to other words in the sentence or paragraph. If the meaning of a sentence does not seem clear, check to make sure you understand what these words refer to. Rereading will often make clear the meaning of words like *they* or *here*.

1. What do the words *their* and *them* stand for in this sentence? *Mike and Lynn stared at the list their father had left for them.*

2. Who does the word *sister* refer to in these sentences? *At last Lynn shouted, "Come here. I've got it!" Mike ran to his sister.*

As you read "Dragon Stew," you will find words that take the place of other words.

Dragon Stew

by Tom McGowen

Once upon a time, there was a kingdom ruled by a fat king. He was so fat that his people called him King Chubby. Eating was so important to the king that it got him into all kinds of trouble. For one thing, he couldn't keep his royal cooks. He would tell every cook how to cook. Each cook would get angry at the king and quit.

So King Chubby decided to have a contest. The person who had the most unusual recipe would become the new royal cook. Many cooks entered the contest. They all failed—until a shabby young man appeared before the king.

"I'm Klaus Dinkelspiel, Your Majesty," the young man said. "I'll bet you've never heard of dragon stew!"

The king was surprised. "That sounds different. What's in it—besides dragon, of course?"

"Oh, I can't tell you!" said Klaus. "It's been a family secret for many years."

"I understand," said the king. "If we can ever find a dragon, you must make it for me. Now you can begin by preparing an ordinary royal feast. You are the new royal cook."

Klaus bowed deeply. "And what would you like for dinner?" he asked.

"How about roast pig?" the king said.

"And would Your Majesty care to show me exactly how you want it cooked?" Klaus asked innocently.

The king stared. "You mean you won't care if I help you cook? Why, you and I are going to get along just fine!"

So off they went to the kitchen. They gathered everything the king needed. Then Klaus said, "Now, how would you prepare this, Your Majesty?"

King Chubby, delighted, stuffed the pig.

"How would you cook this, Your Majesty?"

The king popped the pig into the oven.

When the pig was brown, Klaus said, "I thank you for all your help, Your Majesty. If you will go to the dining hall, I'll serve you the feast I have prepared."

The king gobbled up the pork. He thought that it was the finest feast he'd ever eaten. He said Klaus was the finest cook he'd ever had. From then on, the king and his new cook were happy.

One morning many months later, Klaus was called to the throne room. When he entered, he was shocked. The Captain of the Guard and a dozen soldiers were guarding a large cage. Inside was a small, fat dragon.

"Surprise!" beamed the king. "I sent them out to find a dragon months ago. It's taken all this time to find one. Now you can cook your dragon stew tonight. I promise I won't try to find out your secret."

The soldiers carried the cage to the kitchen. They set it down and marched out. The captain said, "Careful of him, Cook. He bites and scratches. He can also shoot fire six inches out of his nose."

Klaus stared at the small dragon. A tear fell down its cheek. "Are you trying to think of the best way to kill me?" it asked. "It isn't fair! I was minding my own business. Suddenly your soldiers attacked me. They carried me here to be made into—into stew."

"I don't want to make you into stew," said Klaus. "I didn't think there was any such thing as a dragon when I made up dragon stew. I just wanted to fool the king into thinking I was a cook. I can't make a stew. The king will have my head chopped off as soon as he finds out that I fooled him."

"Oh, making stew is easy," said the dragon.

Suddenly, Klaus began to smile. He nodded his head as though he had thought of something.

At seven o'clock, the king hurried into the dining hall. He watched eagerly as Klaus carried in a steaming bowl. The cook spooned browned meat and vegetables onto the king's plate. King Chubby began to gobble.

After four helpings, he leaned back with a sigh. "That's the best stew I've ever eaten. What a shame we can never have it again. That might have been the world's last dragon."

"We can have it as often as you like," Klaus said. "The thing that makes dragon stew so different is that it can only be cooked by a dragon! Allow me to present my helper."

Klaus whistled. In came the dragon. It was wearing a tall, white cook's hat. The dragon bowed deeply.

"Under my direction," said Klaus, "my helper will be happy to make dragon stew. You can have it whenever you want it."

So everything turned out very well. King Chubby was able to cook his own feasts just as he liked them. He could also have dragon stew (made from beef) as often as he wanted it. Klaus was happy to be the royal cook. The dragon was delighted to be the royal cook's helper. And now no one got scorched fingers from lighting the big stove. For the helper lit his own stove by shooting fire out his nose.

Checking Comprehension and Skills

1. How did Klaus Dinkelspiel become King Chubby's cook? (98)
2. Why did King Chubby think Klaus was the finest cook he had ever had? (99 and 100)
•3. On page 100, Klaus says: "How would you cook this, Your Majesty?" To what do the words *Your Majesty* refer?
4. How do you think Klaus felt when King Chubby first presented the dragon? Why do you think he felt this way?
•5. On page 102, King Chubby says: "That's the best stew I've ever eaten. What a shame we can never have it again." To what does the word *it* refer?
6. How was Klaus able to call his dragon stew by that name when he used no dragon meat? (103)
7. Would you call Klaus a clever man? Why or why not?

Tell the root word, the ending, and the spelling change of the underlined word.
○8. The king hurried into the dining hall.

• Referents
○ Structure: Endings

Riddles

You have been reading about clever people.
Now it's your turn to see how clever you are.
Here are some riddles for you to figure out.

1. Why does a humming bird hum?

1. He doesn't know the words

2. What quacks louder than a duck?

2. two ducks

3. What is green, noisy, and extremely dangerous?

3. a stampeding herd of pickles

4. What color is a hiccup?

4. burple

5. Why do birds fly south?

5. because it's too far to walk

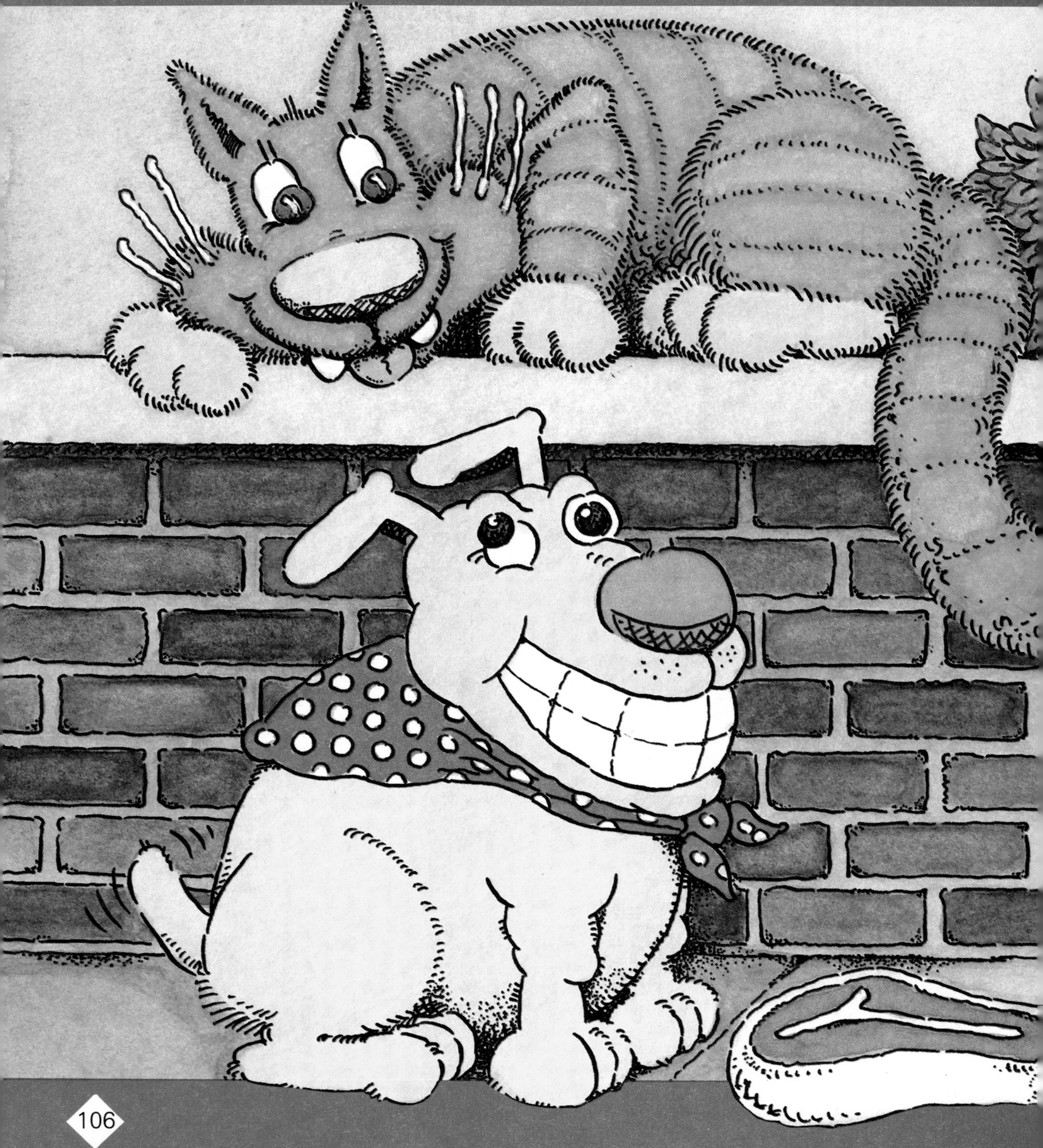

The Cat That Fooled the Dog

A young dog was walking along with a bit of food in its mouth. The food made the dog very happy because it had looked all day for something to eat. The dog suddenly came upon an old and wise cat. The cat eyed the food with great interest.

"I say," said the cat. "You certainly have beautiful white teeth. They are the prettiest teeth I have ever seen."

The dog, feeling very proud, opened its mouth wide so that the cat could get a better look. When the dog opened its mouth, the food fell out onto the ground. The cat quickly grabbed the food with its mouth and ran off, leaving the dog with nothing but an empty, opened mouth.

Sometimes it is better to be wise than it is to be proud.

Small but Important Words

In the picture at the left, the lady-in-waiting thought the queen said, "Brush your teeth <u>while</u> you stand here." But the queen had really said, "Brush your teeth <u>before</u> you stand here." Changing one little word can make a big difference in the meaning of a sentence.

Sharpen Your Skills

The words *while* and *before* are connecting words. Other connecting words are *though, and, but, because,* and *after.* Watch out for some of these small but important words as you read the first part of the story.

Once, long ago, there lived a clever girl named Priscilla. Yes, Priscilla was smart, but she was unhappy. You see, Priscilla was a lady-in-waiting who hated waiting.

All day long, Priscilla had to stand and smile at the queen. The queen talked on and on because she loved the sound of her own voice. But Priscilla hated it.

1. One sentence in the story says, "Priscilla was smart, but she was unhappy." Which of these sentences means the same thing?

   Priscilla was smart, although she was unhappy.
   Priscilla was smart because she was unhappy.

   The first sentence means the same thing as the sentence from the story. *But* and *although* have about the same meaning. As you finish the story, keep watching out for connecting words.

   One day Priscilla grumbled, "I may just as well be a dummy—the kind you see in store windows." That gave Priscilla an idea!
   The next day, Priscilla went to work before the queen came to court. Priscilla put a dummy that looked just like herself at her place behind the throne. Then she dashed off to play.
   Every day Priscilla played this trick. The queen never noticed. She talked and talked, happy to see Priscilla smiling—always smiling.

2. "Priscilla went to work before the queen came to court." Tell how the scene would change if *after* took the place of *before.*

   Don't skip over the little words as you read the next story.

THE WOMAN WHO FLUMMOXED THE LITTLE PEOPLE

by Sorche Nic Leodhas

There was a woman once who was a master baker. There wasn't a wedding or birthday for miles around that she wasn't called on to make the cakes for.

Not only was the woman a master baker. She was also the cleverest woman in the world. It was the first that got her into trouble. It was the second that got her out of it.

Now, the little people dearly love a bit of cake. They often steal a slice from a kitchen while all in the house are sleeping.

Of all cakes, the ones the little people liked best were those this baker made. The trouble was, a taste of her cake was hard to come by. Her cakes were so good that hardly a crumb was ever left over.

So the little people planned to carry the woman away. They would keep her with them always just to bake cakes for them.

Their chance came soon. There was to be a wedding with hundreds of guests. The woman was to make the cakes. She would have to spend the whole day before the wedding doing nothing but baking.

The little people learned about the wedding. They found out, too, what road she'd be taking home.

When the night came, the little people waited by the road. They hid in all kinds of places.

When the baker came by, the little people drifted fern seed into her eyes. All of a sudden she was sleepy!

"Mercy me!" she said with a yawn. "It's worn myself out I have this day!" And she sank down on a grassy bank to sleep. But it wasn't a bank at all. It was the place where the little people lived. Once she lay upon it, she was in their power.

The baker knew nothing till she woke in the land of the little people. Being a clever woman, she didn't have to be told where she was. "Well now," she said happily, "and did you ever! It's all my life I've wanted to get a peep into the land of the little people. And here I am!"

They told her what they wanted. Well, she didn't intend to stay there the rest of her life! But she didn't tell the little people.

"To be sure!" she said, "Why you poor wee things! To think of me baking cakes for everyone else, and not a one for you! So let's be at it."

"Let me see now," said she, looking about. "It is plain you have nothing for me to be baking with. You'll have to be going to my own kitchen to bring back what I'll need."

The little people said they would. So the baker sent some for eggs and some for sugar. She sent some for flour and some for butter. When all was ready for the mixing, she asked for a bowl. But the biggest they could find was the size of a teacup.

Well, there was nothing to do but to have the little people get the woman's own blue bowl. After that it was her wooden spoons. Then it was one thing and another till the little people were all tired out.

At last everything was at hand. The woman began to mix. But all of a sudden she stopped. "'Tis no use!" she sighed, "I can't mix a cake without my cat beside me."

"Go after the cat!" said the king of the little people.

So the little people got the cat. It lay at the woman's feet and purred. The woman stirred away, but not for long.

"Well now," the woman sighed. "I'm used to my dog setting the time of my beating with his snores. I can't seem to get the beat right without him."

"Go after the dog!" cried the king.

So they got the dog. He curled up at the baker's feet beside the cat. The dog snored. The cat purred. All seemed to be well.

But no! The woman stopped again! "I'm worried about my babe," said she. "Away from him all night! It seems I just can't mix."

"Go after that babe!" roared the king.

So the little people got the babe. But when they brought him, he began to scream, for he was hungry. The woman knew he would be, for the baby never let anyone feed him but her.

"I'm sorry to trouble you," said the woman. "But I can't stop beating, or the cake may go wrong. Perhaps my husband can quiet the baby."

The little people didn't wait for the king to tell them. Off they flew for the husband. He, poor man, was all in a whirl. Things had been taken one after another. Then he had been carried through the air himself. But here was his wife. He knew that where she was things couldn't go far wrong.

So the woman beat the batter. The baby screamed. The cat purred. The dog snored. And the man watched to see what his wife was up to. The little people settled down. Though it was plain to see that the screaming upset them.

Then the woman gave the wooden spoon to the baby. He began to bang away with it. Under cover of the screaming and the banging, the woman whispered to her husband. "Pinch the dog!"

"What?" he said. But he did it.

"TOW! ROW! ROW!" barked the dog.

"Step on the cat's tail!" whispered the woman to her husband. He did, for he knew now what she was trying to do. He kept his foot on the cat's tail, and the cat kept howling.

So the woman swished! The baby screamed! The spoon banged! The dog barked! The cat howled! And the little people flew round with their hands over their ears. If there is one thing little people can't bear it's noise. What's more, the woman knew it!

Then the woman poured batter into two pans. She popped a lump of sugar into the baby's mouth, and he stopped screaming. She nodded to her husband. He stopped pinching the dog and took his foot off the cat's tail. Soon all was quiet. The little people sank down too tired to move.

"Where's the oven?" said the woman.

The little people looked at each other sadly. "There isn't an oven," one said.

"What!" said the woman. "Then you'll have to be taking me home to bake it in my oven. You can bring me back when the cake's all done."

The little people looked at the baby and the spoon and the dog and the cat and the man. Then they all shuddered.

"You may all go!" said the king. "But don't ask us to be taking you. We're all too tired!"

Well, the woman began feeling sorry for the little people. "I'll tell you what I'll do. After the cake is baked, I'll be leaving it for you beside the road. What's more, I'll put one there every single weekend."

At that the little people felt better. "I'll do as much!" cried the king. "What you find in that same place shall be your own!"

Then the king raised an arm and the hill broke open. Out they all walked.

So that's the way the woman flummoxed the little people. When the cake was baked, she put it by the road. And when she set it down, she saw a little brown bag. She took the bag up and opened it. It was full of gold pieces.

And so it went, week after week. A cake for the little people, a bag of gold for the woman and her husband. So of course the baker and her husband lived, as why should they not, happily ever after.

Checking Comprehension and Skills

1. Why did the little people carry the baker away? (110)
2. What was the baker's main goal once she was in the land of the little people?
3. How did the baker reach her goal?
4. Do you like the way the story ended? Why?
•5. On page 113, which sentence tells why the baby screamed? (113)
•6. On page 116, which sentence tells when the baker would put the cake by the road? (116)

Answer the questions about these two words: *we're* and *weekend.*
○7. Which word is a contraction?
○8. What words make up the compound word?

• Connecting Words   ○ Structure: Compounds and Contractions

Josh McBroom, his wife, Melissa, and their eleven red-headed youngsters were heading West. They had given up their farm in Connecticut because it was half rocks and half tree stumps. Now they were looking for a new farm. In Iowa they met Hector Jones. He had eighty acres of land that he would sell cheap. McBroom bought Jones's land for ten dollars. In this story, Josh tells what happened next.

Mr. Heck Jones jumped on the running board and guided us a mile up the road. My youngsters tried to make him laugh along the way. Will wiggled his ears, and Jill crossed her eyes. Chester moved his nose like a rabbit. Hester flapped her arms like a bird. Peter whistled through his front teeth, which were missing, and Tom tried to stand on his head in the back of the car. Mr. Heck Jones ignored them all.

Finally he raised his long arm and pointed. "There's your land, neighbor," he said.

Didn't we tumble out of the car in a hurry? We stared with delight at our new farm. It was broad and sunny, with an oak tree on a gentle hill. There was one fault to be sure. A boggy-looking pond spread across an acre beside the road. You could lose a cow in a place like that, but we had a deal—no doubt about it.

"Mama," I said to my dear Melissa. "See that fine old oak on the hill? That's where we'll build our house."

"No you won't," said Mr. Heck Jones. "That oak isn't on your land."

"But, sir—"

"All that's yours is what you see under water. Not a rock or a tree stump in it."

I thought he must be having his little joke, except that there wasn't a smile to be found on his face. "But, sir!" I said. "You clearly stated that the farm was eighty acres."

"That's right."

"That marshy pond hardly covers an acre."

"That's wrong," he said. "There are a full eighty acres—one piled on the other, like hot cakes. I didn't say your farm was all on the surface. It's eighty acres deep, McBroom. Read the deed."

I read the deed. It was true.

"Hee-haw! Hee-haw!" he laughed. "I got the best of you, McBroom! Good day, neighbor."

He hurried away, laughing up his sleeve all the way home. I soon learned that Mr. Heck was always laughing up his sleeve. Folks told me that when he'd hang up his coat and go to bed, all that stored-up laughter would pour out his sleeve and keep him awake nights. But there's no truth to that.

Well, there we stood looking at our one-acre farm that wasn't good for anything but jumping into on a hot day. And that day was the hottest I could remember. The hottest on record, as it turned out. That was the day, three minutes before noon, when the cornfields all over Iowa burst into popcorn. That's history. You must have read about that. There are pictures to prove it.

I turned to our children. "WillJillHester ChesterPeterPollyTimTomMaryLarryandlittle Clarinda," I said. "There's always a bright side to things. That pond we bought is a little muddy, but it's wet. Let's jump in and cool off."

That idea met with favor, and we were soon in our swimming togs. I gave the sign, and we took a running jump. At that moment such a dry spell hit that we landed in an acre of dry earth. The pond had dried up. It was very surprising.

My boys had jumped in head first and there was nothing to be seen of them but their legs kicking in the air. I had to pick them out of the earth like carrots. Some of my girls were still holding their noses. Of course, they were sorely disappointed to have that swimming hole pulled out from under them.

But the moment I ran the soil through my fingers, my farmer's heart skipped a beat. That pond bottom felt as soft and rich as black silk. "My dear Melissa!" I called. "Come look! This soil is so rich it ought to be kept in a bank."

I was in a sudden fever of excitement. That wonderful soil seemed to cry out for seed. My dear Melissa had a sack of dried beans along, and I sent Will and Chester to get it. I saw no need to bother plowing the field. I directed Polly to draw a straight line with a stick and Tim to follow her, poking holes in the ground. Then I came along. I dropped a bean in each hole and stamped on it with my heel.

Well, I had hardly gone a few yards when something green caught my foot. I looked behind me. There was a beanstalk moving along in a hurry and looking for a pole to climb on. The stems were spreading out all over. I had to rush along to keep ahead of them.

By the time I got to the end of the line, the first stems had blossomed, and the pods had formed, and they were ready for picking.

You can guess how excited we were. Will's ears wiggled. Jill's eyes crossed. Chester's nose moved. Hester's arms flapped. Peter's missing front teeth whistled. And Tom stood on his head.

"WillJillHesterChesterPeterPollyTimTomMary LarryandlittleClarinda," I shouted. "Harvest those beans!"

Inside of an hour we had planted and harvested that whole crop of beans. But was it hot working in the sun! I sent Larry to find a good acorn along the road. We planted it, but it didn't grow as fast as I had expected. We had to wait a whole three hours for a shade tree.

We made camp under our oak tree, and the next day we drove to Barnsville with our crop of beans. I traded it for different seeds— carrot and beet and cabbage and other things. The clerk found a few kernels of corn that hadn't popped, at the very bottom of the bin.

But we found out that the corn was surely dangerous to plant. The stalk shot up so fast it would skin your nose.

Of course, there was a secret to that soil. A government man came out and made a study of the matter. He said there had once been a huge lake in that part of Iowa. It had taken thousands of years to become our little pond, as you can guess. The lake fish must have got packed in worse than sardines. There's nothing like fish to put nitrogen in the soil. That's a scientific fact. Nitrogen makes things grow to beat all. And sometimes we did turn up a fish bone.

Using the Dictionary

**Skill
Bonus**

Jane read this clue during the treasure hunt: *Remember the house with the portico? That's where the treasure is. Now go!* But Jane didn't know what a *portico* was. Neither did the other kids on the hunt. But clever Jane knew how to find out. She used the dictionary.

Sharpen Your Skills

The dictionary can help you as you read. When you come to a word you don't know, first try to figure out a meaning that makes sense in the sentence. Then you can check the meaning in a dictionary.

Here are some tips to remember when you use the dictionary—and the glossary too.

- Words in a dictionary are listed in alphabetical order. Jane looked in the *P*s near the middle of the dictionary to find *portico.*
- **Guide words** help you find the right page quickly. Guide words appear in large, dark print at the top of every page. The word you are looking up should

po·rous (pôr′əs), full of pores or tiny holes: *Cloth is porous. Aluminum is not porous.* adjective.

por·poise (pôr′pəs), a sea animal with a blunt, rounded snout. It looks like a small whale. *noun, plural* **por·pois·es** or **por·poise.**

port·a·ble (pôr′tə bəl), capable of being carried or moved; easily carried: *a portable typewriter. adjective*

por·tage (pôr′tij), **1** carrying of boats or provisions overland from one river or lake to another. **2** place over which this is done. *noun.*

por·tal (pôr′tl), door, gate, or entrance, usually an impressive one. *noun.*

por·tend (pôr tend′), indicate beforehand; give warning of: *Black clouds portend a storm. verb.*

por·tent (pôr′tent), a warning, usually of coming evil; sign; omen: *The black clouds were a portent of bad weather. noun.*

por·ti·co (pôr′tə kō), roof supported by columns, forming a porch or a covered walk. See picture. *noun, plural* **por·ti·coes** or **por·ti·cos.**

por·tray (pôr trā′), **1** make a likeness of in a drawing or painting; make a picture of: *portray a historical scene.* **2** picture in words: describe: *The book "Black Beauty" portrays the life of a horse.* **3** act the part of in a play or motion picture: *The actor portrayed a newspaper reporter. verb.*

entry word

a hat	i it	oi oil	ch child	(a in about
ā age	ī ice	ou out	ng long	e in taken
ä far	o hot	u cup	sh she	ə = { i in pencil
e let	ō open	u̇ put	th thin	o in lemon
ē equal	ô order	ü rule	ŦH then	(u in circus
ėr term			zh measure	

portico

definition

come in alphabetical order between the two guide words. What are the guide words on the sample page?

• The words you look up are called **entry words.** They are shown in dark type. Do you see the entry word *portico* on the sample page?

• Entry words are usually root words. Remember that a root word is a word without an ending. If the word you are looking up has an ending, look up its root word. If you wanted to find *porticoes,* what root word would you look up?

- A **definition** tells what an entry word means. Sometimes a word has more than one definition. The definitions are numbered. If there is more than one definition, read them all. Then choose the one that makes the most sense in the sentence where you read the word.
- Often the dictionary gives a sentence that uses the entry word. It shows how the word may be used. Read the definition and the sentence for *portend* on the sample page.
- Sometimes a picture goes with an entry word. Do you see the picture of a portico on the sample page?
- An **entry** is an entry word and all the information about it.

Use the sample dictionary page on page 128 to answer these questions:
1. If the word *porridge* appeared on the page, between what two entry words would it be?
2. Which definition of *portray* makes sense in this sentence: The part of Lassie has been portrayed by several different dogs.

Use your dictionary. It's the best word book!

Books to Read

Brother Anansi and the Cattle Ranch told by James De Sauza. Adapted by Harriet Rohmer. Children's Book Press.

Brother Anansi, the spider, is always very tricky. When Brother Tiger wins some money, they go into business together. Will Brother Anansi fool Brother Tiger once again?

The Family Under the Bridge by Natalie Savage Carlson. Harper.

Armand is a poor old man without a home. Yet he gets along in one of the world's most beautiful cities—Paris, France—by living under a bridge. Three homeless children decide to move in with Armand and change his life forever.

Stone Soup retold by John Warren Stewig. Holiday House.

Young Grethel leaves home because her poor family is starving. She comes to a village, but the people have no food to spare. Clever Grethel makes a fine feast for everyone from a stone!

Search for the Past

THE CLIFF DWELLERS

A group of people called *archaeologists* study the past. They use special tools to dig in the earth. They look for very old objects, or relics, buried in the ground. By studying these relics the archaeologists find out how people lived long ago.

Archaeologists have learned a great deal about a group of Native Americans who were cliff dwellers. These people once lived in what is now Arizona and Colorado. From the years 1000 to 1300 they built their homes high up in rock cliffs. By studying the remains of the cliff villages, archaeologists have discovered much about these people.

THE GREAT PUEBLO PERIOD

Picture yourself in a deep canyon in southwest Colorado. On both sides of you there are steep cliffs. You look up and see houses that have been built right into the cliffs. You are looking at one of the large cliff villages that were built during the Great Pueblo[1] Period.

That period lasted from the years 1000 to 1300. A group of Native Americans called the **Anasazi** built these cliff dwellings. Archaeologists believe the Anasazi began building them around 1019. Before moving to the cliffs, the Anasazi lived in small villages on the plains nearby. Some archaeologists think the Anasazi may have moved to the cliffs to protect their families from enemies.

Anasazi,
(ä′nä sä′zē)
ancient ones

Large cliff villages were built by the Anasazi. But sometime around 1274 the building stopped. No one really knows why. However, from 1276 to 1293, there was a terrible dry spell. Crops did not grow well. Soon afterward the Anasazi left their cliff dwellings. Perhaps the Anasazi had to leave because they had no food. Or they may have been driven away by their enemies.

---

1. pueblo (pweb′lō), houses in a Native American town

Sharpen Your Skills

When you read about real people or events in history, it is important to understand the sequence of events. The dates given in an article can help you keep track of the sequence. A time line, such as this one, can help you.

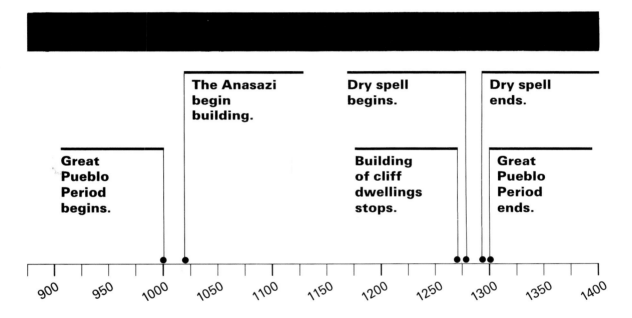

1. About how many hundreds of years did the Great Pueblo Period last?
2. Were any buildings built after the dry spell began?

As you read the next two selections, use the time lines to help you figure out the sequence.

Esteban's Journey

by Louis Tiadore

Esteban

Esteban[1] was a fearless explorer who was born in Morocco, a country in Africa. From 1528 to 1539, Esteban journeyed across the southern part of the United States with Spaniards. He helped the Spaniards discover new land.

Esteban sailed to the New World in June of 1527. He was one of six hundred people who were led by a Spaniard named Narváez.[2] Narváez had been ordered by the King of Spain to explore all the land from Florida to Mexico. The Spaniards wanted to make the land theirs. They also hoped to find gold.

On May 2, 1528, Esteban began a trip across the New World. Narváez had heard about a Native American village in the northern part of Florida. It was supposed to be full of gold. Narváez, Esteban, and three hundred soldiers set out to find it.

For six weeks Esteban and the others walked through swamps, swam across rivers,

---

1. Esteban (es tā'bän)   2. Narváez (när vä'es)

and made their way through thick forests. Finally they found the village they were looking for. But they found no gold.

The Spaniards attacked the village. The Native Americans who lived in the village defended themselves. Esteban and the others were no match for the Native Americans, who knew the land around the village so well. The Spaniards were forced to run for their lives.

For the next six years Esteban and the Spaniards faced hardships. They were still trying to get to Mexico. For a few months they journeyed in five small boats that they had made. Then three of the boats sank in a hurricane, and all the people on board were lost. The other two boats were dashed on shore. Esteban was on one of those boats. He and the remaining Spaniards began to walk.

By 1534 only Esteban and three of the Spaniards were still alive. The rest had been killed or had died from sicknesses. Finally, in 1536, the four men reached Mexico City.

Spaniards in Mexico City had heard about seven cities filled with gold. Esteban had journeyed over much of the land where the cities were supposed to be. So the Spaniards asked him to find the cities. Friar Marcos de Niza[1]

---

1. Marcos de Niza (mär′kōs dā nē′sä)

led the group. Esteban was their guide. The Spaniards and a few Native Americans headed north from Mexico in March, 1539.

The land was wild and the journey was long. On March 23 the Spaniards stopped. They were too tired to go any farther. Friar Marcos asked Esteban to go on. Several Native American runners went with him. Four days after Esteban left, the runners returned. They told the Spaniards that Esteban had found a great land.

The Spaniards followed the Native Americans toward the new land. They never found Esteban or any golden cities. But he had led them to a new land that is now called Arizona and New Mexico.

The time line at right shows you some of the important events in Esteban's journey.

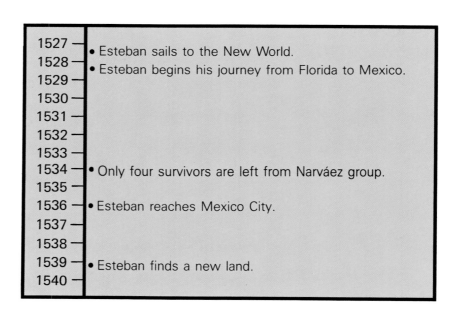

1527	• Esteban sails to the New World.
1528	• Esteban begins his journey from Florida to Mexico.
1529	
1530	
1531	
1532	
1533	
1534	• Only four survivors are left from Narváez group.
1535	
1536	• Esteban reaches Mexico City.
1537	
1538	
1539	• Esteban finds a new land.
1540	

Boy of the Canyon Rim

by Anne Morris

Jonathon John, whose nickname is Tonto,[1] might look just like you today. He is sitting in front of the television and eating a sandwich. But yesterday the Navaho boy ate fry bread and mutton stew.

Tonto lives on the rim of Canyon de Chelly[2] National Monument in Arizona. The cliff dwellings along the canyon walls once belonged to the Anasazi, or "ancient ones." When Tonto wants to escape today's world, he can go down into the canyon. There, in the middle of towering cliff walls, time doesn't seem to be important.

One day while climbing in the canyon, Tonto fell and broke his leg. "I fell off a cliff," he said. His parents carried him in their truck to a small hospital for care. Later, they had a Navaho healing ceremony for him. They

---

1. Tonto (tän′tō)
2. Canyon de Chelly (kan′yən   də   shā)

believed that would help too. In Tonto's life, new and old go together.

Tonto's school day might be much like yours. He awakens to an alarm clock instead of the morning sun. Then Tonto puts on a shirt, pants, and running shoes. After having his oatmeal and orange juice and carrying out the garbage for his mother, he gets on the school bus. Tonto is in the ninth grade.

After school Tonto is home by 3:30 P.M. At home he plays baseball with his friends until it's time for supper. Afterward, he does his homework or watches television until bedtime at 8:30 P.M.

"Just like me," you say.

Well, maybe not. Tonto has other things he does too. Every day he must help his older brothers haul water. Their house has electricity and gas, but no running water. So they must fill barrels with all that they use from a water supply two miles away. With nine people, a horse, two dogs, and a cat living at home, that is a lot of water.

At home, everyone speaks Navaho. English is a second language, learned at school. In summer Tonto speaks Navaho most of the time because his life is spent with his family. They fish together, and the boys swim every day at a water hole on the canyon rim.

"My favorite thing to do is ride horses," Tonto said. He rides with his brother, Jerome. They race each other on the mesa.

The part of summer Tonto hates is herding sheep. Sometimes his aunt asks him to take her flock of sheep and a few goats down into the canyon from the rim. The canyon floods every spring when snow melts on the nearby mountains. Because of the deep shadows of the canyon, water stays a long time. So even in summer the sheep can always find food and water at the bottom of the canyon, even when it is dry up on the rim.

Sometimes Tonto and Jerome go together to herd the flock. With two sharing the work, the job is not so bad. At the bottom of the canyon they can climb trees and make whistles out of the leaves while the sheep graze.

Tonto has fun in summer, but he expects to work too. His mother, Liz John, says children today do not work as much as they used to. Maybe that sounds like your mother.

"We used to make small wagons and dolls out of clay," Liz John said. "I guess those were the only games we used to know. These days they have a lot of toys. I think my kids have changed in a lot of ways from the way I was."

Tonto is a mixture of old and new. He is different from his parents when they were his age. When Tonto grows up, he will probably be different from the way his parents are now. He will always be part of two worlds.

The timeline below shows what a day might be like for Tonto.

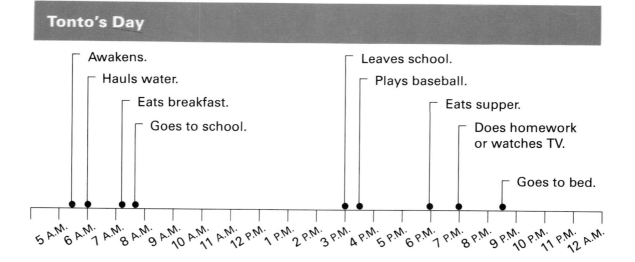

Tonto's Day

Awakens.
Hauls water.
Eats breakfast.
Goes to school.
Leaves school.
Plays baseball.
Eats supper.
Does homework or watches TV.
Goes to bed.

5 A.M. 6 A.M. 7 A.M. 8 A.M. 9 A.M. 10 A.M. 11 A.M. 12 P.M. 1 P.M. 2 P.M. 3 P.M. 4 P.M. 5 P.M. 6 P.M. 7 P.M. 8 P.M. 9 P.M. 10 P.M. 11 P.M. 12 A.M.

Checking Comprehension and Skills

1. Where was Esteban's homeland? (136)
2. Did Esteban come to North America in the 1500s or the 1600s? (136)
3. Why did the king of Spain send people to North America? (136)
- 4. About how many months did it take Esteban to sail from Spain to the New World? (136)
- 5. About how many years passed between the time when Esteban reached Florida and the time when he reached Mexico City? (138)
6. Would you call Esteban's exploration successful or not? Why do you say so?
7. Is it possible that Esteban traveled in the area where Tonto would live one day? Explain your answer.
- 8. According to the time line, about how much time does Tonto have for hauling water? (142)
- 9. Does Tonto haul water before or after breakfast? (142)
10. How is Jonathon John a mixture of old and new?

With a slanted line, show where the first syllable ends and the second one begins in each word.

○11. middle   ○12. whistle

- Sequence: Time Sequence   ○ Structure: Syllables

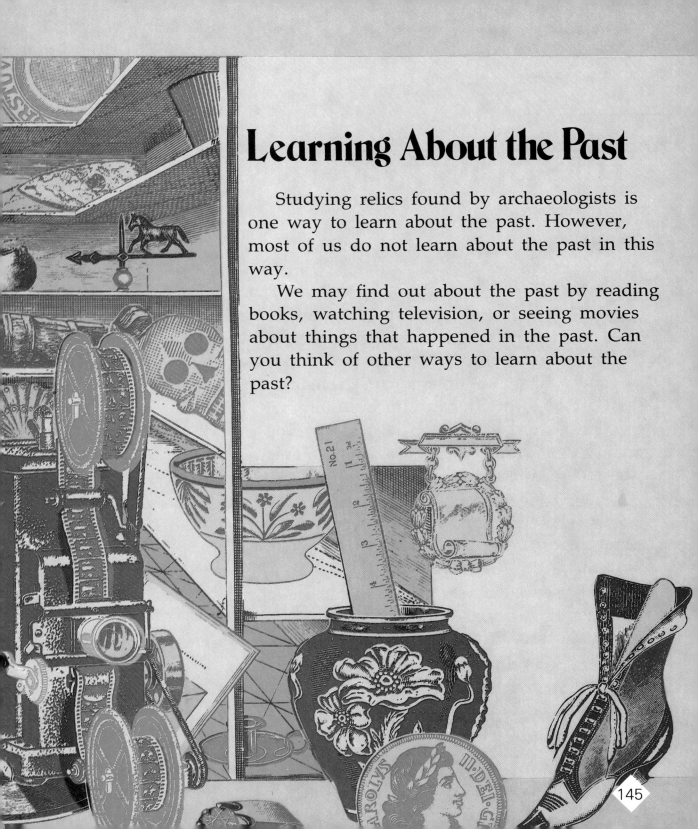

Learning About the Past

Studying relics found by archaeologists is one way to learn about the past. However, most of us do not learn about the past in this way.

We may find out about the past by reading books, watching television, or seeing movies about things that happened in the past. Can you think of other ways to learn about the past?

TREASURE HUNTING

Rosa Cortes spends most of her time digging. Rosa is an archaeologist. She works for the Southwest Desert Museum. Part of her job is looking for buried treasure.

The treasures she looks for are not gold or silver. They are very old things. They show how people used to live. Rosa has found several Native American arrows, cooking pots, and masks. Now they are in the museum.

One Saturday morning Rosa decided to dig in her own yard. Rosa hoped she would find something interesting.

First, Rosa took out her tools. She laid them on the ground. Then she marked off a small place to dig. Next, she carefully began to remove the sand.

She used a tiny shovel to dig. It was about the size of a spoon. Rosa had to be careful when she was digging. If she worked too quickly, she might break something hidden in the earth.

Suddenly Rosa's shovel hit something hard. She dug a little more. Soon Rosa saw the top of a metal chest. Then she used both her shovel and a small brush to remove the rest of the sand. At last she pulled the chest up from the hole and opened it.

Inside the chest Rosa found some clothes. She also found a small box. When she opened it, she saw some old medals. There was a name written inside the cover of the box.

"Ramon Diego Cortes!" Rosa said. "He was my great-grandfather. These things must have belonged to him." Rosa was very pleased to have found this family treasure.

Sharpen Your Skills

Often it is important to keep track of the sequence of events or steps to understand a story or part of a story. Clue words like *first, then,* and *at last* can help you to understand the sequence of events or steps.

1. What was the first thing Rosa did after she marked off a small place to dig? What clue word helped you?
2. When did Rosa begin to use a small brush to help remove the sand?

As you read the next story, notice what steps the children must take in order to enter the art fair.

A Link with the Past

by Kate Holland

One day seemed much like any other out on the Arizona desert—hot! The sun beat down on George's broad straw hat. He could feel the heat soaking into his back as he bent over a patch of rabbit weed.

George was gathering a collection of desert plants. As soon as his basket was full, he would rush home to meet his sister, Susan. Together they would make dye from the plants. They hoped to have enough dye to color the blanket they were going to weave.

George and Susan Lonewolf were going to enter their blanket in the Desert Natural Art Fair. The rules of the fair said that everything entered had to be made from natural things. That was why they were making their own dyes.

While George gathered his plants, Susan was gathering other kinds of plants. She was working at a spot near her home.

Susan stood up to leave. Just then she saw something sticking up out of the ground. She

bent down and looked at it. It was an old pot. She dug it up. Carefully, Susan rubbed the pot with her sleeve. Under the dirt was a very interesting design. Susan knew the pot was very old and that it might be valuable. She decided to take it home. She wanted to show it to George.

Susan walked into the house shortly after her brother. After looking at his plants, Susan showed him what she had found.

"Where did you get that pot?" he asked.

"I found it while I was gathering plants," Susan answered. "If we shine it up and fill it with dry flowers, I think we can use it in the art fair."

Just then there was a knock on the door. It was their Uncle Philip. He had brought along some white, fluffy wool from his sheep. Now George and Susan had everything they would need to make the blanket.

First, the children had to prepare the wool. They began by using brushes to comb the wool. Next they spun the combed wool into smooth, fine yarn.

Then the children were ready to color the wool. Uncle Philip watched them make the dyes. Susan and George gave him an explanation of what they were doing. Susan filled pots with water and set them on the stove. While waiting for the water to boil, George and Susan got the plants ready. Some plants were chopped into pieces. Some were crushed into a fine powder. Others were left whole. At just the right time, George and Susan added the plants to the water. In a few hours, each pot would hold pools of bright red, soft yellow, or deep blue.

At last George lined up the pots of dye one beside the other. Uncle Philip helped put the wool into the dye. Now and then Susan and George would carefully stir the wool so that the color would be even.

Finally the yarn was ready for weaving. George and Uncle Philip helped Susan set up the loom. She and George would use it to weave the yarn into a blanket.

Several weeks passed. The day of the Desert Natural Art Fair finally arrived. Susan

and George had finished the blanket the night before. They were proud of their work.

At the fair, Susan and George carefully lifted the blanket out of the box it was in. The children took their time hanging it up so that it would look just right.

Then Susan reached into the box and brought out some dried desert flowers and a shiny black pot. George could hardly believe it was the same pot that Susan had found. He put the flowers into the pot and set it next to the blanket.

"You did a great job cleaning up that pot," George told Susan. "I never would have thought anything so old could end up looking so good. Everything looks great! All we have to do now is wait for the judges to arrive."

An hour passed. At last the judges came to look at George and Susan's blanket. They asked Susan about weaving the blanket. Then they asked George about gathering the plants.

"Your blanket is very well made," said one judge. "And this old pot is really a good link with the past. I'd say this pot is from the early 1800s. You're lucky to have such a fine old relic. By using it here with your blanket, you have done a good job of mixing the old and the new in a beautiful, natural way. That's why we've decided that the first-prize ribbon will go to you two."

George and Susan looked at each other. They glanced at the gleaming pot resting on their blanket. The old pot had been buried and forgotten far too long. Susan and George were happy they had given it a new home.

Checking Comprehension and Skills

1. Why were Susan and George gathering desert plants in the beginning of "A Link to the Past"? (148)

•2. Did Susan find the pot before or after she was finished looking for plants? (148–149)

•3. When did Susan show George the pot she had found? (149)

•4. Susan and George had to do three things to the wool before it was ready for weaving. Describe these things in the order in which they occurred. (150)

5. How did the objects that Susan and George entered in the fair mix the old and the new?

6. Why could the objects Susan and George entered in the fair both be called natural objects?

7. If you had to make an art object from natural materials, what would you choose to make?

Use a slanted line to show where one syllable ends and another begins in each word.

○8. forgotten   ○9. powder

• Sequence: Time Sequence
○ Structure: Syllables

◆ Getting Started

Several Steps Maria Followed to Make Her Pottery

Maria made every pot in several steps. She began by mixing clay, sand, and water. She worked the clay with her hands. When all the lumps were gone, she rolled the clay into a ball.

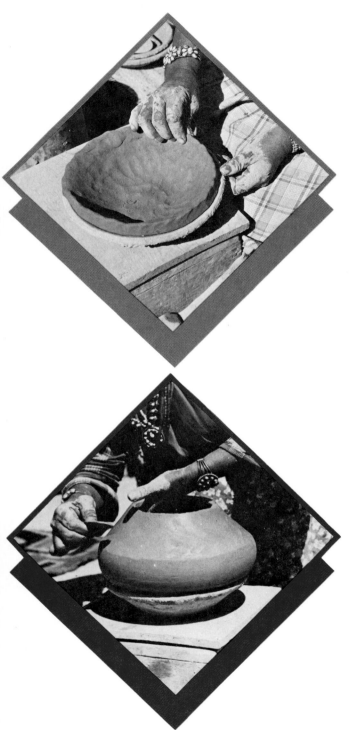

After the clay was in the shape of a ball, Maria formed the bottom of the pot. She pushed the clay ball onto a mold that was made from a broken pot. The mold would shape the clay. This clay in the mold would then become the bottom of the pot.

Once the bottom was formed, Maria built the sides up from the bottom. The sides were made from coils of clay. The coils had to be smoothed. Maria used a spoon, and she used her fingers. She smoothed the sides of the pot from the inside out and from the bottom to the top. During this step, Maria gave the pot its shape.

Maria let the pot dry in the sun before she put a coating on it. The coating was made of thin, watery clay. She covered the pot's surface with the coating and let it dry again.

When the pot was dry, Maria chose the places on the pot that were to be shiny. After she made her selection, she used a smooth stone to polish those places. She did not polish the places that she wanted to be dull.

To finish the pot, Maria fired it. A fire was set all around the pot. Both the fire and the ashes changed the surface of the pot. The polished parts came out shiny black. The unpolished parts came out dull black.

Checking Comprehension and Skills

1. What sort of art work was Maria Martinez known for? (158)
2. How did pottery found by archaeologists change Maria's life?
3. Why did Maria have to use a different kind of clay when she began to make thinner pots? (160)
•4. Which of these did Maria do first whenever she made pottery? She formed the bottom of the pot. She made the sides of the pot. (162)
•5. Which of these did Maria do first when she made a pot? She polished the places that were meant to be shiny. She coated the pot with watery clay. (163)
•6. What was the last thing Maria did when making a pot? (163)
7. Do you think Maria was someone who worked very carefully? Explain your answer.
8. Is there something that you are willing to give the kind of attention that Maria gave her pottery? What is it?

Use a slanted line to show where one syllable ends and the next begins in each word.
○9. polish   ○10. cover

• Sequence: Steps in a Process
○ Structure: Syllables

Buffalo Skin History

In the past, some Native Americans recorded, or showed, their history by painting pictures on buffalo skins. The pictures showed the different things that had happened over a number of years. Each year the Native Americans drew one picture to show the most important thing that happened that year. After many years, the buffalo skin might look like the one shown here.

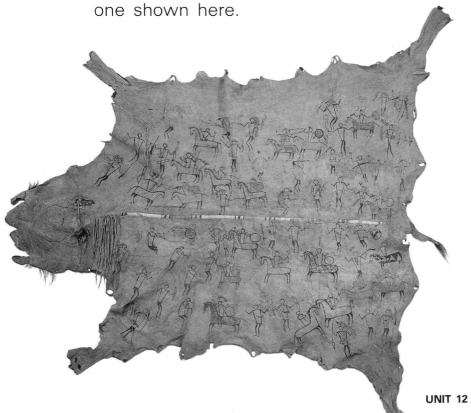

Just for fun, draw the shape of a buffalo skin on a large sheet of paper. Then draw pictures on your buffalo skin. Let each picture show the most important thing that happens in your class during one week.

One week the most important thing in your class might be a history project. The next week the most important thing might be a field trip. Look at the picture below to see how these two things have been shown.

Facts from the Past Can Help

One day Elmo and Elroy, the twins, decided to make clay pots for Grandmother's birthday. The pictures below show how they worked. Which boy do you think used what he already knew about clay pots? What advice would you give the other boy?

Elmo had an easier time because he used what he already knew. Using what you already know can help you do many things. It can also help you get more from your reading.

Understanding articles and stories is easier when you think about what you already

know. Before you read an article or story, ask yourself the questions that follow.

1. Have I already read something about this topic? If so, what?
2. What are some facts I already know about the topic?
3. Which of these facts might be most important for understanding what I am about to read?

Sometimes you might want to make a list of facts to remember before you begin to read. You could write the list down or just keep it in your mind.

You can also use what you already know *while* you read. The facts you know can help you predict what will come next.

Remember Elmo and Elroy the next time you read an article or story. Be like Elmo. Use what you already know to help you get more from what you read.

MEETING CHALLENGES
HEAD ON

They Challenge Nature

Men and women slowly climb up the sides of mountains. They try not to pay attention to the sweat, dirt, pain, heat, and cold that are a part of mountain climbing. When they reach the mountain top, they are alone. There are no crowds to cheer their victory. There are no trophies or first-place ribbons. Their bodies ache, and they are tired. Still ahead is the hard climb back down the mountain. Why do they do it?

Why do other people race down wild rivers in canoes? Why do others sail across seas in small sailboats? Why would anyone try to fly around the world in a hot-air balloon?

These people like to challenge nature. They want to find out if they can defeat a mountain, a river, the sea, or the air.

The Search

When the Girl Scout leader had handed out directions and a map, Pam and Sue knew the course would be hard. They were supposed to leave from the base camp. Then, by using the directions and the map, they were to find the three flags their leader had hidden along the course. The problem was that they had to finish the course in less than an hour. And the course went through some rough country. Pam and Sue would have to go through thick woods and cross a wide stream.

They had found the first two flags easily, but their search for the last flag was not going well. Pam had been trying to cross the stream when she slipped on a rock. She got soaking wet. Pam had to spend time drying herself off. Pam and Sue lost valuable time. They were afraid they would fail.

At last the girls went on with their search. Pam and Sue looked at the map.

"This is where we are," Pam said, pointing to a spot on the map. "We have to get to this bridge and cross it. The flag should be sitting by a stump on the other side of the bridge."

Because they read the map carefully, the girls were able to find the bridge. Once they crossed the bridge, they found the flag easily.

They raced back to the starting point. Their leader smiled at them as they handed her the flags. "Good job, girls. You finished in just under an hour."

Sharpen Your Skills

The **cause** is the reason why something happens. What happens is called the **effect.** Words such as *because, so,* and *since* sometimes signal the cause of something that happens. Sometimes these words do not appear. Then you have to figure out the causes and effects.

1. What caused Pam and Sue to lose time?
2. What caused the girls to be able to find the bridge?

When you read "Hillary Conquers Everest" and "Lost on a Mountain," find out what happens to the mountain climbers in each selection and why it happens.

Hillary Conquers Everest

by May Lewis

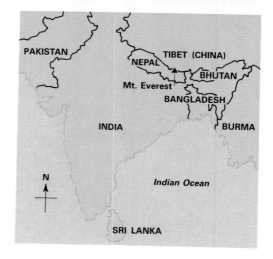

Mt. Everest is the king of the mountains. It sits where the countries called Nepal and Tibet meet. Everest stands so tall that sometimes its top is invisible in the clouds. People can't agree on its exact height. But a widely used figure is 29,141 feet.[1] That is as high as airplanes fly.

Everest's sides are steep and sharp. They are always covered with snow and ice. Wide cracks in the ice can open and close without warning. Huge pieces of ice and snow weighing thousands of pounds sometimes crash down the mountain. Everything in their path is crushed. Temperatures on Everest can fall to forty below zero. Winds reach ninety miles an hour. Near the top of the mountain the air becomes thin. It is difficult for people to breathe.

---

1. 8,882 meters

Up until 1953, no one had reached the top of Everest. Between 1921 and 1953 eight teams of climbers had tried. All eight teams failed. Some of the people died trying.

Then on March 10, 1953, a team of ten people began to climb Mt. Everest. They were led by Sir John Hunt.

Starting the Climb

The team spent months planning the climb. Several tons of clothing, climbing tools, and food were shipped to Nepal. Hundreds of guides helped the team carry the supplies up the mountain.

As the members of the team climbed Everest's steep south side, they set up camps. Equipment was left at each camp. Some members of the team stayed behind at each camp while others climbed on. When the team members climbed back down the mountain, they would be able to stop at each camp to rest and eat before going on. If any of the climbers got into trouble, the people who were left behind at these camps could help them.

One of Mount Everest's steep, snow-covered slopes.

Reaching the Top

On May 29, 1953, after two months of battling Everest, Edmund Hillary and Tenzing

Edmund Hillary (at right) and Tenzing Norgay (at left) were the first people to reach the top of Mt. Everest.

In Greater Detail
On the night before Hillary and Norgay climbed to the top of Everest, they got little rest. In order to sleep, they needed to breathe from their oxygen tanks. Because they had little oxygen left, they could use the tanks for only four hours each. During the remaining hours, they lay awake in the freezing air of their wind-whipped tent.

Norgay were the only two members of the team still climbing. They had set up their final camp at the 27,900-foot[1] level. It had taken them two hours to carve out a place in the ice for their tent.

At six-thirty in the morning, the two men began to climb the final 1,200 feet.[2] Each man carried an air tank on his back to help him breathe in the thin air. The wind whirled about the men. The cold caused their hands and feet to become numb.

Shortly before noon, Hillary dragged himself over the last hump of snow. He looked down the other side of Everest. Hillary had done the impossible. He had reached the top of the king of mountains. Soon Norgay joined him. They shook hands on the very top of the world. Hillary and Norgay had won a victory over Everest.

---

1. 8,504 meters (m)   2. about 366 m

Lost on a Mountain

by Alan Bickley

Gail Naguchi knew she was lost. "Help, help!" she yelled. But no one answered. It was late afternoon. A cold, white mist rolled across the mountain. The only sounds she could hear were the tap-tap of frozen rain on the rocks and the beating of her heart.

Gail thought of her mother and her brother Steve. She guessed about an hour had passed since she and Steve had argued. They had been on the path from the mountain top to the base camp in the valley. "Steve," Gail had said. "Let's leave the path and look around."

"No!" Steve had answered. "It's dangerous and it's getting late."

They argued for a few minutes. Finally, Steve said that he was going to continue down the mountain path. He walked away from her. Gail, angry and hurt, walked into the thick woods. Now she was lost.

Even though it was July, it was like early March on the mountain. Gail was chilly and wet. She was having trouble seeing through the thick fog. Gail was wearing a light jacket. It was quite impractical for this weather.

Gail walked for what seemed like hours, but she couldn't find the path. She knew her sense of direction must be imperfect. "Why didn't I stay with Steve?" she said to herself.

Darkness began to settle over the mountain. Soon Gail would have to find a place to rest for the night. She was hungry and thirsty, but still she walked on.

Suddenly, she came to a stream. Gail drank her fill of water. Then she looked around for something to eat. Some wild berries were growing not far from the stream. Gail picked a handful of berries and ate them quickly. Then she sat down to think.

Gail decided it would be best to follow the stream. A search party could spot her there more easily than in the thick woods. And she'd be sure to have enough water to stay alive until help arrived.

The air was warmer here by the stream, but clouds of flies made comfort impossible. Gail wrapped her jacket around her head to keep the flies away. Soon she fell asleep.

As soon as Steve realized that Gail hadn't followed him down the path, he started to look for her. He called her name loudly, but Gail was already deep into the woods and could not hear him. Steve rushed back to the base camp. He told his mother what had happened. Mrs. Naguchi quickly formed a search party. They began to look for Gail.

During the next three days hundreds of people looked for Gail. Dogs were brought in to help. However, their paws became so badly cut by sharp stones that they could not walk. They could no longer be used in the search. On the fourth day a search plane circled the mountain. Gail was nowhere in sight.

Gail had been lost for four days. Mrs. Naguchi was beginning to think she might never see Gail alive again. Few people thought Gail could still be alive. Yet no one was ready to give up hope.

Finally, the weather turned warm and dry. Soon hundreds of searchers covered the west side of the mountain. They looked under every tree and bush and in every large crack in the rocks. None of them knew they were looking in the wrong place. Gail was on the other side of the mountain.

For seven days Gail had followed the stream. She had been living on the water from the stream and any berries she could find. Under the rags of her clothes, her skin was burned from the sun. Her feet were bleeding. The flies made a feast of Gail, and everything hurt.

Gail dropped down by the stream. She felt too weak to go on. For the first time, she thought she might not be found.

Suddenly Gail heard something. Slowly she looked up. She couldn't believe what she saw on the other side of the stream. A man was coming toward her in a canoe.

Gail stood beside the stream and watched as the man paddled his canoe toward her. When he was close enough to hear, she yelled, "I'm Gail Naguchi. I've been lost on this mountain."

Eight days had passed since Gail had wandered from the mountain path and lost sight of her brother. At last she was safe.

Checking Comprehension and Skills

1. Why is Mt. Everest called the king of mountains? (174)
● 2. As John Hunt's group climbed Mt. Everest, they set up camps. For what two reasons did they do this? (175)
3. Who were the first two people to reach the top of Mt. Everest? (176)
● 4. What caused Gail to become lost in "Lost on a Mountain"?
5. What did Mrs. Naguchi do when she got the news of her daughter's disappearance? (179)
6. Was it wise of Gail to stay by the stream? Give evidence to support your answer.
7. If you had to find someone lost in a forest, how would you go about it?
8. Do you think members of the group that climbed Mt. Everest would have gone off by themselves as Gail did? Explain your answer.

Choose the definition for each underlined word.
○ 9. She knew she would get lost because her sense of direction was <u>imperfect</u>.
nearly perfect   not perfect
○10. The light jacket was <u>impractical</u> for this weather.
very practical   not practical

● Cause and Effect Relationships   ○ Structure: Prefixes (in-, im-)

Doing It Their Way

Sometimes people feel the need to test themselves. They need to find out how much they can improve their bodies, their minds, or both.

People might test their bodies by running or swimming marathons. They might test their minds by solving problems or writing books. These are just a few ways that people test themselves. Can you think of other ways?

Figuring Out Causes and Effects

Michael takes piano lessons once a week.

He practices every day.

Michael plays well for both these reasons.

Sharpen Your Skills

The pictures show two causes of Michael's playing the piano well. One effect can have more than one cause. To find causes and effects in a story, follow these tips:

- To find an effect, ask yourself "What happened?"
- To find causes, ask "Why did it happen?"
- Remember that there may be causes and effects in a story even when you don't see clue words such as *because, so,* and *since.*

Watch for causes in this true story.

Jill Robertson was always on the go. She loved dancing and playing ball. She took swimming lessons when she was only five.

When Jill was twelve, she fell and broke her arm in many places. Her arm became badly infected. Doctors couldn't save it, and Jill lost her left arm.

1. Give three causes of Jill losing her arm. Did you say that (1) the arm was broken in many places, (2) it became badly infected, and (3) doctors couldn't save it? If so, you were correct. As you read the rest of the story, watch for several causes having one good effect.

Jill didn't allow losing an arm to change her life very much. Jill learned to use one arm to do many things she had done with two. She expected to be treated like everyone else. Jill kept playing sports. In fact, her eighth-grade class voted her "Most Athletic."

2. Jill's life didn't change much after she lost her arm. What were three causes of this?

As you read the next selection, look for the causes of Diana Nyad's success.

DIANA

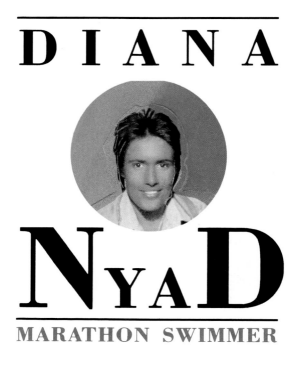

NYAD

MARATHON SWIMMER

by Martha Weintraub

Diana Nyad grew up in Florida. She learned to swim when she was less than a year old. When Diana was eleven, she joined the school swimming team. The team coach was Jack Nelson. He was thought to be a very good coach. Nelson had already coached several young women who later went on to win United States titles.

Nelson could see that Diana was a born swimmer because of her powerful shoulders and arms. He was also excited by her desire to work hard. Coach Nelson worked with the young girl. Diana put up with countless hours of training. She wanted to be the best swimmer in the world.

When Diana trained with Coach Nelson, every day began early. Diana was up at five in the morning. She swam for two hours before school. Diana also swam for an hour at noon. Then, after school, she swam for two more hours. During the summer Diana spent even more hours in the pool.

Diana also learned to live with pain during her training. Sometimes she was in the pool so long that the water made her eyes sore. This was before people wore swimming goggles to protect their eyes from the water.

After her first year of training with Nelson, Diana won two state swimming titles in short-distance racing. By 1966, when Diana was sixteen, she was already a great swimmer. She was looking forward to the 1968 Olympics. Diana wanted to be on that year's United States Olympic swimming team.

In the summer of 1966, Diana felt a bad chest pain during one of her training swims. She became very ill. Doctors told Diana that to get better she had to rest. At the end of three months, Diana was still very weak. She had lost a lot of weight.

It was 1967 before Diana gained back her health. By then she knew that making the 1968 Olympic team was hopeless. Her sickness had caused her to get out of shape. It would take Diana several years of training to be able to swim as well as she did before she got ill. Diana decided to give up swimming. She went to college instead.

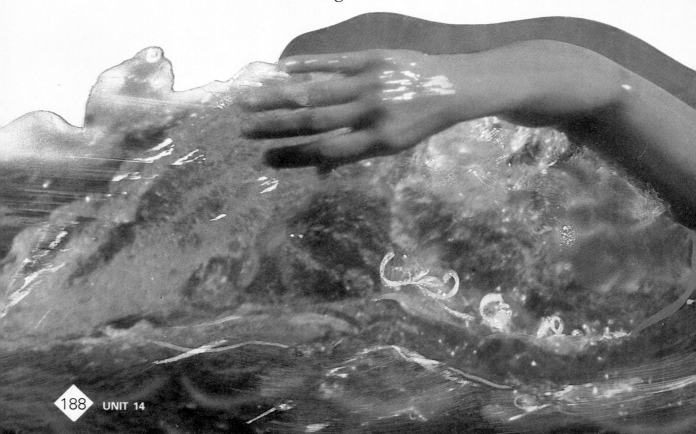

Diana went to a college in Georgia. However, she left school before her first year of college was over. Diana went home to earn some money. She also wanted to think about what to do with her life. In 1970 Diana was ready to return to college. She chose a school in Illinois. She studied hard. She also started swimming again—this time as a marathoner.

Marathon swimming was different for Diana. Diana had been swimming in short races in swimming pools. Now she would be swimming in long races in open water. It was a great test. But Diana accepted the challenge. In the spring of 1970, she began training once again.

Diana raced against men and women from all over the world. In Lake Ontario, she raced

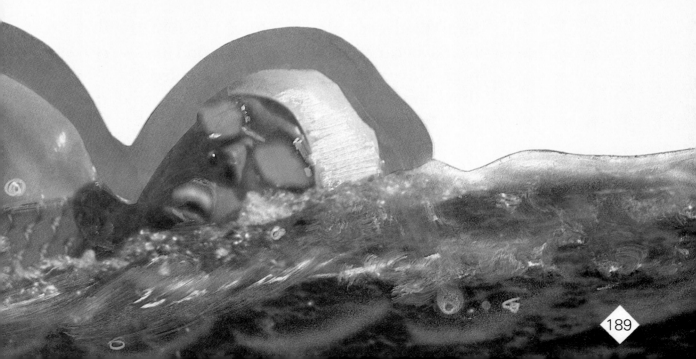

for ten miles.[1] In the Suez Canal, she raced for twenty-five miles.[2] Then Diana raced fifty miles[3] from the Great Barrier Reef to Australia.

By 1974, Diana was the women's world champion in marathon swimming. By then she had also finished college with honors.

Next, Diana decided to try some swims in which she would not be racing against anyone else. Instead, she would be racing against the clock. Diana would try to swim long distances faster than anyone had before. Her first swim against the clock was around Manhattan Island in New York. Her swim around the island was the fastest ever.

Swimming the English Channel (between England and France) is a well-known marathon swim. Diana tried it three times. She failed each time. During her first try, Diana became sick. On the second try, very high waves stopped her. Diana failed the third time because the water was so cold. Her skin turned bluish. She passed out.

She didn't let failing to swim the English Channel stop her. Soon she decided to do something no other person had ever done.

---

1. about 16 kilometers (km)   2. about 40 km
3. about 80 km

Diana is shown inside the cage that protected her from sharks in her Cuba to Florida swim.

She wanted to set a record that could not be broken for years and years. So in 1978, she tried to swim the 103 miles[1] from Cuba to Florida. The swim was to take sixty hours.

Diana tried very hard. She trained for months. Sometimes Diana swam twelve hours a day to get ready for the swim.

On August 13, 1978, Diana began the long swim from Cuba to Florida. She had to swim inside a cage that floated and had a motor on it. The cage protected Diana from sharks. She

1. about 165 km

swam for more than forty hours. Strong winds and a strong current caused her to swim off course. She finally saw that it would be impossible to reach her goal. Diana was forced to give up after having swum 50 miles.[1]

Diana did not let this stop her. She refused to think that all her training was useless. The next summer she did set a world record. Diana swam from the Bimini Islands to Florida. It was eighty-nine miles.[2] She did it in twenty-seven hours and forty-three minutes.

Diana has suffered a number of defeats in her life. But she has learned from each one. After sickness kept her from being in the 1968 Olympics, Diana became a champion in marathon swimming. After leaving one college in less than a year, she returned to school and graduated with honors. After failing to swim from Cuba to Florida, Diana set a world record by swimming from the Bimini Islands to Florida.

Diana is a champion because she has been willing to train long and hard. She is a success because she refuses to accept defeat.

---

1. about 80 km   2. about 143 km

Checking Comprehension and Skills

1. When she was in her early teens, how did Diana Nyad show that she wanted to become a champion swimmer? (187)

•2. What caused Diana to give up all hope of entering the 1968 Olympics? (188)

3. What important championship did Diana win in 1974? (190)

•4. What things caused Diana to fail in her attempt to swim the English Channel? (190)

5. What does the author mean when she says Diana Nyad is a success because she refuses to accept defeat?

6. Do you agree that Diana Nyad has been a success? Explain your answer.

7. What did you find most interesting about Diana?

Which word or group of words tells the meaning of the underlined word?

○8. Diana refused to think that all her training was <u>useless</u>.
of no use   of much use   over

○9. The water was so cold it turned her skin <u>bluish</u>.
somewhat blue   cold   dark blue

• Cause and Effect Relationships
○ Structure: Suffixes *(-less, -ish)*

Keeping Track of Records

Who was the first person to fly around the world in an airplane? Who has scored the most points in a football game? What is the farthest a person has ever swum? Who holds the record for ski jumping the farthest? Why do people even care about these things?

People have been keeping records for years and years. It is one way for us to challenge each other.

Looking for Adventure

While Marcella Hayes was still in college, she decided she wanted an Army career. After finishing college, Marcella joined the Army. She trained very hard and finally became an officer.

Marcella thought flying would be an adventure. So she decided to try to earn her pilot's wings while she was in the Army.

Marcella had to work very hard. Before she could train in an airplane, she went to classes and studied for many hours. Like everyone else in the Army, Marcella also worked out to get her body in good shape.

Then it was time to begin training in an airplane. Marcella began to wonder if she could do it.

1. Do you think Marcella Hayes will learn to fly an airplane? Why or why not?

First, Marcella had to learn about the instruments in the airplane. This was one of the hardest and most important parts of her training. You can safely land an airplane that is in trouble if you know how to use the instruments.

There were still more things to learn. Marcella had to be able to fly different kinds of airplanes. She also had to learn to jump from an airplane.

Marcella Hayes did all these things well. In 1979 she earned her wings. She became the first black woman pilot in the United States Army.

Sharpen Your Skills

When you are reading a selection, stop to predict what you think is going to happen next in the selection. To make your prediction, think about what has already happened in the selection.

2. Were you right about Marcella's learning to fly an airplane? If not, what details could you have used?

As you read the next selection, try to predict whether or not Harold will be able to set a record.

Harold Sets a Record

by Thomas Woldum

It was a beautiful summer morning, but Harold had nothing to do. No one was outside playing. His friends were either sick or they were busy. Harold was bored.

"Hi, Harold," his mother said as Harold walked into the house. "Couldn't you find anyone to play with?"

"No! I've never been so bored in my life!"

"Why don't you read a book?"

Harold picked up a book, *The Guinness Book of World Records.* On page 162 it said: "Swinging: the record time for continuous swinging is one hundred twenty hours."

Suddenly Harold got an idea. He leaped up in the air and ran to the kitchen.

"I have to make a bunch of peanut-butter-and-jelly sandwiches," he said. "I'm going to need them. I'd better make a million of them."

Harold ran out and leaped onto the swing in his back yard. But after a few minutes, he stopped swinging and ran back in.

"Mom," he yelled. "What time will it be in one hundred twenty hours?"

"Let's see," answered his mother. "It's 12:17. Today is July 12. That means it will be 12:17, July 17. Why?"

Harold didn't answer. He had already run back to the swing set. He started swinging and swinging and swinging. After what seemed like hours, Harold called his mother.

"Mom, what time is it?"

"12:52, dear."

"Only thirty-five minutes. I have a feeling this is going to take a while," Harold thought.

Just then his mother walked out.

"What are you doing?" she asked.

"Swinging," answered Harold.

"Swinging for half an hour?" asked his mom.

"Yes. I'm going to set a record! All I have to do is swing for one hundred nineteen and one-half more hours."

"Well, have fun!" said his mother. She walked away with a half-worried, half-wondering look.

Harold just kept on swinging. About 5:30 P.M. his dad arrived home from work. His dad said "Hi" and walked into the house. But in about a minute, he was right back out.

"I hear you've been swinging since lunchtime, Harold," he said. "Do you really expect to break the world's swinging record?"

"You bet! I'll be in the *Guinness* book and all kinds of great stuff!" said Harold. "Oh, by the way, would you please bring out some more peanut-butter sandwiches?"

Dinnertime passed, then bedtime. Harold's parents got tired of waiting up for him. The light in their bedroom went out. One by one, lights went off in other houses. It was pitch dark.

Harold was getting very tired. He dragged his feet back and forth. He struggled to keep his eyes open. His whole body felt like it had been stepped on by an elephant.

At 11:00 P.M. Harold fell asleep.

At 11:02 P.M. Harold fell off the swing. He quickly jumped back on, determined not to fall asleep again.

Harold was beginning to think the night would never end. But at last he saw the sun coming up. Later, he could hear cars starting as people drove off to work. His dad came out to say good-by. Then he went to work too.

At about 9:30 A.M. Harold saw two men walking toward him. One of them was carrying a camera.

"We're from the *Hendricksville Star*," the men said. "You're going to be in the newspaper!"

"Me?" exclaimed Harold excitedly. "Yes. No. I was bored. Yes." Harold eagerly answered all their questions as he got his picture taken. By the time they left, he was wide awake.

Harold was getting bored swinging. He finally found something to do. Harold listened to a baseball game on the radio.

At about 5:00 P.M. Fats Flemming walked over.

"What are you doing?"

"I'm swinging. I'm going to be in the paper."

"You are going to be in the paper?"

"Yup."

"No way. You always say stuff like that."

Just then Harold's dad drove up. He jumped out of his car, waving a newspaper.

"Hey, kids, look at this!" Harold's dad shouted. He held out the paper. The headline said, "Twelve-Year-Old Goes for Record." Harold's dad read the rest of the story out loud: "Harold Skibly, age 12, of Hendricksville, set the Rhode Island state swinging record today. He's been swinging for over twenty-four hours now and is still going strong. . . ."

"The Rhode Island record!" exclaimed Harold.

"Wow!" said Fats. "I didn't think you were really going to break the record."

Just then Harold heard his mother calling, "It's time for supper. Are you coming, Harold?"

"I'm still swinging."

"It's spaghetti!"

Harold was faced with a hard choice. Did he really want to go for the world record? He knew what it meant: four more days of swinging, sleepless nights, boring days, no playing, peanut butter. Or he could have spaghetti.

After all, he'd already set one record. All Hendricksville knew it. Soon all Rhode Island would know it.

"Coming!" Harold yelled happily.

"Time!" shouted his parents at the same time. "Twenty-nine hours, thirteen minutes."

As Harold jumped off the swing, he felt as if he were walking on air.

"I'm never going to sit on another swing in all my life," Harold told his parents later. "It's good to be free again."

Checking Comprehension and Skills

- 1. By the time Harold makes peanut butter sandwiches, you have already been given clues that he might try for a new swinging record. What are two of those clues? (199)
  2. Why did two men come to visit Harold? (202)
  3. What record did Harold break? (203)
  4. What caused Harold to stop swinging? (204)
  5. What did Harold mean when he said, at the end of the story, "It's good to be free again"?
- 6. Did you predict that Harold would give up on his attempt to win the world's record? If so, what clues suggested to you that Harold would decide to stop?
  7. If you were going to try to break a record, what kind of record would you try for?

Here are some words and word parts. Use them to make two words that fit in the blanks.

sleep   wonder   excite

–ing   –ed   –less   –ly

- ○ 8. "I'm going to be in the newspaper!" Harold yelled ____.
- ○ 9. Harold didn't want to face four more ____ nights.

- • Predicting Outcomes
- ○ Structure: Prefixes, Suffixes, and Endings

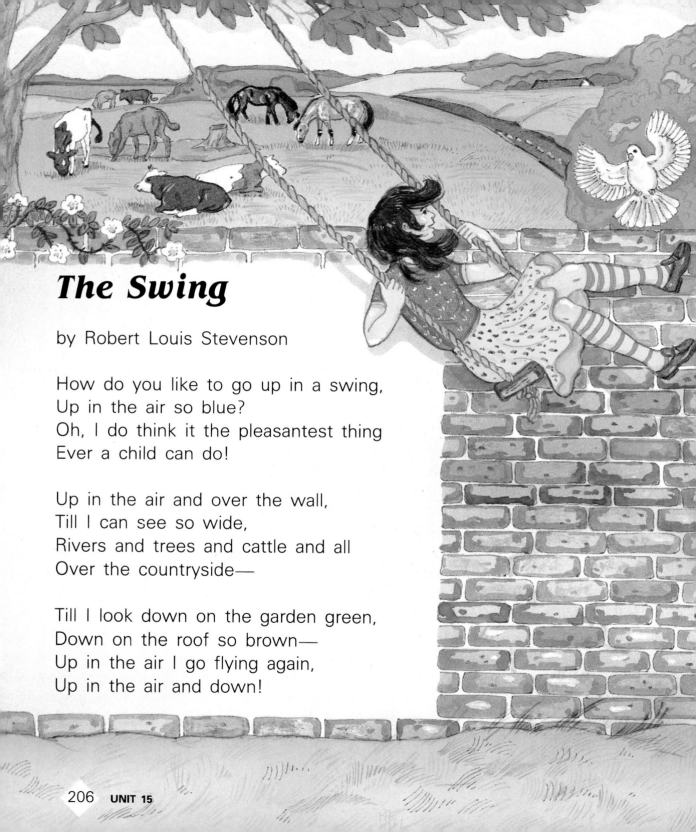

The Swing

by Robert Louis Stevenson

How do you like to go up in a swing,
Up in the air so blue?
Oh, I do think it the pleasantest thing
Ever a child can do!

Up in the air and over the wall,
Till I can see so wide,
Rivers and trees and cattle and all
Over the countryside—

Till I look down on the garden green,
Down on the roof so brown—
Up in the air I go flying again,
Up in the air and down!

YOUNG RECORDBREAKERS

Did you think that swinging for one hundred twenty hours was a strange thing to do? Here are some other unusual records from the *Guinness Book of Young Recordbreakers.*

In March, 1975, nine people pushed a hospital bed 1,000 miles.[1] It took them 308 hours to set this record.

Alan Maki set a record by balancing on one foot for eight hours and five minutes. He didn't rest his raised foot once during that time.

---

1. 1,609 kilometers (km)

Fourteen high-school students leapfrogged one hundred miles.[1] It took more than twenty-three hours.

Two high-school boys crawled more than seven miles.[2] It took them six hours and twenty-six minutes to set their record.

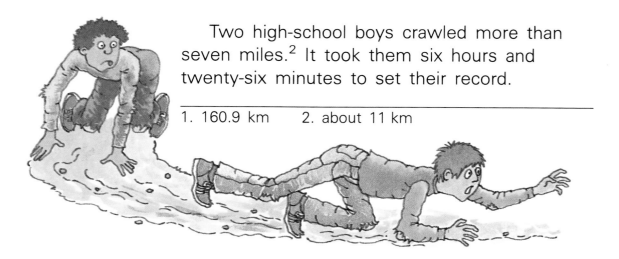

1. 160.9 km   2. about 11 km

Warm Up for Reading

Before a race, runners prepare their bodies and their minds. They stretch to get their bodies ready. They think about the race to get their minds ready. What is the track like? Who else is running? What can they do to win?

Like a runner before a race, you can get ready to read by asking yourself questions. What are you going to read about? What would you like to find out? As you read, some of your questions will be answered. Some won't be. New ones may come up. There are no right and wrong questions to ask.

Look at the article on the next page. You can tell by the title that it's about a marathon, or running race. Here are some questions you might have.

1. When and where was the marathon?
2. How long was the race?
3. Who ran in the race? Who won it?

What other questions can you think of? Read the article to see if your questions are answered.

The Most Exciting Marathon

One of the most exciting races in Olympic history was the marathon of 1908 in London. The race was over 26 miles[1] long. It ended almost three hours after it started.

The first runner to reach the finish line was Dorando Pietri[2] of Italy. He was in bad shape from the run. He fell several times near the end. The second runner was Johnny Hayes of the United States. He had run more carefully and saved his energy. He pushed on, seeing Pietri only thirty yards[3] from the finish.

Pietri fell again. Two officials finally helped him across the finish line. A few seconds later, Hayes crossed.

Runners who get help automatically lose. But because of the confusion, Pietri was named the winner. The American team protested. The decision was changed and Hayes won.

Did the author answer your questions? Do you have any other questions? If so, look up the answers in an encyclopedia or an almanac.

Look through the next section, "Lost and Found." What questions might you ask about the section?

---

1. 42.2 kilometers   2. Dorando Pietri (dô rän′dō pyä′trē)
3. 27.4 meters

Lost and Found

How could you lose a gold mine? 212–221
Are sunken treasures lost forever? 222–239
What's round and safe and shiny and big? 240–252

Looking for Lost Mines

Gold and silver—people have searched for them, fought for them, and died for them. People still look for the gold and silver that is in the mountains and deserts of the southwestern United States.

Sometimes people look for gold and silver where it has never been found before. But often people look for old mines that were rich in gold and silver but are now "lost."

Sometimes mines are lost because they were carefully hidden by the early miners. These miners didn't want others to find their gold and silver. Some of the mines may not even exist. There are few maps that show where these mines are supposed to be. Most of the maps aren't drawn very well, so it is hard to use them. Some of the maps are false. They don't lead to any mines.

To some people, it doesn't matter how hard it is to find these lost mines. It doesn't matter that they may not even exist. These people keep searching. They aren't just looking for gold and silver. They also want to answer the riddles of the lost mines.

The Search for Lost Treasure

One of the oldest lost mines in the Southwest is said to be in Texas. Years ago a man rode west from the Lampasas River. He crossed the Colorado River and headed toward the San Saba River. He was close to the town of Menard. Look at the map to see where the man had journeyed.

Suddenly he saw a cave. He stopped to look inside the cave. The walls were made of silver. The man decided to come back for the silver later. He was never able to find the cave again.

The map on the next page shows where many people have searched for this lost mine. They looked near the town of Menard, around the San Saba River, along the upper Colorado River, and south of the Llano River.

Another treasure is said to lie about eight miles from Brownsville. Some people say that gold was buried there by Mexican soldiers in the 1800s. Forty years later, treasure hunters found the gold. The gold sank into quicksand while they were digging it up.

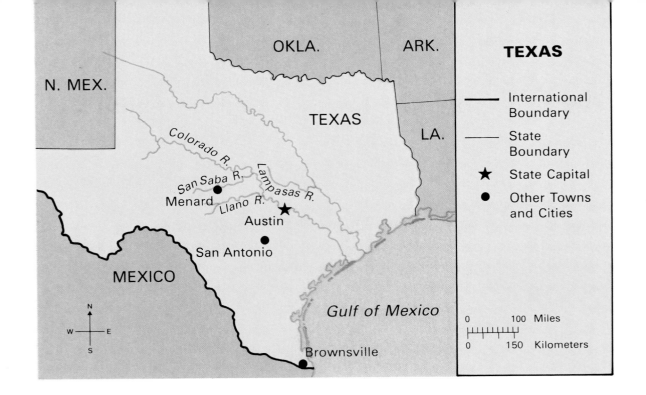

Sharpen Your Skills

Maps can help you find the places or trace the journeys described in an article. Maps show where places are in relation to each other. The arrows show which way is north, south, east, and west. The scale of miles helps you figure out how far it is from one place to another.

1. Is the Llano River north or south of Brownsville?
2. About how many miles is Brownsville from Menard?

As you read the next selection, use the maps to find the places that are mentioned.

The Lost Gold of the Superstition Mountains

by Marianne von Meerwall

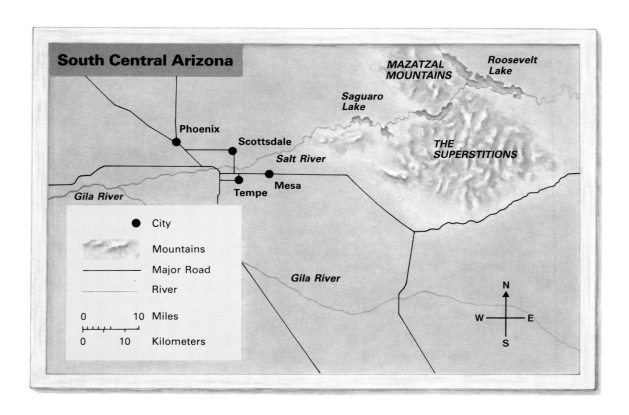

South Central Arizona

MAZATZAL MOUNTAINS

Roosevelt Lake

Saguaro Lake

Phoenix

Scottsdale

THE SUPERSTITIONS

Salt River

Tempe

Mesa

Gila River

● City

Mountains

Major Road

River

Gila River

0   10   Miles

0   10   Kilometers

N
W — E
S

The map above shows how close the Superstition Mountains are to Phoenix, Arizona. Yet the mountains are very different from Phoenix. More than a million people live, work, and shop in and around Phoenix. But, the Superstitions are part of a true wilderness.

The Superstitions rise sharply from the desert. There are no roads through these mountains. The Superstitions are wild and dangerous. Almost no people live there. The Superstitions are also a place about which stories are told.

The most well-known stories are about gold in the mountains. These stories seem to have begun in the 1800s. Prospectors, or miners, have dreamed of the gold that they heard about in the stories. That dream has led miners to their deaths in the rough country. One of the stories is about the Peralta family.

Don Miguel Peralta of Sonora, Mexico, had grown rich from ranching and mining silver in Mexico. He also owned a large piece of land in the Superstition Mountains.

In the early 1800s Don Miguel's mines in Mexico began to run out of silver. Three of his sons went north to see what they could find in the Superstitions. They found gold.

The Peraltas made several trips from Mexico to the Superstitions. Each time they returned home with as much gold as they could carry. It is thought that their mines were near a mountain peak that is now called Weaver's Needle.

The Peraltas were not the only ones who cared about the land where the gold was being mined. The Apaches had lived on that land for many years. They felt the land belonged to them.

At first, there was no trouble between the Peraltas and the Apaches. However, in the middle 1800s the Peraltas made another journey for the gold. By then the Apaches had become angry because the Peraltas were mining on Apache land. The Peraltas began their trip home. They were loaded with gold. The Apaches attacked the Peraltas and killed nearly all of them.

Another story about lost gold in the Superstition Mountains is the story of the Lost Dutchman Mine.

There were really two men in this story. They were Jacob Walz and his best friend, Jacob Weiser. It is thought that they journeyed to Mexico. While there, they are supposed to have met one of the Peraltas, who told them where the Peralta mine was. Walz and Weiser went to the Superstitions to look for the gold. It is believed that they found the Peralta mine. In any case, it seems they did find gold.

After a few years of mining the gold, Weiser disappeared. Some say he was killed by Walz for the gold.

Walz lived to be over eighty years old. He died in 1891. For the last few months of his life, he was cared for by a woman named Julia Thomas. Walz is supposed to have told her where the gold mine was. Walz said the mine would be very hard to find. It is believed that he went to a lot of trouble to hide it.

Soon after Jacob Walz died, Julia Thomas went into the Superstitions. She searched and searched for the mine. But, she never found it. Most of her digging was around Weaver's Needle, which is near Peralta Canyon. The map shows how far people would have had to journey into the mountains to get to Weaver's Needle. Notice the X's on the map. They show where other people have searched for gold.

Some people think they have found the Lost Dutchman Mine. Others think there never was a mine. But today some prospectors still go to the Superstitions. They still believe in the lost gold of the Superstition Mountains.

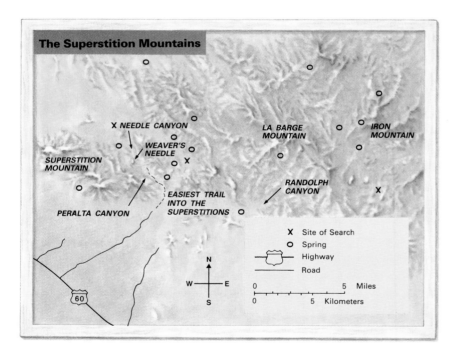

The Superstition Mountains

X NEEDLE CANYON

WEAVER'S NEEDLE

LA BARGE MOUNTAIN

IRON MOUNTAIN

SUPERSTITION MOUNTAIN

RANDOLPH CANYON

EASIEST TRAIL INTO THE SUPERSTITIONS

PERALTA CANYON

X Site of Search
O Spring
Highway
Road

N
W — E
S

0   5 Miles
0   5 Kilometers

60

Checking Comprehension and Skills

- 1. In what state are the Superstition Mountains located? (216)
  2. Why did the Peralta sons go to the Superstition Mountains? (218)
- 3. The Peralta mines were said to be near the Weaver's Needle. What two canyons are near this mountain? (220)
  4. How did Walz and Weiser find out about the Peraltas' mine? (219)
  5. Why do you think Julia Thomas searched for gold near Weaver's Needle? (219)
- 6. According to the map on page 220, which direction would you travel to get from Superstition Mountain to Weaver's Needle? (220)
  7. Do you think the Peralta mines really existed? Explain your answer.
  8. How could you draw a map that would tell you where a mine was but tell others nothing?

  Choose the word that fits each sentence.
  journeyed   attacked   peak

- 9. People think the mine was near a mountain ____ called Weaver's Needle.
- 10. The Apaches ____ the Peraltas and killed nearly all of them.

- Graphic Aids: Maps   ○ Context: Unfamiliar Words

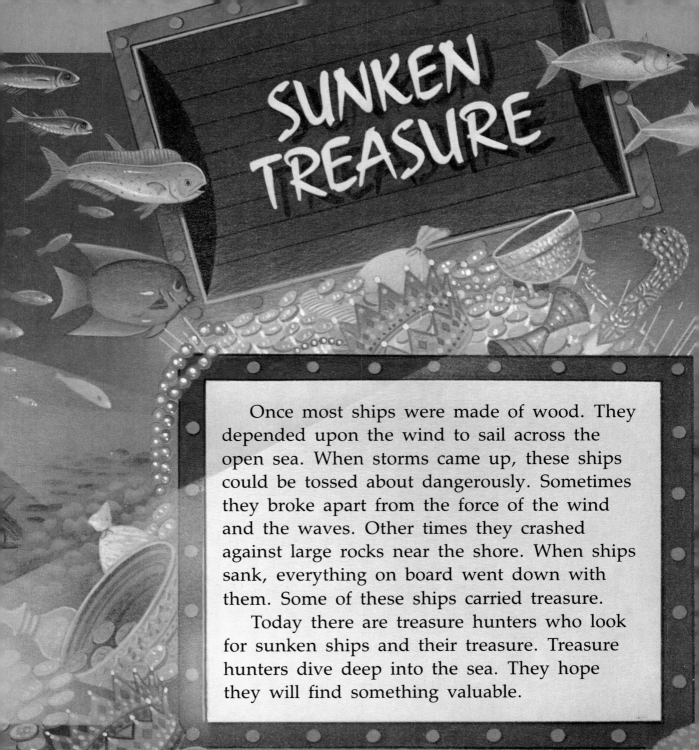

SUNKEN TREASURE

Once most ships were made of wood. They depended upon the wind to sail across the open sea. When storms came up, these ships could be tossed about dangerously. Sometimes they broke apart from the force of the wind and the waves. Other times they crashed against large rocks near the shore. When ships sank, everything on board went down with them. Some of these ships carried treasure.

Today there are treasure hunters who look for sunken ships and their treasure. Treasure hunters dive deep into the sea. They hope they will find something valuable.

Using What You Know

You know several ways to look for treasure. You also know ways to figure out new words.

Sharpen Your Skills

Here are several ways you've learned to figure out words.

- **Context and consonants** Think of a word that makes sense in the sentence. Then see if the consonants in your word match the consonants in the new word. What words can fit in the sentence below—*last, large,* or *lost?*

    The treasure chest is on the l_st ship.

- **Vowels** Sometimes you can't be sure of a word just from figuring out a word that makes sense and matches the consonants. Either *last* or *lost* fits the sentence above. You need to know the vowel letter and the sound it stands for.

    The treasure chest is on the last ship.

- **Syllables** Another way you know to figure out a word is to break it into syllables, figure out the parts, and put the parts together again. Where do you break the underlined words in this sentence?

The <u>letter</u> in the <u>cabin</u> said that the gold was hidden in the <u>jungle</u>.

- **Meaning** Sometimes you may be able to read a word but still not know what it means. Use the context, or the meaning of the words around the unknown word, to figure out what it means. Can you figure out what *bangles* means below?

In the treasure chest were gold <u>bangles</u>. They would look pretty on someone's wrist.

Use one or more of these ways to figure out the underlined words below.

Long ago a ship sailed from China. In the ship were many rings and bracelets made of green <u>jade</u>. This stone is pretty and costs a lot. The ship got caught in a <u>typhoon</u>. That terrible storm made the ship sink. The <u>wreckage</u> of the ship is still at the bottom of the sea. The storm was probably <u>fatal</u> to all people on board. None of them was heard from again.

Use what you know to figure out words as you read "The *Mary Rose* Returns to England" and "Treasure from the Sea."

DIVING INTO ADVENTURE

In order to look for a sunken ship, treasure hunters must know where to dive. First, they look at old maps to figure out about where the ship sank. Even after the treasure hunters find out where the ship sank, they still don't know exactly where the wreck lies. The movement of the water causes wrecks to move about.

Some treasure hunters search around the spot where the ship sank. They may sail over the spot in a glass-bottom boat. Or they may ride over the spot in a plane or hot-air balloon. Sometimes they are lucky enough to find a trace of the wreck from above.

Once the treasure hunters think they know where the wreck lies, they prepare their boat and diving gear for the search. They may also make a schedule for their dive. It may look like the one on the next page.

8:00 A.M.	Divers check the boat and diving gear. They make needed repairs.
9:30 A.M.	Divers put on their gear.
10:00 A.M.	Divers 1 and 2 swim down and search for the wreck.
11:00 A.M.	Divers 1 and 2 return to the boat. They describe their findings.
11:30 A.M.	Divers 3 and 4 swim over the same spot and look for traces of the ship.
12:30 P.M.	Divers 3 and 4 return for a rest.
1:00 P.M.	All divers tell what they found.

Sharpen Your Skills

A **schedule** is a list of events and times that show when the events take place. A schedule can tell you when a bus, train, or plane is arriving or leaving. It can also tell you when different television programs are on. Or, like the schedule in this selection, it can tell you when someone is going to do something.

1. At what time did divers 1 and 2 plan to swim down and search for the wreck?
2. What was to happen at 11:30?

As you read the next selection, notice how long it took to bring up one sunken ship. When you read "Treasure from the Sea," notice how long a trip from Cuba to Spain took in 1733.

The Mary Rose Returns to England

by May Lewis

The warship *Mary Rose* finally returned home to England on October 11, 1982. It had been gone since July 19, 1545! For over four hundred years, the *Mary Rose* had rested at the bottom of the sea about one mile[1] from the coast of Portsmouth, England.

---

1. 1.6 kilometers

The *Mary Rose* as it looked in the 1500s.

The *Mary Rose* had been the pride of King Henry VIII's[1] navy. With ninety-one cannons and seven hundred men aboard, the ship had set sail from Portsmouth with other English ships. The English were on their way to battle the French. The *Mary Rose* never made it into battle. It sank about a mile from shore. Only thirty-six men were saved.

No one knows why the *Mary Rose* sank. Some people think the cannons were not fastened to the deck. A strong breeze made the *Mary Rose* lean to one side. Then the heavy cannons rolled across the deck. When the cannons hit the side of the ship, they crashed through. Water rushed through the hole made by the cannons. The ship flooded and sank.

Finding the Mary Rose

The wreck of the *Mary Rose* was found in 1970 by Alexander McKee. However, at that time he didn't know the name of the ship he had found. In 1971 he and Margaret Rule, who was working with him, were looking at an old chart. They discovered that McKee had found the *Mary Rose.*

1. King of England from 1509-1547

When the ship was found, one of its sides was covered with silt. This covering kept the frame and that side of the ship from rotting.

Studying the Mary Rose

From 1971 to 1982 about five hundred divers made thirty-five thousand dives to study the *Mary Rose*. They brought up seventeen thousand **artifacts** from the ship.

Among the things the divers brought up was a gun that weighed several tons. The gun had been made in 1537. The divers also brought up clothing, games, fishing gear, and a sword.

During the summer of 1982, a team of people prepared to raise the *Mary Rose* from the sea. First, divers dug the wreck out of the silt. Then a large metal frame was connected

artifact, any thing made by human skill.

A gun found on the *Mary Rose* is lifted out of the water.

The *Mary Rose* is lifted from the water.

to the ship. The frame was placed above and around the *Mary Rose*. A week later, the ship and the frame were placed in a metal cradle. The cradle was lined with padding so that it would not damage the ship.

Rebuilding the Mary Rose

Finally, on October 11, 1982, the *Mary Rose* was brought to the surface. It was loaded onto a barge. Then it was towed to the same dry dock in Portsmouth where it had been built in 1509.

The *Mary Rose* will stay in the dry dock for about three years. At the end of the three years, workers will begin to rebuild the ship. It will take about twenty years to finish the job. When the work is done, the *Mary Rose* will look like it did when it was first built.

Once the ship is ready, many of the artifacts will be returned to it. The *Mary Rose* will be opened to the public. People will be able to go aboard the ship. Once on board, they will see what life was like on an early English ship.

The schedule below will help you see how long it takes to raise and rebuild the warship *Mary Rose.*

Summer of 1982:	Divers dig out the wreck of the *Mary Rose.*
Week of October 3, 1982:	A large metal frame is connected to the ship.
October 9, 1982:	The ship and the metal frame are placed in a padded metal cradle.
October 11, 1982:	The *Mary Rose* is brought to the surface, loaded onto a barge, and towed to a dry dock in Portsmouth.
October, 1982, to 1985:	The *Mary Rose* sits in dry dock waiting to be rebuilt.
1985 to 2005:	Workers rebuild the *Mary Rose* to look like new.
2005:	The *Mary Rose* is opened to the public.

Treasure from the Sea

by Pat Magaw

Rod Torres splashed joyfully into the warm waves. Sparkling drops flew everywhere. Rod loved sunlight. He loved summer. Most of all, he loved the sea.

Carmen Torres stopped painting for a moment and watched her son as he ran through the water. Rod and his mother often went to the seashore together. She was an artist who loved to paint pictures of the sea.

During those times when she wasn't painting, Rod's mother would tell him stories about the sea and the ships that used to sail upon it. And he would show her the shells, old bottles, and other things that he had found on the beach.

As Rod was splashing through the water, a glint of shiny metal caught his eye. He reached for it. Rod looked at it closely. The edges were rough. A king's crown was stamped on one side above the date 1731. Rod ran toward his mother with his find.

"Treasure, real treasure!" he shouted.

His mother watched Rod as he ran toward her. "Let me see what you have found, Rod," she said.

Mrs. Torres studied the old coin. She thought about the old ship that had sunk nearby.

"Rod, sometimes old coins from a wreck lie buried in an iron box," Mrs. Torres said. "Many years of storms can break open the box and finally wash the coins to shore. That may be what happened to this coin."

"But what ship could it have come from?" Rod asked his mother.

"Well, in 1733 a group of ships left Veracruz, Mexico, to sail for Spain. They carried goods and treasures from the New World," she said. "One of the ships was called *El Poder*.[1] On board the ship was a load of silver.

---

1. El Poder (el' pō der')

"The sailors on board *El Poder* were restless. They were upset because the ship was supposed to have left for Spain many months earlier. Now they would have to worry about summer storms.

"On July 15 the ship and its crew were caught in a terrible storm. The men on the ship fought hard to keep it from sinking. But high winds and strong waves lashed the ship. *El Poder* broke apart and sank. It carried its load of silver to the bottom of the sea. Treasure hunters have been searching for the ship ever since. The coin you have found may have come from the wreck of *El Poder*."

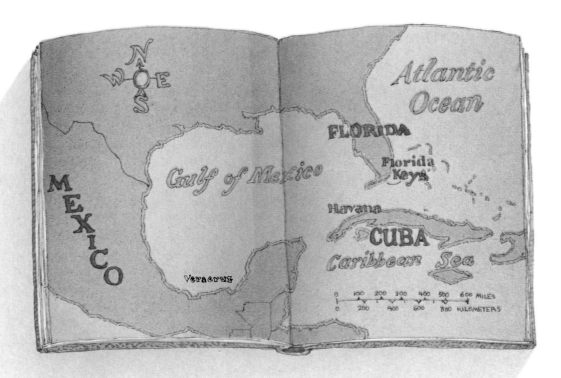

Rod thought for a minute. Then he said, "I would like to know more about *El Poder*. Tomorrow I'll go to the library. Maybe I can find some books about the ship."

At the library the next day, Rod found several books that told the story of *El Poder*. From his reading, Rod knew that if there had been a schedule for *El Poder*, it would have looked something like this:

May, 1733:	Finish loading silver. Leave Veracruz, Mexico.
June, 1733:	Arrive in Havana, Cuba, for a short stay to load food, water, and other goods for trip across the Atlantic.
July 13, 1733:	Leave Havana.
Mid-July, 1733:	Sail past Florida Keys, north past Florida, and then out across the Atlantic Ocean toward Spain.
September, 1733:	Arrive in Spain.

Rod was pleased. He had learned much about *El Poder*. Rod was looking forward to returning to the library and learning more.

Checking Comprehension and Skills

1. Where was the *Mary Rose* from 1545 to 1982? (228)
2. Why did the *Mary Rose* sink? (229)
3. In what year will work on the *Mary Rose* be completed? (231)
- 4. How many days did it take to bring the *Mary Rose* to the surface once it had been placed in its padded metal cradle? (232)
5. In "Treasure from the Sea," how do you think Rod felt when he found the old coin? Explain your answer.
6. How did Rod's discovery of a coin on the beach lead him to the library?
7. Why do you think Rod's mother knew about *El Poder?*
- 8. Use the story and the schedule to figure out where the *El Poder* was when it sank.
9. Why do you think divers are willing to take the risk and expense of searching for ships like the *Mary Rose?*

Choose the word that fits each sentence.
date   glint   seashore

- 10. A ___ of shiny metal caught Rod's eye.
- 11. A king's crown was stamped above the ___ 1731.

- Graphic Aids: Schedules   ○ Word Study Strategies

Flag Talk

Long ago, before the days of radio and telephone, sailors used flags to "talk" to each other across a stretch of ocean.

A yellow flag meant that there was illness on the ship.

A green flag on a wrecked ship warned other ships of sharp rocks.

Can you guess why most sailors would hate to see this flag?

Six more flags are shown below. See what each one means.

stop instantly

carrying mails

doctor on board

disabled

keep clear

about to sail; lights out

Just for fun, you and your friends might make up your own set of flags. See what kinds of messages you can send back and forth without using words.

Nate the Great and the Missing Key

This is a story about a missing key. It may not be gold or silver or sunken treasure, but it is very valuable to a girl named Annie.

by
Marjorie
Weinman
Sharmat

Reading
Bonus

I, Nate the Great, am a detective. I am not afraid of anything. Except for one thing. It's Annie's dog Fang. Today I am going to a birthday party for Fang.

This morning my dog Sludge and I were getting ready for the party. The doorbell rang. I opened the door. Annie and Fang were standing there.

Fang looked bigger than ever and so did his teeth. But he looked like a birthday dog. He was wearing a silly sweater and a new collar.

"I need help," Annie said. "I can't find the key to my house. So I can't get inside to have the birthday party for Fang."

I, Nate the Great, was sorry about the key and glad about the party. I said, "Tell me about your key."

"Well," Annie said, "the last time I saw it was when I went out to get Fang a birthday surprise to eat."

"To eat?" I said.

"Yes," Annie said. "It's the one present I had forgotten to buy. I got Fang lots of presents. A striped sweater, a new collar with a license number, a name tag, a little silver dog dish, and a little silver bone to hang from the collar."

"Tell me more," I said.

"Well, Rosamond and her four cats were at my house," Annie said. "She was helping me get ready for the party. When I went to the store, I left Rosamond and the cats in my house. I left Fang in the yard. I left the key to my house on a table. That is the last time I saw the key. When I got back, Fang was still in the yard. But the house was locked, and Rosamond and her cats were gone. Rosamond left this note stuck to my front door."

Your key can be found
At a place that is round,
A place that is safe,
And where things are shiny,
A place that is big
Because it's not tiny.
And this is a poem.
And I went home.

"You must go to Rosamond's house and ask her where she put your key," I said.

"I went to her house," Annie said. "But it was locked too. I rang the bell, but no one was at home."

"Who else has a key to your house?" I said.

"My parents. But they went out for the day. They don't like dog parties," Annie said.

I, Nate the Great, knew that dog parties were very easy not to like. But I said, "I will take your case." I wrote a note to my mother.

Dear Mother,
I am on a case. I am looking for a round, safe, shiny, big place. I do not know where or what a round, safe, shiny, big place is. But when I find it, I will be back.
Love,
Nate the Great

Annie, Fang, Sludge, and I went to Annie's house to look for the key.

"What does your key look like?" I asked.

"It is silver and shiny," Annie said.

Sludge and I looked around. There were many places to leave a key. But they were not round, safe, shiny, and big.

"I will have to look somewhere else," I said.

"I will wait for you here," Annie said.

Sludge and I went to Oliver's house. Oliver is a pest, but I had a job to do. I knew that Oliver collected shiny things. Like tin cans, safety pins, badges, poison ivy, and pictures of the sun. Each week he collected one new, shiny thing. Perhaps this week it was a key.

"Did Rosamond leave a shiny key with you in a big, round, safe place?" I asked.

"No," Oliver said. "This is not my key week. This is my week for shiny snakes. Would you like to see my new snake?"

I, Nate the Great, did not want to see a new snake or an old snake. I started to leave.

"May I follow you?" Oliver asked.

"No," I said.

"I will help you look for the key," he said.

"All right," I said.

Sludge and I left Oliver's house.

I, Nate the Great, was busy thinking and looking. All at once I saw a big, safe place. A bank. I knew there were many round, shiny things in a bank. Like pennies and nickels and dimes and quarters. Sludge and I walked inside. Oliver followed us.

Sludge and I looked on desks and behind counters. Then we crawled on the floor. If Rosamond had been here, there would be cat hairs all over the floor. I saw paper clips and a broken pen and a penny and mud. And a bank guard. First his feet, then the rest of him.

"Do you want to make a deposit?" he asked.

I said, "Did anyone strange with four cats leave a key here?"

The guard pointed to the door.

Sludge and I left. Now I, Nate the Great, knew where I should not look for the key. A bank was not a strange place to leave a key. I had to think of a strange place.

I thought of a kitchen with bottles of syrup, hunks of butter, and stacks of pancakes. It was not a strange place. But it was a good place to think of because I, Nate the Great, was hungry.

Sludge and I started for home. I felt something breathing on the back of my neck. I turned around. It was Oliver.

"I will follow you forever," Oliver said.

I, Nate the Great, knew that forever was far too long to be followed by anyone. Sludge and I started to run. We ran down the street, up a hill, around five corners, and into an alley. We lost Oliver. I, Nate the Great, still had not solved the case. Sludge and I went home. I was very hungry.

I gave Sludge a bone. I made many pancakes. I sat down to eat them. But I did not have a fork. I opened a drawer. It was full of spoons and knives and forks all together in a shiny silver pile. I had to pick up many spoons and knives before I found a fork. It is hard to find something silver and shiny when it is mixed in with other things that are silver and shiny.

I, Nate the Great, thought about that. Maybe Annie's key was someplace where nobody would see it because it was with

other shiny silver things. A strange place. A round place. A big place. A safe place. Now I, Nate the Great, knew the place! Sludge and I went back to Annie's house. Annie was sitting in front with Fang. She looked sad. Fang looked big. I ran up to Annie.

"I know where your key is," I said.

"Where?" Annie asked.

"Look at Fang's collar," I said.

Annie looked. "I see Fang's name tag hanging from his collar," she said. "And his license. And his silver dog dish. And his silver bone and—my key!"

"Yes," I said. "I, Nate the Great, say that Rosamond hung your key from Fang's collar. We did not notice it because there were other silver things there."

"But why did she hang it there?" Annie asked.

"Well, it is a very strange place," I said. "And remember Rosamond's poem. A round place. A big and safe place where things are shiny. Well, Fang's collar is round. The things hanging from it are shiny. Fang is big. And safe. There is no place more safe to leave a key than a few inches from Fang's teeth. No one would try to take off that key. Including me." I started to leave.

"Wait!" Annie said. She took the key from Fang's collar. "Now I can have my party and you can come!"

I, Nate the Great, was glad for Annie and sorry for me.

Just then Rosamond and her four cats came up the walk. "You found the key!" she said. "I knew I left it in the perfect place."

I, Nate the Great, had many things to say to Rosamond. But the party was starting. Annie unlocked the door. We all went inside. We sat around the birthday table. Annie gave me the seat of honor because I had solved the case. It was next to Fang.

Previewing and Skimming

Skill Bonus

Suppose you were meeting a friend at a crowded beach. When you got there, you glanced quickly at the crowd. You knew your friend had a yellow beach towel. When you saw the yellow towel, you found your friend.

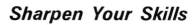

Sharpen Your Skills

You can read the same way you look for a friend. You can look over the pages of a book or an article—or preview the pages—as you look over a crowd. To **preview**, you glance over some pages to see what they are about. Then you may look a second time, or skim the pages, to find a certain fact or idea. To **skim**, you read quickly, looking for important words or dates.

Page 250 comes from a science book. Preview the page to answer these questions.

1. What is the page about?
2. What do you see on the bottom of the page?

4 What Is Known About the Moon?

satellite (sat′l ĭt), a smaller object that revolves around a larger object.

crater (krā′tər), a bowl-shaped hole ranging in size from tiny to very large.

meteorite (mē′tē ə rīt′), a piece of rock, often containing metals, that strikes a planet or a satellite.

The moon as seen from space

The moon is the earth's **satellite**—it revolves around the earth. Astronauts took this picture of the moon from space. The dark patches are large, flat plains. The light patches are mountains and rough hills.

The moon is covered with billions of bowl-shaped pits called **craters.** Some craters are as small as dinner plates. Other craters are much bigger. The crater shown is 112 kilometers wide.

Scientists think these craters formed when rocks called **meteorites** struck the moon. Meteorites often contain large amounts of metals.

On July 20, 1969, American astronaut Neil Armstrong became the first person to step onto the moon. Since that first time, several astronauts have walked on the moon. They left the tracks shown. Notice that the moon's surface is made of rocky and glassy bits and chunks.

An astronaut's footprint on the moon

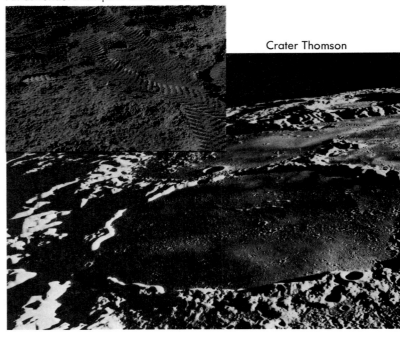

Crater Thomson

Now skim the science book page at left to answer these questions.

3. What are craters?
4. When did Neil Armstrong step on the moon?

Now preview the next section of this book, from pages 253 to 292, to answer the following questions.

1. What is the section about?
2. Which stories and articles look most interesting to you?

Turn to pages 280 and 28l. Skim these pages to answer these questions.

3. To whom is the first letter addressed? Who wrote it?
4. To whom is the second letter addressed? Who wrote it?

When you start to read a book or an article, remember to preview it. Glance at the pages to see what they are about. If you need to find a certain fact or idea, skim the pages. Read quickly, looking for important words or dates.

Books to Read

Family Pictures paintings and stories by Carmen Lomas Garza as told to Harriet Rohmer. Children's Book Press.

The paintings, and stories in both Spanish and English, tell of the life of a Mexican American family in Kingsville, Texas. You will get to know the author as a young girl. You will also see her relatives and friends and the neighborhood kids as they work and play together.

Go Fish by Mary Stolz. Harper.

"Let's go fishing!" says Thomas's grandfather after Thomas stops him from reading for the tenth time that morning. Back home that night after a day of fishing, Grandfather tells Thomas a wonderful story passed down from his "great-great-great-and-one-more-great" grandfather, who lived long ago in Africa.

The Gold Coin by Alma Flor Ada. Atheneum.

Juan has been a thief for many years. When he spies a gold coin, through a crack in Doña Josefa's door, he must have it. Read what happens when Juan finally catches up with the old woman and her treasure.

Decide for Yourself

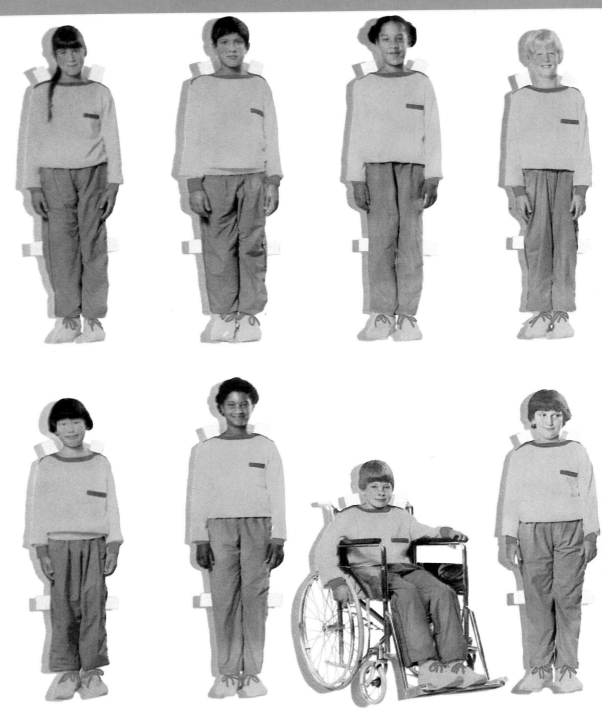

Do Friends Influence You?

Jeff and his mother were spending the day shopping. They had stopped in front of a rack of pants. Jeff checked the rack. When he found the pants he wanted, he grabbed them.

"Why do you have to own pants that look exactly like that?" Jeff's mother asked.

"Because all of my friends are wearing them," Jeff said.

Do you understand how Jeff felt? Sometimes you may feel you need to have something because your friends have it. Or sometimes you may feel as if you should do something because your friends are doing it.

Drawing Conclusions as You Read

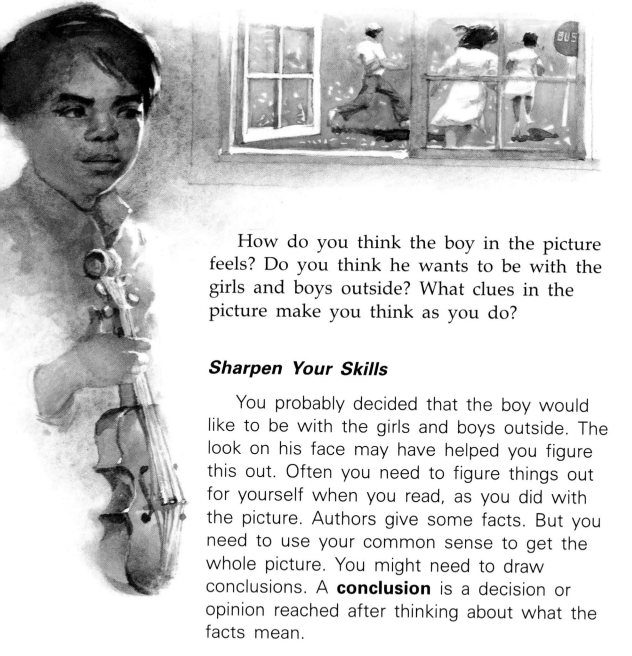

How do you think the boy in the picture feels? Do you think he wants to be with the girls and boys outside? What clues in the picture make you think as you do?

Sharpen Your Skills

You probably decided that the boy would like to be with the girls and boys outside. The look on his face may have helped you figure this out. Often you need to figure things out for yourself when you read, as you did with the picture. Authors give some facts. But you need to use your common sense to get the whole picture. You might need to draw conclusions. A **conclusion** is a decision or opinion reached after thinking about what the facts mean.

Read the following story to find out why the boy in the picture is staying inside.

IMC
SUNNYVALE SCHOOL DISTRICT
DEC 2 0, 1997

Marcos didn't have to look at the clock to know what time it was—four o'clock. That was the time when he played his violin.

Just then the doorbell rang. It was Greg and some of his friends. "We're going to see the circus people set up their tents," said Greg. "Want to come along?"

How great that would be! But Marcos knew what he had to say. "I'm sorry, but it's my time to practice."

That day Marcos played a slow, sad song on his violin. The beautiful music made him feel better about staying inside.

1. Do you think Marcos practiced every school day?
2. What facts helped you draw this conclusion?

Marcos probably practiced every day. You can tell because he knew it was time to play without looking at the clock. Read the story again to see how Marcos felt about Greg's idea.

3. Did Marcos want to go with Greg at first?
4. What facts helped you draw this conclusion?

As you read the next story, draw conclusions about how Angie feels about Mr. O'Connor.

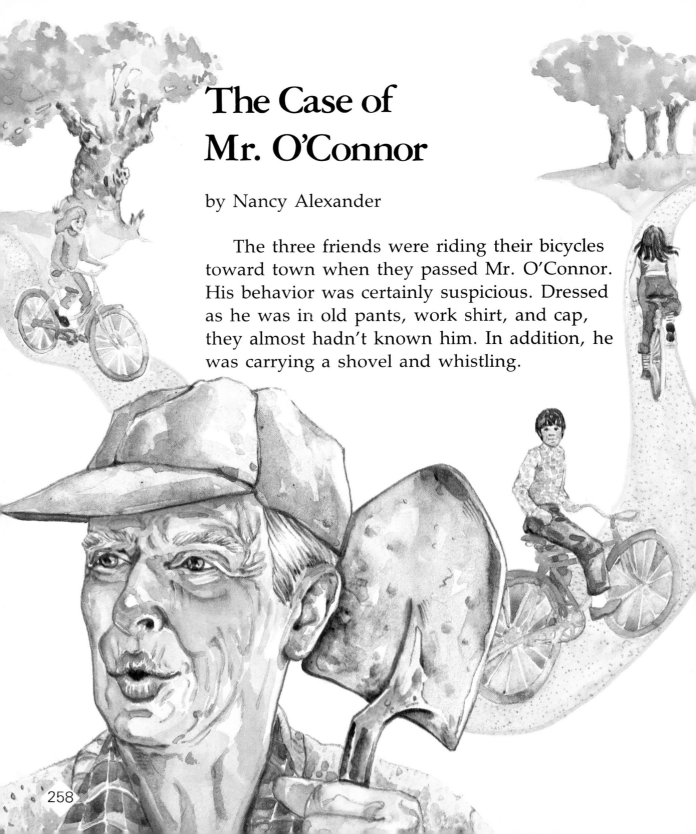

The Case of Mr. O'Connor

by Nancy Alexander

The three friends were riding their bicycles toward town when they passed Mr. O'Connor. His behavior was certainly suspicious. Dressed as he was in old pants, work shirt, and cap, they almost hadn't known him. In addition, he was carrying a shovel and whistling.

258

"That's funny," said Dan.

"You mean Mr. O'Connor?" said Louise.

"He looked so strange," said Angie. "But why?"

Later they figured it out. They had never seen Mr. O'Connor wear anything but a suit. They had never seen him work with a shovel. And they had never ever heard him whistle. In fact, they'd almost never heard him speak above a whisper. Until last week, he had been the town librarian.

"He retired from the library," said Angie. "So he can do anything he wants."

That should have been the end of it. But two days later Dan and Louise came running into Angie's yard. They looked like cats who had cornered a mouse.

"Guess where we saw O'Connor!" said Louise. "He was out at the edge of town, where those old fallen-down houses are. He was digging! I'll bet he's burying something. I wonder what? Maybe it's treasure, or . . . ."

"Hold it! Did you see him bury anything?" asked Angie.

"Well, no," said Louise.

"Come on, then. Maybe he was looking for something," Angie said.

"Or maybe he's cracking up," said Dan.

Angie laughed. "No he isn't. Mr. O'Connor always makes sense." But she did wonder about it.

Then, riding out to the creek one day, Dan, Louise, and Angie saw Mr. O'Connor again. He was carrying a shovel—just like before. The three friends saw him leave the road and head for the old houses.

They hid their bicycles and followed. For half an hour they watched him dig around the bits of crumbling stone wall. He didn't find anything. But he didn't seem to mind.

"He *is* looking for something," said Louise. "It's money that he stole and hid. I'll bet he's just coming back for it."

"Don't be silly," said Angie. "Once he got too much change at the grocery store. As soon as he saw what had happened, he gave it back. Some thief he'd make!"

"Besides," said Dan. "If he were digging up stolen loot, he'd look upset when he didn't find it. Instead, he looked happy. I just think he's gone soft up here." Dan tapped his forehead.

"Mr. O'Connor has always been sharp," said Angie.

"People change," said Dan.

Angie sighed. She had to admit it. Mr. O'Connor was acting strange.

The next day, Dan and Louise had something even more unusual to report. "He's in the cemetery," said Louise.

"Doing what?" Angie asked.

"Creeping around," said Louise. "He has some terrible secret. I think we should tell the police!"

"He might not be up to anything bad," said Dan. "But I do think he's gone weird. I'm going to talk to my folks."

Angie got angry. "How can you two say these things! Just a week ago Mr. O'Connor was his usual self. People don't change that fast. And another thing. You'd better stop following him. It's . . . It's not right!"

Louise and Dan didn't give in at first. But they finally agreed to stop looking and talking.

Angie felt better. She knew she was right in what she'd said. She was certain there must be a good reason for what Mr. O'Connor was doing. And yet, she was curious—too curious to do what she knew she should do. The next day she looked for Mr. O'Connor.

Mr. O'Connor was back in the cemetery. Angie noticed two things. He was interested only in the oldest gravestones, and he was writing in a notebook. Now that seemed more like Mr. O'Connor. He took more notes and left.

Angie followed Mr. O'Connor toward the old houses. When he got there, he took his notebook, a pen, and a tape measure out of a bag. For a long time, he walked, measured, and wrote in the notebook. At last he laid down the notebook and walked out of sight.

Angie decided to take a chance. She jumped up from her hiding place behind a low stone wall, ran to the open notebook, and took a look.

It was a drawing. No, a map. Taking notes and making maps? Was he studying something?

"Hello, Angie," said Mr. O'Connor. "That map isn't finished yet. But it gives you some idea of what this place used to look like."

"Oh, hi, Mr. O'Connor." Angie hadn't heard him come back. "It . . . . It looks like a town."

"It was a town. It was one of the first settlements in this county. As a matter of fact . . ."

Mr. O'Connor picked up the notebook. He turned to something he had written in the cemetery. "Someone with the same last name as

yours," he said, "was born right here in 1881. An ancestor of yours, I'll bet."

"No kidding!" said Angie. "Did you learn that at the cemetery?"

"Well, yes. How did you know?" he asked.

Angie explained that she and some friends had seen him doing some unusual things. "But I still don't know why you were digging."

"I was making sure there aren't any buildings completely covered up. I didn't find any. I'm certain we can see part of every building that was once here."

"I see," said Angie. "Now it all makes sense. When I saw you taking notes and measuring, I was pretty sure you were . . . What do you call it?"

"Doing research?" he said.

"Yes!" she said. "It's the kind of thing you would do. Something to do with books, I mean."

"Well, you were right," he said. "Only this time I'm writing a book of my own. It's a history of our county. One whole chapter will be about this settlement."

"Boy!" said Angie. "Dan and Louise will be so surprised. They were really fooled. They couldn't think what you were up to!"

"But you could," said Mr. O'Connor. He seemed to think for a minute. Then he said, "Perhaps you could help me with my research. You know, history is full of puzzles. You might help me solve some of them. What do you think?"

"I think I'd like that," said Angie. "Yes, I think I would. Wait till I tell Louise and Dan! Or maybe," she went on, "I won't tell them. I'll let them figure it out for themselves."

Checking Comprehension and Skills

•1. Do you think "The Case of Mr. O'Connor" takes place in a small town or in a large city? Explain your answer.

2. Why did it seem odd to the three friends that Mr. O'Connor was wearing old clothes and whistling? (259)

•3. Why was Louise convinced that Mr. O'Connor had done something illegal? (260)

•4. Why do you think Angie got angry right after her friends said that they were going to tell others about Mr. O'Connor? (261)

5. Did it seem odd to you that Angie followed Mr. O'Connor after her friends had stopped? Why or why not?

6. Why had Mr. O'Connor been digging near old houses and standing in the cemetery? (264)

7. Why did Mr. O'Connor think Angie would make a good researcher? (264)

Use your glossary to answer the questions.

○8. Which pronunciation key symbol shows how to pronounce the *ea* in *measure*—ē, ə, or e?

○9. Which pronunciation key symbol shows how to pronounce the *o* in *ancestor*—ə, ō, or o?

• Drawing Conclusions
○ Dictionary: Pronunciation

Making a Hard Decision

Sometimes decisions are easy for you to make on your own. But there are other times when you may need help in deciding.

Adults can often give you help when you have a hard decision to make. Sometimes just talking things over with an older person will give you good ideas. Parents, teachers, aunts, and uncles are just some of the people who may be able to help you.

The Paper Route

"Elissa, Mom and I are really happy that you like your new paper route," Dad said. "But we miss having breakfast with you in the mornings."

"I miss having breakfast with you too," Elissa said.

Elissa had a new job. She also had a new problem. She didn't get to see her parents at breakfast anymore. She also didn't get to see them much during the week. Elissa had to go to school, and her parents had to go to work. They had all enjoyed sitting down to breakfast together. But Elissa enjoyed her morning paper route too. She also liked earning her own money. Now Elissa wasn't sure what to do.

"Maybe we can think of a way to spend more time together on Saturdays or Sundays," Mom said.

Elissa thought about that for a while. Her mother's idea seemed to be a good one.

"I know what we can do," Elissa said. "We can spend every Sunday afternoon together. I'll make sure I have all my school work finished, and I'll play with my friends on other days."

"That's wonderful," Elissa's mother said. "That's a good idea."

Sharpen Your Skills

An author gives you facts and details in a story, but you must often figure things out on your own, or draw conclusions. A **conclusion** is a decision or opinion reached after thinking about the facts and details in a story.

1. How do you think Elissa's parents feel about Elissa's new job?
2. Does Elissa seem to be lazy or do you think she has lots of energy? Why?

As you read "Jacob and Owl," notice which people and events help Jacob make a difficult decision.

Jacob and Owl

by Ada and Frank Graham

One day Jacob found an injured barred owl. He brought it home and named it Owl. Soon Jacob and Owl became close friends. Jacob knew he shouldn't keep a wild animal as a pet. Besides, Jacob had learned that he would soon be going to California for a few months. So he had to decide what to do with Owl.

Jacob's mother introduced him to Mr. Redmond, who ran a sanctuary—a place where wild birds are protected. Jacob began to help Mr. Redmond. In this story, Jacob learns about the care wild animals need, friendship, and the rewards that come from making a good decision.

It was a very busy Saturday morning for Jacob. He was bringing food and water to all the birds in their cages at the sanctuary. Jacob looked forward to working there each week.

Mr. Redmond did his best to care for all the wild animals that were brought to him. He treated their wounds and made good homes for them. What gave him the greatest satisfaction was watching a bird get well. Then he could give it back its freedom.

Someone had brought a barred owl to the sanctuary the night before. The bird had been hit by a car. Mr. Redmond fixed its broken wing. But the owl refused to eat.

"I could try to open its beak and push in some food," Mr. Redmond told Jacob. "But I would rather have the owl really want to eat by itself. Sometimes you can play tricks on a bird."

Jacob remembered how much trouble he had gone through getting Owl to eat. He watched as Mr. Redmond played a trick on the owl.

The older man held a dead mouse. He put it on the floor of the owl's cage. He partly covered the mouse with some leaves. The mouse looked as if it were hiding in the leaves, ready to run away.

Mr. Redmond made a sound like a squeaking mouse. The owl stared hard at the mouse.

"The owl knows the sound I made isn't coming from the mouse," Mr. Redmond whispered. "But I am hoping that the sound will get the owl thinking about the taste of mice. It might even think that the mouse is going to escape."

Suddenly the bird dropped from its perch. It landed squarely on the mouse. Then the owl hopped back to its perch with the mouse and swallowed it.

"Owls are like people in some ways," Mr. Redmond said. "They want to feel they can be on their own just like we do. If an owl is able to do something it is supposed to do in the wild—like catch a mouse—it is sure to feel better."

Jacob watched the owl in the big cage. "Do you think this owl will get better?" he asked.

Mr. Redmond nodded. "I think it will," he said. "That is not a bad break in its wing. I think that in a few weeks we can turn the bird loose, as good as new."

"But Owl can never be turned loose," Jacob said.

"No, because from what you tell me, Owl can't really fly," the man said. "But there are birds like Owl right here at the sanctuary that can never leave. They are valuable too. People come from all over to look at them. Then people begin to think more about liking and protecting birds."

Jacob went back to his chores around the big cages. At the end of the day he stopped at the house to say good-by to Mr. Redmond.

"I won't be able to help you for a while," he told him. "I'm going to California in a few weeks."

Jacob had become so fond of Owl that it hurt to think they would have to be separated. But Owl needed special care. Jacob knew that Mr. Redmond would be able to give Owl the care it needed. Jacob had made the hardest decision of his life, and had taken Owl to the sanctuary. Now the day arrived for Jacob to leave for California. He was stopping at the sanctuary to say good-by to Owl and to Mr. Redmond.

Jacob stopped at the sanctuary on his way to the airport. His mother remained in the car while he ran up the path to the house. His spirits were high.

"You're just in time," Mr. Redmond called to him.

The man stood on the lawn, holding one of the barred owls from the cage. Mr. Redmond held the owl in both hands. He turned in the direction of the river and tossed the bird lightly into the air. It flew away toward the river.

"I think that's the most beautiful sight in the world," Mr. Redmond said. "It always gives me a thrill to be able to send a bird back to its life in the wild."

A look of wonder came over Jacob's face. "Oh!" was all that he could say. He watched the bird fly on slowly beating wings across the nearby river.

"Well, you are going on a flight of your own, young man," Mr. Redmond said to him.

"I have my ticket in my pocket," Jacob said. "Mother gave me twenty dollars for spending money. And Nelson, my new friend at school, loaned me a book about African animals to read on the plane."

Jacob walked to the large cage where four barred owls sat on perches. One barred owl had just flown to freedom. But Owl sat on a perch taking its place.

When Jacob reached the cage, Owl hopped to the wire. Jacob petted the feathers on his throat through the wire. Owl nibbled at the boy's fingers.

"He looks good," Jacob said to Mr. Redmond. "Better than ever."

It was Jacob's way of saying "thank you" to the older man.

"I've been giving Owl some vitamins with his mice," Mr. Redmond said. "He's been living a good life here, these last two weeks. Owls live a long time, and he is still young. I'll bet that even when you are grown up, you will come back and visit Owl here."

"I wish he could fly back to the woods," Jacob said.

"Owls learn how to make the best of things, just like we do," Mr. Redmond said. "Owl was lucky that he had you for a friend when he needed one."

Jacob looked down as Owl nibbled his finger again.

"I was lucky too," he said.

Checking Comprehension and Skills

1. What did Mr. Redmond do with the birds that were brought to his sanctuary? (271)
2. How are owls like people, according to Mr. Redmond? (273)
3. Why couldn't Owl, Jacob's pet bird, be allowed to go free? (273)
4. Do you agree with Mr. Redmond that seeing birds in captivity makes people want to protect them in the wild? Explain your answer.
- 5. At the end of the story, what do you think Jacob meant when he said he was lucky too?
6. Which word best describes Jacob's behavior toward Owl: *caring, mean, lazy*. Explain your choice.
- 7. Do you think Mr. Redmond enjoyed his work? Why or why not?
8. Why do the people you know keep pets?

Use your glossary to answer the questions.
○ 9. Jacob's spirits were high.
 Which pronunciation symbol shows how to pronounce the second *i* in *spirit*—*i, ī,* or *ə?*
○10. Jacob went back to his chores.
 Does *chores* mean *food, work,* or *music?*

- Drawing Conclusions
○ Dictionary: Pronunciation and Definition

Words Can Influence You

The words in one ad tell you that if you eat one kind of cereal, you will grow up to be big and strong. Another ad tells you that a different kind of cereal tastes great. Ads like these try to make you decide to buy something.

Sometimes people who write articles also may try to get you to buy or do something. Every day people try to get you to make decisions about something. But, in the end, the decisions are up to you. You probably want to make the best decisions you can.

Where Should We Go?

Each year at Public School 53, the fifth-grade class chooses where they want to go on a field trip. Anyone with an idea can write a letter to the school newspaper suggesting where the class should go. Then everyone in the class votes for the trip they think will be the best. Here are two of the letters.

Dear Fifth Graders:

Usually our class goes to a place that we can go to anytime. This year let's do something different. Let's go to a play. Most of us have never been to a play. It will be lots of fun, and the play is sure to be interesting too. Vote for this field trip. It'll be the best one ever!

Donna Smith

Classmates:

There are three good reasons why this year's field trip should be to Red Rock State Park. First, it would be nice to be outdoors. Second, guides will teach us about the things that we will see. Third, there is a great nature center there. Vote for this trip and have a great time.

Mary Langford

Sharpen Your Skills

An **author's purpose** is the reason the author has for writing. An author may want to inform you, entertain you, or persuade you. An author usually has one of these main purposes for writing. For example, when the purpose is to persuade you, the author tries to convince you to think or act a certain way.

1. Authors Donna and Mary have the same main purpose for writing. What is it?
   a. to entertain their classmates—to tell funny stories about field trips
   b. to persuade their classmates—to make them want to vote for a certain field trip
   c. to inform their classmates—to describe where the field trip will be
2. Which of the following explains your answer?
   a. The letters give facts and figures.
   b. The letters give reasons for doing something.
   c. The letters make you laugh.

As you read the next two selections, decide what each writer's main purpose is.

What Do You Think?

Would you prefer to go to school five days a week or only four? The pupils at Wildwood School have been asked to answer that question. Here are two opinions. What do you think?

Four Days a Week—That's Enough!
by Renaldo Lopez

I believe we should have only four days of school a week. School is not the only place where we can learn. We should have one day for learning away from school. Think of all the fascinating adventures we could have!

Some people might think we would spend our extra day just playing and watching television. I think we would use it to learn more than we would at school. The best part is, we could all study the things that we are interested in.

Some pupils would go to the library and use the computer there. Others would go there to read about their favorite subjects. Someone interested in nature might take a walk outdoors to study birds and plants. Pupils who like animals might help out at a pet shop or animal hospital. Those who want to learn about machines could visit factories.

Our town could save money too. It costs a lot to run a school. On the day that the school was closed, school buses wouldn't have to run. And the school would save money on electricity and fuel too.

I believe that if we had one day a week to learn outside of school, we would work harder the four days that we were in school.

We Need All the School We Can Get
by Allison Wicks

I am glad we are in school five days a week. Here at school the teachers can give us help with subjects we don't understand. Who would help us on the day that we weren't in school? I don't think most of us would even try to learn if we weren't in school.

Just being with other people can make learning more fun. In school we can get together for things such as sports or music.

At school we have all we need for learning. Our school library has books on all subjects. We also have materials for projects. We even have films about faraway places. At school we are always busy with interesting things to do—writing book reports, putting on plays, going on field trips, and reading books. At home all I do is take care of my baby sister and keep her out of mischief.

Many of us have parents who both work. Who would take care of us on the day that the school wasn't open? If one of us got hurt or needed help, where would we turn?

My grandmother is right. She always says, "Allison, learn all you can at school, and don't miss a single day. It's the best way to make a good life for yourself!"

SUMMER DAZE

by Lois Kuek

Sometimes I wish people would just leave me alone. All I really want to do this summer is have fun. But I can't decide how to do it. Maybe if people would leave me alone, I would have time to figure it out.

My parents are insisting that I do something interesting. "You can't lie around the house all day and do nothing," is how my mother put it.

Well, that's easy for her to say. But what is there for me to do in this boring town?

"Why don't you play baseball?" my mother asked.

"Don't you remember what happened to me the last time I tried playing baseball?" I asked. "It took me two months to get the kids to stop laughing at me. The first ball hit to me smacked me right between the eyes. I walked around for days with the stitches of the baseball stamped on my forehead."

Then my father suggested that I take piano lessons. "You've always loved music," he said. "I think you would really enjoy learning how to play the piano."

That's true. I do love *listening* to music. But the last time I tried playing a horn, our dog Frazzle nearly made sawdust out of our front door trying to escape the noise.

No, neither of those ideas would work. But I had to find something to do this summer. There were only two weeks of school left. If I didn't choose something soon, my parents would decide for me.

I was having trouble getting my work done in school. I had spent most of the morning trying to decide what I really wanted to do this summer. I spent so much time thinking about it that my teacher, Mr. Ross, asked, "Jane, do you have your work done?"

"No," I said.

"Well, please stop dreaming and finish your work," he said.

My morning was rotten. I decided not to go out for lunch recess. Instead I sat in the library. I practiced with the school's computer and then read the school newspaper.

There it was in black and white—the solution to my problem! Someone had written a letter to the paper. The person who wrote the letter was trying to talk kids into going to computer camp. The letter said you would learn to use computers. It also said there would be time for swimming and taking field trips. It sounded like great fun! Why hadn't I thought of that before?

Boy, was I excited! I decided right there in the library what I was going to do this summer. I was going to go to computer camp. This was going to be my best summer ever. I couldn't wait to get home and tell my parents the news. I just hoped they would be as excited about my summer plans as I was.

Checking Comprehension and Skills

•1. In "What Do You Think?" was Renaldo Lopez's main purpose in writing to entertain, inform or persuade? Support your answer with evidence. (282–283)

2. How many days a week does Allison Wicks think children should go to school? (283)

•3. Was Allison Wicks's purpose to inform, to persuade, or to entertain? Support your answer with evidence. (283–284)

4. In the beginning of "Summer Daze," what does Jane need or want to do? (285)

5. How do Jane's parents try to help? (285–286)

6. By the end of "Summer Daze" has Jane done what she needed to do in the beginning of the story? Explain your answer.

•7. Did the author of "Summer Daze" want to persuade, to inform, or to entertain? Explain your answer.

Answer the questions about these words:
boring   practiced

○8. Is -ring, -ing, or -ng the ending of boring?

○9. Is -ed or -ced the ending of practiced?

• Author's Purpose
○ Structure: Endings

Try It, You'll Like It

Here are some ads like those you might see in a newspaper or a magazine. After you read them, draw an ad of your own. You may even want to make up your own product.

The person who made this ad thinks you'll like the "after" hair better than the "before" hair. The ad maker hopes you'll believe that the difference is caused by Hair Glow.

This ad tells you that Frosty is a very popular fruit drink. It also suggests that young people have fun while they drink it. The ad maker hopes you'll believe the ad and want Frosty too.

In this ad, a tennis star tells you that she eats a cereal called Great Grains. The ad maker wants you to believe that you'll do well at sports if you eat Great Grains.

Give Yourself a Checkup

"Vocabulary, good. Sentence meaning, excellent. Understanding of main idea . . . ."

Have you ever been to the doctor's office for a checkup? If you're like most people, you have. Maybe you wondered why you had to take the time for a checkup when you were feeling fine. The main reason for checkups is that checkups can keep you from having health problems later on. Did you ever think of giving yourself a checkup? "Oh, come on!" you say. "I'm no doctor!"

But you can give yourself a checkup when you read. Everyone who reads runs into a problem now and then. When this happens to you, stop for a checkup. By checking yourself as you read, you can cut down on those problems.

On the next page is a list of questions you can ask yourself. Think of the list as a reading checkup! Keep it in mind as you read.

Your Reading Checkup

- Does this story or article make sense to me? Do I understand what it is about?
- Is there any part I don't understand? How important is this part?
- Are there any parts of this article or story I should read again? Would that help me understand them better?
- Am I reading too fast or too slowly?
- Do I need to check the meaning of a word?
- Is there someone who could help me understand this better—a teacher or librarian? Where can I go to get more help?

You can use questions like these to help you with many of your reading problems. You can even use them before you have a problem.

It's not hard to give yourself a reading checkup. Get into the checkup habit and see if you understand more of what you read.

PRESCRIPTION

"Take one dictionary three times a day."

Section Eight

Do You Believe It?

Far-Fetched **FUN**

In the riddles below, the truth has been stretched to make the answers seem funny. Can you find the exaggeration in each riddle?

Question: How do you fit six elephants in a small car?
Answer: You put three in the front seat and three in the back seat.

Question: How many balls of string would it take to reach the moon?
Answer: It would take just one if the string were long enough.

Finding the Meaning in a Dictionary

What do you do if you're trying to find your way in a strange place? Chances are you start by looking around. If that doesn't help, you stop and ask for information.

Sharpen Your Skills

To figure out the meaning of a word, follow the same steps as when you're lost. First look around. Look at the sentence where the word appears. Also look at the sentences that come before and after. See if this helps you get the meaning. If you still need help, you can get the meaning by looking up the word in a dictionary or glossary.

Read the following sentences:

1. You'll bump your head if you don't <u>duck</u>.
2. She put on her <u>spectacles</u> to see better.

Could you figure out the meanings of the underlined words from the sentences? If not, you could look up the words in the dictionary. You might find entries like these:

> **duck**[1] (duk), a swimming bird with a flat bill, short neck, short legs, and webbed feet. *noun.*
> **duck**[2] (duk), lower the head or bend the body quickly to keep from being hit or seen: *She ducked to avoid a low branch. verb.*
> **spec·ta·cle** (spek′tə kəl), **1** things to look at; sight: *A quarrrel is an unpleasant spectacle.* **2 spectacles,** eye-glasses. *noun.*

Sometimes the dictionary gives more than one meaning for an entry word. When this happens, as in *spectacle,* read each definition. Then choose the one that makes the best sense. There may be more than one entry word with the same spelling, as in *duck*[1] and *duck*[2]. You may have to read the definitions for both entries before you find the right meaning.

1. Which meaning for *duck* fits sentence 1 above?
2. Which meaning for *spectacles* fits sentence 2?

You may need to use your dictionary or glossary as you read the selections that follow.

SKILL: CHARACTER

Murray's New Friend

Murray went into the living room, where his mother and father were reading.

"Excuse me," he said politely. "An alien from another world has asked me to visit his spaceship. May I go—just for a little while?"

His mother looked up from her book. "Murray," she said with a sigh. "Remember when you saw a sea serpent in the pond, and it turned out to be a large fish? And remember the time you found pirate treasure, and it turned out to be just a jar of pennies?"

His father looked up from his newspaper. "And remember when you were three and you lost your teddy bear? You told us that it had run away."

Murray looked down at his feet and said nothing to his parents.

"You promised to stop telling those tales," his father said. "Now if you want to visit one of your friends for a while, just say so."

"Yes, Dad. May I go then?"

"Just be back for dinner," his mother said.

"Thanks." Murray went out the back door and across the yard to the big elm tree where his new friend stood waiting.

His friend was just over three feet tall and had four eyes. Silvery fur covered his face and the backs of his hands, each of which had four fingers.

"Can you come with me?" Murray's friend asked.

"Yes, but I have to be home for dinner."

"All right," the alien said. "Let's go."

Sharpen Your Skills

Characters are the people in stories. The main character in a story is the most important character in that story. You can find out a lot about the characters in a story by what they do, what they say, and how other characters feel about them.

1. Why don't Murray's mother and father believe his story about the alien?

2. Based on the story, which of these words describe Murray—imaginative, lazy, friendly, fearless, rude? Explain your choices.

As you read the next story, "Gorilla," look for ways in which Murray is like the girl who is telling that story.

GORILLA!

by Robert Ruddick

If you always expect to get the truth, the whole truth, and nothing but the truth, then my Uncle Carlos is not for you. But if you don't mind your truth baked, boiled, and scrambled, then you would like him as much as I do.

You see, Uncle Carlos is my favorite uncle. But he has been known to tell tall tales.

Today I was ready for him. I had a plan. I was going to beat him at his own game.

I had just arrived at Uncle Carlos's farm for the weekend. He had, as usual, asked me about school. I wasn't fooled. Any time Uncle Carlos asks me an innocent question, it means that he is just waiting for the chance to tell me one of his wild tales.

I repeated his question. "What's been happening in school? Nothing much really. . . ."

"Nothing much, eh," Uncle Carlos said. "Reminds me of that slow summer. . . ."

"Except for the gorilla," I added.

That surprised him. "Gorilla?" he asked, puzzled.

"Yes," I said. "The gorilla who came into our classroom."

"What?" he cried. "A gorilla in your classroom?"

"He was just an ordinary sort of gorilla," I said. "He was about six feet or so tall—until he stood up, that is."

"You mean a gorilla just opened the door of your classroom and walked right in?" he asked.

"Of course not, Uncle Carlos. Gorillas don't know how to open doors." I shook my head as though I'd never heard of such a ridiculous idea. "He just tore the door down and carried it in under his arm."

"Oh, I see," said Uncle Carlos, nodding. I could see a faint trace of suspicion on his face. "But," he said, "were you afraid? What did your teacher do?"

"Oh, Mr. Johnson was sort of upset. He yelled, 'TAKE COVER, EVERYONE!' and then he tried to climb into his desk drawer."

Uncle Carlos looked at me. He wasn't sure what I was up to, but he had a pretty good idea.

I hurried on. "Now you know how small a desk drawer can be. Mr. Johnson just couldn't seem to fit his head in, so he gave up and screamed, 'EVERYONE INTO THE CLOSET! QUICK!'

"Well, I was quick, but not quick enough. After all the running and yelling were over and the dust had cleared, I looked around and found that I was the only one who hadn't made it into the closet. Thirty-four kids and one teacher were squeezed into that closet. But there I was on the wrong side of the door!"

"Just you and the gorilla?" asked Uncle Carlos.

"That's right," I said, "and that gorilla meant business too. First he pounded his chest. Then he threw a desk in my direction. Luckily, I ducked, and it crashed against the wall. I hit him with an eraser, but that only made him mad. He reached for me, but I ducked through his legs and ran to the other side of the room.

"He was closing in on me when I happened to pick up the stick that Mr. Johnson uses as a map pointer. Suddenly, the gorilla stopped. He looked at me, walked over to a desk, and quietly sat down!"

Uncle Carlos smiled. "Do you mean to tell me that a great big gorilla was afraid of a little old stick?" He thought he had me.

"A gorilla afraid of a stick? Of course not! He was just taking his seat. He thought it was time for geography!"

When I told Uncle Carlos that the gorilla thought it was time for geography, Uncle Carlos laughed and slapped his leg. "That makes good sense, I guess. But what did you do then?"

"Well, I had a big problem. You see, I don't know anything about geography! I mean, I hardly know which is North America and which is West America."

"It's North America and South America," said Uncle Carlos helpfully.

"Oh, that's right," I said. "South America. Anyway, now you can see the spot I was in. Here was this eight-hundred-pound gorilla

squeezed into a desk, with his hands folded in front of him. And he was waiting for me to tell him about the Panama Canal!"

"I see what you mean," said Uncle Carlos. "You were in a real fix all right. How did you get out of it?"

"I thought fast, that's how! I figured it this way. I didn't know anything about geography, but maybe the gorilla did. So I handed him the stick and invited him up to the map.

"Well, I was never so happy in my life as when I found out that that gorilla was an absolute expert on geography. I mean, did you know that Borneo is the third largest island in the world?"

Uncle Carlos laughed. "The gorilla knew that?" he asked.

"You bet! I learned a lot from that ape. By the time Mr. Johnson and the kids crept out of the closet, the gorilla was busy tracing Marco Polo's route to China."

Uncle Carlos tried to keep a straight face, but his mouth moved and his eyes watered the way they do when he's trying not to laugh. "What happened to the gorilla?" he asked. "I guess they came and took him back to the zoo?"

"No," I said. "They took him to the principal's office. They hired him full time to teach geography. Except for lunch, of course—that's when he keeps order in the cafeteria. And you've never seen such order. How can you throw food at your friends when half a ton of gorilla is staring at you?"

That did it! Uncle Carlos cracked up. He leaned back and roared. He uses a lot of energy when he laughs. For a while there, I thought the chair would give way under him.

Finally he quieted down, wiped his eyes, and put his glasses back on. He looked at me over the top of them.

"Lucky for you he was a smart gorilla," said Uncle Carlos. "Yes sir, a mighty smart ape, if you ask me. Reminds me of a goat I used to have. A genius he was, and he knew it too. That goat used to play jokes on my other animals, but one day a hippopotamus walked by and. . . ."

Uncle Carlos settled back and told me a tale about that goat that was a little hard to believe. But I just smiled and swallowed it. I had no choice. After all, goats are smaller than gorillas, and if Uncle Carlos could swallow my gorilla, it was the least I could do to swallow his goat.

Checking Comprehension and Skills

1. What did the narrator of "Gorilla" mean when she said that Uncle Carlos's truth was baked, boiled, and scrambled? (300)
2. At the beginning of the story, the narrator said she was ready for her Uncle Carlos. What was the narrator's plan? (300)
3. Who does the narrator say came into her classroom? (301)
4. When does Uncle Carlos begin to suspect that his niece is telling a tall tale? How do you know? (302)
•5. What does Uncle Carlos do while his niece is talking that shows he has a sense of humor?
•6. How do you think Uncle Carlos and the narrator feel about each other? Why do you think so?
7. Name a relative or an adult friend about whom you could tell an interesting story. Tell why you picked this person.

Choose the definition of each underlined word.
◦8. They took the gorilla to the principal's office.
   amount of money   head of a school
◦9. Uncle Carlos leaned back and roared.
   bent from an upright position   thin

• Story Elements: Character   ◦ Dictionary: Word Meaning

Is She EXAGGERATING?

© 1956 United Feature Syndicate, Inc.

Imagine That!

Can you picture a huge purple monster? Would you like to flap your arms and go flying up into the sky? Can you imagine meeting a mouse that talked? If you answer *yes* to any of these questions, you're using your imagination.

With a good imagination, you can picture people and places that never really existed. You can imagine events that never really happened. Sometimes the imaginary things you think or read about can almost seem real.

THE DEAL

Once there was a very small island. On this island was a very small village. The people in this village had children, the cats had kittens, and the cows had calves. It was crowded. There was barely enough food for everyone.

To make matters worse, a monster lived in the sea around the island. Every so often he came to the island and stole the people's food.

The people talked of leaving the island. Across the sea there was plenty of land. There they could grow more wheat for bread. They could raise more cows to make more milk.

"But the monster would never let us go," someone was always saying. One young man wasn't so sure. He decided to visit the monster and talk to him.

"Don't go," said the monster. "I need your bread and milk. I can't eat anything else."

"Soon," said the young man, "we won't be able to feed ourselves, let alone you. So let us make a deal." He told the monster his plan. The monster thought the plan made sense.

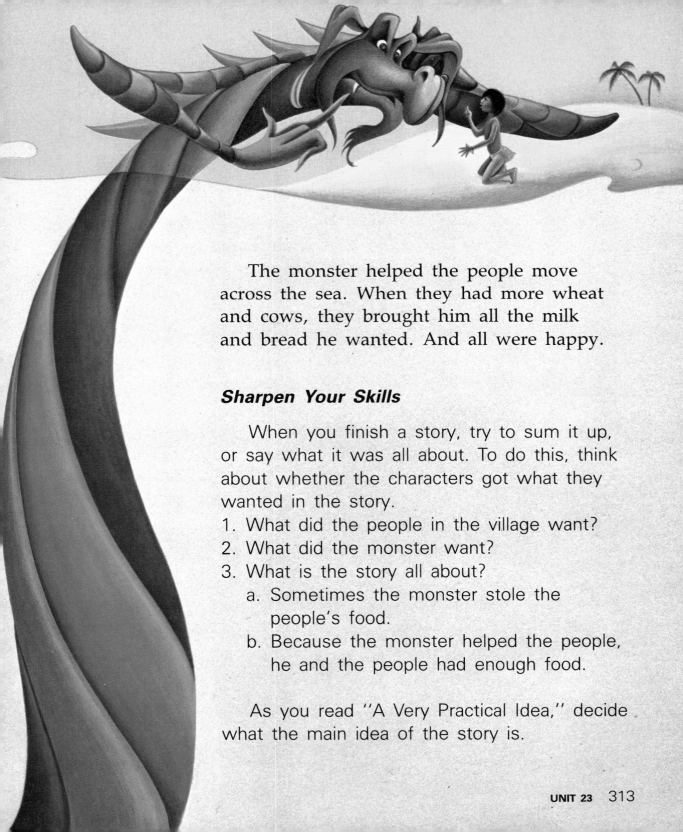

The monster helped the people move across the sea. When they had more wheat and cows, they brought him all the milk and bread he wanted. And all were happy.

Sharpen Your Skills

When you finish a story, try to sum it up, or say what it was all about. To do this, think about whether the characters got what they wanted in the story.

1. What did the people in the village want?
2. What did the monster want?
3. What is the story all about?
   a. Sometimes the monster stole the people's food.
   b. Because the monster helped the people, he and the people had enough food.

As you read "A Very Practical Idea," decide what the main idea of the story is.

A Very Practical Idea

by Tom Llewellyn

Rosalie was sitting on her bed reading a book. Suddenly she had an odd feeling. Rosalie could hear strange noises. They seemed to be coming from far away. Then her bed began to shake, and there was a puff of smoke.

When the smoke cleared, Rosalie found herself in a different place. She was no longer in her own bedroom. She was standing in a small room. It had old-fashioned furniture. The room was packed with things—jars, wires, machines. Stacks of paper sat on tables, and other papers were spread out all over the floor. Shelves filled with books covered the walls.

Then Rosalie noticed she wasn't alone. Watching her was a man in a brown suit and buckled shoes. He was bald, and his eyes were wide with surprise.

He walked over to Rosalie and studied her closely. Then he walked around her, rubbing his bald spot and talking to himself. Finally he stopped in front of Rosalie and gave her arm a little pinch.

"Hey! Stop that!" she yelled.

The man jumped back. "You are real!" he said. "You speak English! You are a . . . girl or boy?"

"Girl!" she said. "Anyone can see that!"

"Yes, yes," he said. "It is only that girls here wear long dresses, bows, and slippers. What do you call those—ah—interesting clothes?"

"I call them jeans, a T-shirt, and running shoes," Rosalie answered.

He bent down to look at her shoes. "Wonderful shoes!" he said. "Please tell me your name, where you come from, and when you were born."

"I'm Rosalie Johnson," she said. "I live in Newton, Massachusetts." Then she told him when she had been born.

"Ah, would you repeat that date?" he asked, as if he couldn't quite hear her.

She did. The man looked shocked.

"And who are *you?*" she asked him.

"Pardon me," he said. "I should have told you before. I am Benjamin Franklin.

"I am a printer," he continued. "I print a newspaper and this little almanac." He showed her a small book. "It is full of interesting stories and words of wisdom, such as 'early to bed and early to rise makes a man healthy, wealthy, and wise.'"

"Mr. Franklin!" she said. "I know about you! You were—ah—are a great inventor." She walked over to a stove to warm herself by the fire. "Is this the stove you made?"

"Yes," he said. "I call it the Pennsylvania fireplace."

"We call it the Franklin stove," Rosalie said.

"Oh, really?" he blushed.

"You made the lightning rod too," she said.

"Why, yes," he said. "How much you know!"

"Well, I read a lot," Rosalie said. "And you are very well-known. But there's something I don't understand. How did I get here?"

"I'm not certain," Mr. Franklin said. "Most of the time I know what I'm doing. I do things for a reason. I made the stove because the old-fashioned fireplace made too much

smoke and used too much wood. I made the lightning rod so lightning would hit it instead of hitting my house and starting a fire here.

"But this," he said, pointing to a large machine, "was just an experiment. All I know is that it brought you here from the future."

Rosalie walked over to the machine. She took a close look. "I think what you have here, Mr. Franklin," she said, "is a time machine."

It was later, when Mr. Franklin told Rosalie he wasn't sure she could go back home, that she felt as if she might cry.

"Since I'm not sure how I got you here," he said, "I'm not sure how to get you back."

"I have to go home," Rosalie said. "Think how my parents will feel if I don't go back."

"Of course you must go home!" Mr. Franklin said. "I have children too, and I know how your parents would feel. But we must be calm and think our way through this."

Mr. Franklin began to pace back and forth, rubbing his bald spot and talking to himself. Rosalie soon joined him, and both of them paced back and forth.

At last Mr. Franklin stopped pacing and walked over to the time machine. He began to tap things. "Rosalie," he said. "please get me that big red book on the top shelf."

"I can't reach it, Mr. Franklin," she said.

"The chair behind you turns into a stepladder," he said.

"What a clever idea," Rosalie said. She climbed up, got the book, and took it to him.

Mr. Franklin began to look at the book and sighed. Rosalie looked at him. Mr. Franklin was moving the book close to his eyes, then farther away, then close again.

"What is it?" she asked.

"Weak eyes," he said. "My spectacles help me see far away. But sometimes I can't see to read."

Rosalie thought about Mr. Franklin's problem. "What if," she said, "you put two kinds of glass in your spectacles? In the top, put glass for seeing far away. In the bottom, put glass for seeing up close."

"A very practical idea," Mr. Franklin said. "Good sense is a thing all need, but few have. It seems you have it, Rosalie. Have you any ideas about the time machine?"

"Only this one," she said. "You did certain things to the machine to bring me here. To send me back, maybe you should do the same things but in reverse order."

"Another good idea!" Mr. Franklin said. "Let's try it. Stand over there."

Rosalie stood beside the time machine.

"If this works," Mr. Franklin said, "I may not see you again. So be a good girl, Rosalie. And keep having those good ideas."

"I'll try, Mr. Franklin," Rosalie said. "And maybe you should leave the time machine alone and stick to making more practical things."

"A word to the wise is enough," he said. "In other words, you don't have to say any more."

They said good-by again. Mr. Franklin went to the machine and began to push and pull and turn things. There was a whirr, a crackle, a sound like tearing cloth, and a puff of smoke. When the smoke cleared, Rosalie was home.

Some years later, Rosalie's mother bought a pair of bifocal glasses. The glass in the top let her see far away. The glass in the bottom let her see up close.

"Did you know," her mother said, "that Benjamin Franklin invented bifocals?"

"I read that somewhere," Rosalie said.

Checking Comprehension and Skills

1. Where was Rosalie before the puff of smoke appeared in paragraph one? After? (314)
2. What did Rosalie know about Ben Franklin when she first met him? (316)
3. According to this story, who had the idea for bifocals? Do you think that is true? Why or why not?
•4. Which of these statements best tells what the story is all about?
   a. Bifocals have two kinds of glass in them.
   b. Rosalie visits Ben Franklin by way of a time machine.
•5. Explain why you picked the answer you did in the last question.
6. What famous person would you most like to meet if you could be taken back in time? Why did you pick that person?

   Choose the definition that fits each underlined word.

   special glasses   stoves   useful

○7. Rosalie invented bifocals to help Mr. Franklin's weak eyes.
○8. Leave the time machine and stick to practical things.

• Story Elements: Main Idea
○ Context: Unfamiliar Words

Mysteries

What is a mystery? It might be a strange sickness without a cure. Or it might be something we see that is hard to explain— like a UFO. Often it's a case to be solved by detectives. Do you think the place shown in this picture would provide a good setting for mysterious events?

Theft at the Circus

by
Donald J. Sobol

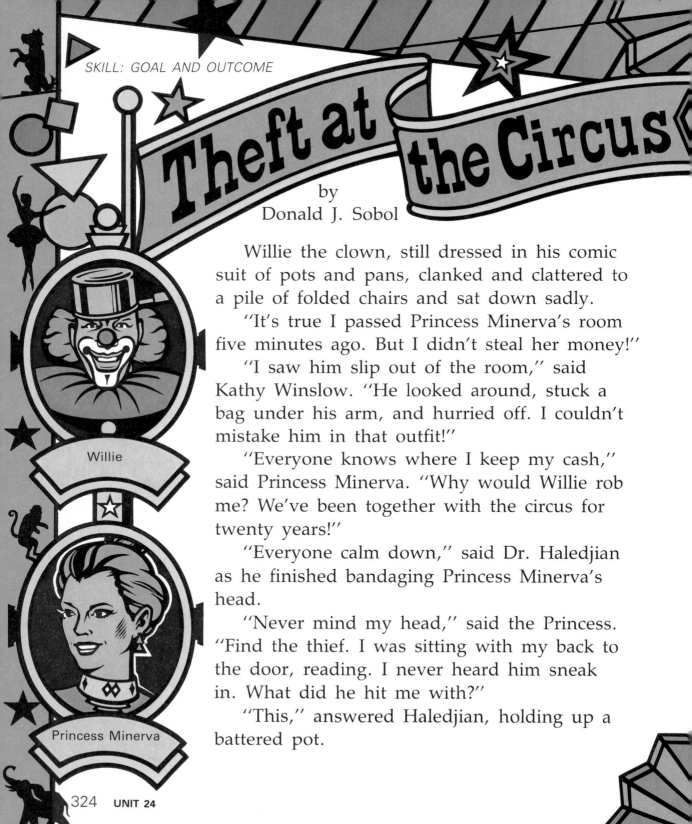

Willie

Princess Minerva

Willie the clown, still dressed in his comic suit of pots and pans, clanked and clattered to a pile of folded chairs and sat down sadly.

"It's true I passed Princess Minerva's room five minutes ago. But I didn't steal her money!"

"I saw him slip out of the room," said Kathy Winslow. "He looked around, stuck a bag under his arm, and hurried off. I couldn't mistake him in that outfit!"

"Everyone knows where I keep my cash," said Princess Minerva. "Why would Willie rob me? We've been together with the circus for twenty years!"

"Everyone calm down," said Dr. Haledjian as he finished bandaging Princess Minerva's head.

"Never mind my head," said the Princess. "Find the thief. I was sitting with my back to the door, reading. I never heard him sneak in. What did he hit me with?"

"This," answered Haledjian, holding up a battered pot.

"It's not mine," said the clown.
"Don't believe him," said Kathy.

Haledjian studied Willie closely. Then he looked at Kathy. "Your attempt to frame Willie won't work," Haledjian told Kathy.

How did Haledjian know Willie wasn't the thief?

Sharpen Your Skills

The **goal** in a story is what the character or characters in the story want. Different characters may have different goals, or one character may have more than one goal. The **outcome** shows whether the character or characters got what they wanted.

1. What was Kathy's goal? Willie's goal?
2. Did Kathy get what she wanted? Did Willie get what he wanted? Why or why not?

As you read "Frightened Town," decide whether or not Burl gets what he wants.

Dr. Haledjian

Kathy Winslow

ANSWER: Princess Minerva said she had not heard the thief enter her room. That ruled out Willie in his clanking and clattering outfit. When Haledjian told Kathy this, she confessed to being the thief.

Frightened Town

by Burl Ives

This is a true story about Burl Ives, a famous singer and actor.

When I was in the sixth grade, our high school decided to put on a play. Since there were only eight or ten students in the school, they had to draw from the grade school to fill out the cast. Because of my singing in public, I was given a part.

The following year the school put on another play. I was given the lead. The play was put on in a hall in the center of our town. Everybody came to see the play. Even people from other towns came to see it. Before we knew it, we were putting on plays in the neighboring towns. Between the acts I played the banjo, cracked jokes, and sang.

I saved money I earned from acting and bought a make-up box. It had greasepaint, eyebrow pencils, and all kinds of make-up.

One night after our play season was over and forgotten, I began to experiment with make-up. I sat before the mirror. I made myself up as an old man with whiskers.

In an old trunk in my father's bedroom, there were a cape and hat. They had belonged to my father's brother.

I took the cape and hat out of the old trunk. I put them on. With my whiskers and gray make-up on, and a cane in my right hand, I stooped over like an old man. I decided it would be fun to have a little adventure.

I walked toward the restaurant in town. On the way I met a neighbor. I walked slowly past her and I saw that she was curious. But she did not recognize me. She went toward her home, looking back over her shoulder as if I were a stranger in town.

I walked past the restaurant. I stayed far enough away so that the people in the restaurant saw only an outline of an old man with a cane, a cape, and a tall hat.

Then I moved away from the light into the darkness. I ripped off the cape and hat, flew home, and took off the make-up. Then I ran back to the restaurant as fast as I could. The place was buzzing with excitement. My neighbor had come in and reported what she had seen on the street. Several people had seen the old man as he passed in front of the restaurant. I could tell in a moment that nobody knew I was the old man. So I said, "Why, I saw him not two or three minutes ago as I came up. He was going toward the church."

That night people who had not locked their doors in years locked them. Children waited to walk home with their parents, and there was an air of mystery around the town.

After a few weeks the old man was forgotten. Then I thought it time that he should return to town. It was in the spring of the year and the roads were muddy. It was difficult for anybody to get around. Horseback and carriage were the only ways in or out of town. So the town had fewer visitors than at other times of the year.

It was a beautiful moonlit night when an old man with a cape, tall hat, and cane again moved slowly down the street. People passed him, but he walked on, saying nothing.

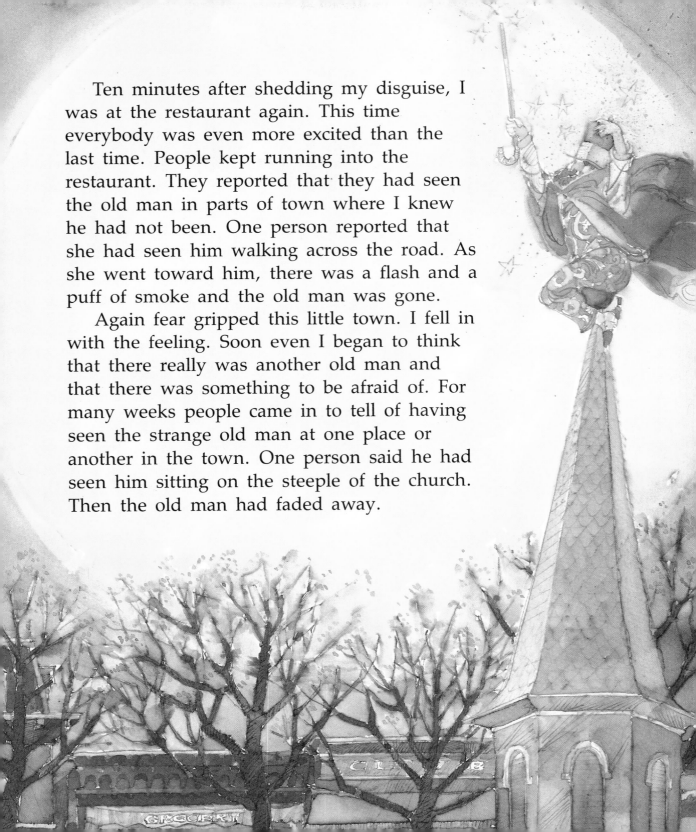

Ten minutes after shedding my disguise, I was at the restaurant again. This time everybody was even more excited than the last time. People kept running into the restaurant. They reported that they had seen the old man in parts of town where I knew he had not been. One person reported that she had seen him walking across the road. As she went toward him, there was a flash and a puff of smoke and the old man was gone.

Again fear gripped this little town. I fell in with the feeling. Soon even I began to think that there really was another old man and that there was something to be afraid of. For many weeks people came in to tell of having seen the strange old man at one place or another in the town. One person said he had seen him sitting on the steeple of the church. Then the old man had faded away.

Summer came. Again the old man had been forgotten except as a story. Then one night, feeling the need for more adventure, I put on my outfit again and went into the streets. Four young men were coming toward me. I thought, should I give ground or should I walk directly past them? I pulled the hat down over my face. I bent on the cane and walked by the four frightened young men. I kept walking and they stopped. One of them said, "Let's catch him!"

They started walking after me. I started walking a little faster. I knew that they intended to catch me. But I also sensed their fear. I turned, with my cape in the same hand as my cane, and lifted them both high in the air. The young men stopped for a second. Then they flew down the street. I ran home and changed. Then I hurried to the restaurant. I reported that I had seen the old man.

The town was stirred up. The old man was reported many times and in many places by many people.

During all of this I became very frightened of getting caught. I did not appear again in this outfit for a long time. Then I appeared again on the street as the old man.

The last few times I appeared were in the fall. There was an empty lot down one of the streets where the weeds had grown eight feet high. We boys had made tunnels through them.

It happened that on the night when the old man appeared, there was a group of men and boys in the street. Somebody said, "Let's get him." All at once they came at me. They were running as fast as they could go. I came to the weed patch. I went through a hole in the fence. I crawled into the weed patch, threw off my cape and hat, and escaped. They did not see where I had gone.

I heard later that some of the men who had chased me said that as the old man flew down the street, his feet had not touched the ground. And as the old man came to the weed patch, he had raised in flight. The men said that they had seen the old man fly into the sky.

I was excited at all these stories and at all the wonderful things that people had made up in their minds about the old man. I felt I wanted to tell somebody that I was the old man. But there was no one to tell. I couldn't let this get out. It had to be a secret. But I was bursting to tell someone. I thought of telling my father. Then I realized he might get angry over what I was doing.

In two weeks I appeared on the street again as the old man. This time I was chased into the weed patch by five or six men. One of them was my father. After I had crawled into the weed patch, I took off the cape and hat and threw them into the weeds. Then I went back by tunnel. I joined those who were seeking the old man.

I started down the street ahead of the men who had been seeking the old man and my father said, "Burl, are you going home?"

I said, "Yes, I think I will."

He said, "Wait, I will come with you."

As we neared our house, he pulled a cape, a hat, and a cane from underneath his coat. He said, "Did you ever see these before?"

I said, "Yes, they were Uncle John's."

He said, "Yes, they were. You might have been killed, pulling a trick like that."

I said, "Yes."

Then he said, "If the old man never appears again I will tell no one. It will be our secret."

We stopped and looked directly into each other's eyes. Until this day it has remained our secret.

Checking Comprehension and Skills

1. Why was Burl Ives given a part in a high school play when he was only in the sixth grade? (326)
2. Do you think Burl was successful in that first play? Why? (326)
3. What led Burl to make himself up as an old man? (327)
•4. What effect did Burl want to have on people as he walked about town in his old-man outfit the first time? (327–328)
•5. Did Burl have the effect that he first wanted to have? Explain your answer.
6. What may have caused people to think they saw the old man when they had not?
7. Do you think what Burl did was funny or mean? Explain your answer.

Choose the definition that fits each underlined word.
  about to give way
  something for carrying people
○8. Horseback and carriage were the only ways out of town.
○9. I couldn't let the secret out, but I was bursting to tell.

• Story Elements: Goal and Outcome
○ Context: Appropriate Word Meaning

Keeping the Meanings Straight

Anna was reading an exciting story. She came across the following sentence: Rex Rabbit took off and headed for the carrot patch.

Anna stopped reading. "That can't be right!" she thought. Here's what Anna pictured in her mind:

You can't blame Anna for being a little confused. Many words have more than one meaning. Sometimes it's hard to keep the meanings straight. But lucky Anna—she knew what to do. She looked at the sentences that came before and after the one above. She tried to figure out a meaning for *patch* that made sense. Then Anna checked the meaning by looking up *patch* in the dictionary. Look below to see the entry she found.

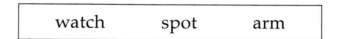

patch (pach), **1** piece put on to mend a hole or a tear, or as a decoration. **2** piece of ground: *a garden patch. noun.*

Which definition of *patch* best fits the sentence about Rex Rabbit on page 335? If you said *definition 2,* you were right.

Now read the words in the box. Each word has two or more meanings. Use the words in the box to answer the riddles below.

watch   spot   arm

1. I am part of a chair. I am also part of your body. What am I?
2. I am a duty soldiers must do. I am also something used to tell time. What am I?
3. I am a small stain. I am also a place. What am I?

Don't forget that some words have more than one meaning. Keep those meanings straight!

Jaws AND Claws

About Bears

by A. Pfleger

Bears come in many shapes, colors, and sizes, but they all have some things that are the same. Their bodies are covered with thick fur. They have short tails. Bears walk on four feet. And each foot has five toes and five long, curved claws.

Bears can live in all kinds of places except deserts. There is not enough food in deserts. Bears can stand up to all kinds of weather. Today, bears live in the few areas of wilderness that are left. Some kinds of bears have died out. Others are almost never seen outside of zoos and national parks.

Understanding Idioms

Yoko has bears on her mind. Does that mean bears are sitting on her head? No. When you *have something on your mind,* you're "thinking about something." Perhaps you have bears on your mind too. Or maybe you have lunch on your mind. Words don't always mean exactly what they say.

Sharpen Your Skills

Groups of words such as *have on your mind* are called idioms. **Idioms** are groups of words whose meanings are different from the usual meaning of the words by themselves. People use idioms to describe things in a different way. You can often figure out what an idiom means by understanding what the sentences around it mean.

Try to figure out what the underlined idiom means in these sentences:

Yoko said, "I've been kept in the dark about the plans to go to the zoo. I don't know when we're leaving. I don't know where the zoo is. I don't even know if the zoo has any bears."

The sentences following *kept in the dark* help you understand what those words mean. *Kept in the dark* means "not told about something." Yoko hadn't been told about the plans to go to the zoo.

Idioms are underlined in the following groups of sentences. Some might be new to you. Use the meaning of the sentences around each idiom to figure out what the idiom means.

1. Sue <u>grinned from ear to ear</u> when she won the race. I'd never seen such a big smile.
2. Myra <u>got a kick out of</u> the movie. She liked it so much she went to see it a second time.
3. I didn't know it was supposed to be a surprise party for Manuel when I asked him about it. I <u>let the cat out of the bag.</u>
4. Kevin <u>chickened out</u> of the bicycle race. He was afraid to ride his new bicycle.
5. You always do what you say you will do. I know we can <u>count on</u> you.

You'll come across many idioms as you read. If you don't know the meaning of a group of words, try to figure it out from the meaning of the sentences around it. Then you'll catch on!

Bear Prints

by A. Pfleger

Bears have five long, curved claws on each foot. Their claws are very sharp. They cannot pull their claws in under their foot pads as cats can. As a bear gets older, its claws get worn down like old shoe soles.

Bears use their claws to dig into tree bark when they are climbing. They also use their claws to fight their enemies.

Bears follow the paths of other bears in the woods. They would rather stay on bear paths than make their own paths. They step carefully into the footprints of the bears that went before them.

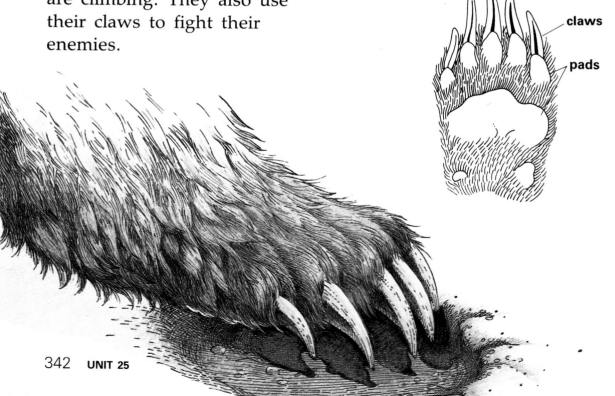

claws

pads

The Singing Bear

by Laura Geringer

Gerry Durrell was a new keeper in a special zoo that was like a big farm.

One day, while bicycling past the bears, Gerry heard a strange noise. He hopped off his bicycle to look. The sound led him to a blackberry clump. There Gerry saw Teddy the bear singing to himself.

Gerry watched for a while. Then he began to sing. To his surprise, Teddy joined in.

From that day on, Gerry and Teddy sang together every day.

Sharpen Your Skills

The writer of a story may want to inform you, persuade you, or entertain you.
1. What information does "Bear Prints" give you about bears' claws?
2. Is "The Singing Bear" meant to entertain you? Why or why not?

See if you can tell what the author's purpose is in "The Story of Yakutat Barry."

The Story of Yakutat Barry

by Laura Geringer

In Yakutat country in Alaska there lives a very rare animal. It is called the blue bear because of the blue shading in its fur. This is a true story about a blue bear named Yakutat Barry.

Yakutat Barry lived alone in the woods. Barry knew how to find grubs and bugs, juicy roots, and berries to eat. He turned rocks over and licked up ants with his tongue. Barry could walk into a stream and grab fish as they swam by.

But life was not easy for Barry. Often his hunting left him hungry. Sometimes Barry cried himself to sleep.

One day Barry followed a scent until he came to a group of huts near a beach. Lined up in front was a neat row of garbage cans. Barry tipped them over, and garbage came spilling out. He ate all he wanted. Barry began to return to the same place every day. At last he had found a home.

Barry did not know it, but the home he had found was a Coast Guard station. The men there were very excited when they saw him. They began to set out bits of the cook's best meals for Barry.

After a while, Barry began to trust them. He let the men come closer and closer to him with food. He was becoming almost tame.

One man at the station, Jim Jenson, was worried about Barry. Jim knew it wasn't safe for a bear to lose his shy ways—especially this bear. Hunting season was in full swing, and Barry was a prize. His blue fur made him very valuable.

Meanwhile, stories about Barry were flying around town. Hunters had already offered a reward for his hide.

The blue bear was safe only as long as he stayed on the land owned by the Coast Guard. The hunters could not get him while he was on Coast Guard land. The Coast Guard would protect him. But how was Barry to know where the safe land began and ended?

One night a guard making the rounds heard a bumping noise. He crept around softly in the dark station. A window in the kitchen was open. Barry stood inside by the sink. He had gobbled up a crate of banana-cream cupcakes.

The men liked Barry. But they did not welcome the thought of Barry in their home. They knew a bear could be very dangerous if it was suddenly frightened. Now the men were sorry they had made friends with Barry. The lieutenant in charge of the post called a meeting.

Plan after plan was discussed. Not one plan seemed right. If they took away Barry's food, he would leave. Then they would be out of danger. But by now Barry trusted people. He would no longer hide from them—even if they were hunters.

Jim knew he would have to do something fast. He remembered reading that some zoos were interested in saving rare animals. He called the San Diego Zoo. The curator was very excited. As far as he knew, there was no blue bear in any zoo in the world.

The zoo workers held a meeting. They formed a crew called Operation Blue Bear. They wanted to save Barry. However, they weren't sure if they could get to Alaska and find Barry before the hunters caught him.

At last a plane carrying the crew landed in Yakutat, Alaska. The curator, a photographer, and Chuck Sedgewick, who would catch Barry, were on board.

The plan was for Chuck to shoot Barry with a dart gun that held a drug. The bear would slow down and then lie still. This would not hurt him and would wear off later, after they had put him into a cage.

By eight o'clock in the evening, the men were all waiting at a window close to the garbage cans. They listened for Barry. The hours passed. No Barry. Midnight came. Still no Barry.

In the morning the crew from the zoo was hopeful once again. They bought two packs of bacon. The men ate one for breakfast and hung the other over the trees to attract Barry. Then the crew flew over Barry's range in airplanes and looked for him. They saw no sign of Barry.

The crew guessed that Barry was looking for a winter den. But where had he gone? Then they heard some good news. Barry had been seen feeding near the home of a state forest ranger.

The men knew this was their last chance because the weather was turning bad. If they didn't find the bear that night, they would have to return to San Diego without him.

Early in the evening, they took their places in a small shed. After only an hour, two of the men were so chilled they called off the watch. Only Chuck stayed up.

Suddenly, Chuck forgot about his fingers getting cold. A bear was peeking around the far corner of the house. It stopped to make sure the coast was clear. Then it walked out into the open.

Just at that moment, a truck drove up. It screeched to a halt. In a flash, the bear was gone. It seemed that Chuck had failed.

But Chuck stayed longer. Huddled up, he stared into the night. The bear peeked around the corner again. This time it was twice as shy. It sniffed for smells and listened for sounds. Then the bear stepped forward. Chuck couldn't be sure it was the right bear, but he knew he had to take a chance. Slowly he brought the dart gun to his shoulder and carefully took aim.

Before Chuck knew what was happening, the bear charged straight at him. Then it turned and jumped into a pine tree. Chuck stepped outside and yelled. The bear climbed higher. Then Chuck shot. A few minutes later, the bear slid slowly down the tree and bumped the ground. Chuck turned his flashlight on. The bear's coat was shining like frost. It was Barry.

When the blue bear next awoke, he was on his way to a safe home in the San Diego Zoo.

Checking Comprehension and Skills

1. In what state is Yakutat country? (344)
2. What caused Yakutat Barry to go to the Coast Guard Station? (345)
3. How did the men of the Coast Guard Station begin to tame Barry? (345)
4. Why was Barry safe only while he was on Coast Guard land? (346)
5. Why did Barry's growing trust of humans endanger his life? (347)
6. How did people from the San Diego Zoo help the people of the Coast Guard Station?
- 7. What do you think this author's main purpose was—to persuade, to inform, or to entertain? Explain your answer.
- 8. Do you think the author had a second purpose in mind? If so, what do you think it was?

Note the underlined idiom in each sentence below. Choose the group of words that you think has the same meaning as the idiom. Rereading page 349 may help you figure out the meaning.

nothing was on the seacoast   very quickly
in a burst of light   no people were in sight

- 9. It stopped to make sure the coast was clear.
- 10. In a flash, the bear was gone.

- Author's Purpose   ○ Context: Idioms

Bears

by Elizabeth Coatsworth

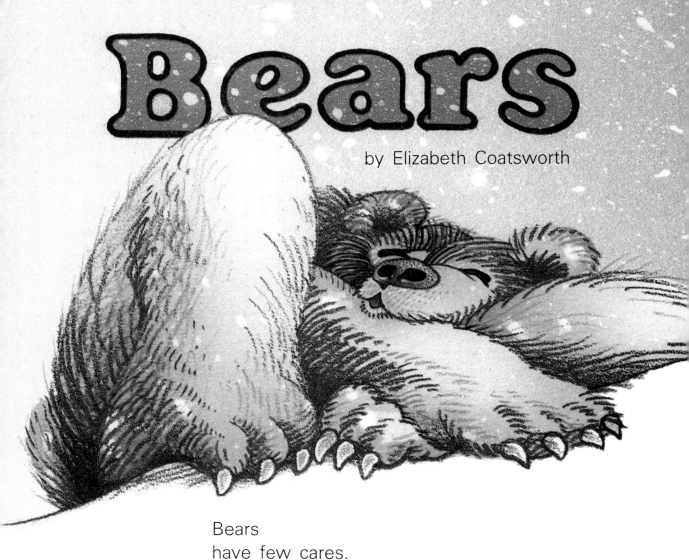

Bears
have few cares.
When the wind blows cold and the snow drifts
deep
they sleep and sleep and sleep and sleep.

Furry Bear

by A. A. Milne

If I were a bear
And a big bear too,
I shouldn't much care
If it froze or snew;
I shouldn't much mind
If it snowed or friz—
I'd be all fur-lined
With a coat like his!

Finding Out About Sharks

How do we find out about sharks? Sometimes sharks are caught in the ocean and taken to a place like Sea World in Florida. Here they are given a new home in a huge tank of water called an aquarium. People can visit Sea World and see how these sharks live.

Sometimes scientists use special gear to dive into the sea and study sharks. These people might even go down deep in a large shark cage. This cage protects people so that they can get near the sharks without being in any danger.

By studying sharks where they live, we can find out why they act the way they do. As we learn more facts about sharks, we will understand them better.

Shark Facts

What do you think of when you hear the word *sharks?* You may be surprised to discover the truth about these fish. Did you know that sharks do not have any bones or that some sharks are tiny, while others are quite large?

Sharks do not have ears like ours, but they notice sounds. Their sight is good, and they notice anything that moves. Sometimes sharks get excited when something nearby moves quickly. They may even attack.

Some sharks feed on ocean plants. Some eat fish or other water animals. You may have heard that sharks are dangerous. The truth is that they do not often attack people.

Both photos above show blue sharks.

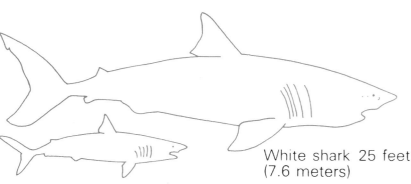

White shark 25 feet (7.6 meters)

Mako shark 12 feet (3.7 meters)

Old Whitecap

Long ago there lived a sailor named Old Whitecap. He wasn't afraid of anything. Some say he looked like a wild monster. His teeth had sharp points from eating hard biscuits.

One evening when Old Whitecap was out in a rowboat, a hungry shark came up to him.

"Best of the evening to you, Shark," said the sailor. "I'm looking for a lovely, juicy shark steak to have for supper." Old Whitecap smiled. His teeth gleamed in the setting sun.

The shark closed its eyes, shuddered, and got away from the sailor as fast as it could.

Sharpen Your Skills

An article or story that gives facts about real people, places, things, and events is **nonfiction. Fiction,** on the other hand, comes mostly from the writer's imagination.
1. Is "Shark Facts" fiction or nonfiction? Why do you think so?
2. Is "Old Whitecap" fiction or nonfiction? Why do you think so?

When you read "The Shape in the Harbor," decide if it is fiction or nonfiction.

The Shape in the Harbor

by Mike Eagle

It was an early morning in July. The sun rose slowly, and the sea began to shine in its light. The harbor was a plate of glass that mirrored the docks, the boats, and the morning sun. The tide was coming in. A gull glided above the water.

Art Hatch was busy checking the gear on his boat. As he worked, he kept an eye on the bird. Suddenly it screamed and flew away out of the harbor. Art didn't see what had alarmed the bird, and he didn't notice the slowly moving shape in the harbor.

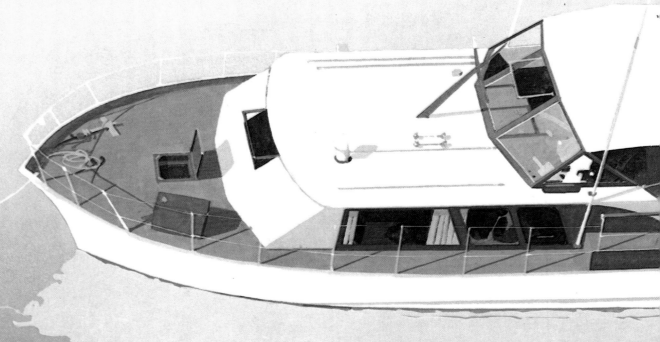

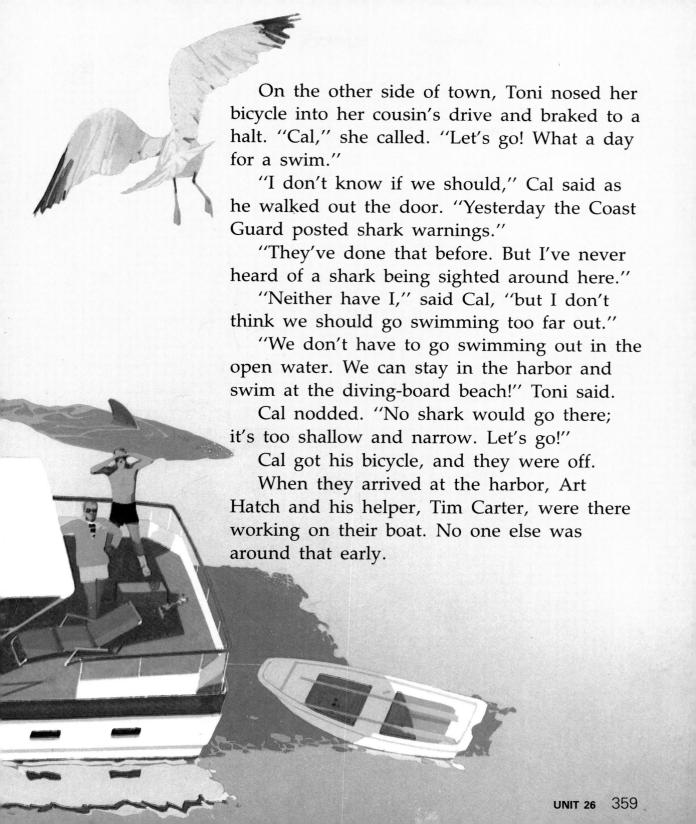

On the other side of town, Toni nosed her bicycle into her cousin's drive and braked to a halt. "Cal," she called. "Let's go! What a day for a swim."

"I don't know if we should," Cal said as he walked out the door. "Yesterday the Coast Guard posted shark warnings."

"They've done that before. But I've never heard of a shark being sighted around here."

"Neither have I," said Cal, "but I don't think we should go swimming too far out."

"We don't have to go swimming out in the open water. We can stay in the harbor and swim at the diving-board beach!" Toni said.

Cal nodded. "No shark would go there; it's too shallow and narrow. Let's go!"

Cal got his bicycle, and they were off.

When they arrived at the harbor, Art Hatch and his helper, Tim Carter, were there working on their boat. No one else was around that early.

Toni and Cal crossed the bridge. Halfway across, Toni slammed on her brakes. Cal, who was following, turned sharply to avoid running into Toni.

"Why did you stop like that?" Cal yelled.

Toni was staring down into the water. "Did you see something big in the water, Cal?"

"I wasn't looking. What did you see?"

"I couldn't make it out. But it looked big and gray!" Toni answered.

"Well, it isn't there now," Cal said. They both rode off the bridge onto the beach.

Cal hopped up on the diving board at one side of the beach. Toni had spotted a big rock crab hurrying across the water bottom just in front of her. She jumped up on the dock and followed it.

The crab disappeared into the deep water twenty yards from shore. Sitting at the end of the dock, Toni caught sight of something else moving in the water below.

"What are you looking for, Toni?" yelled Cal. Just then, Art Hatch turned over the boat's engine.

Toni shouted back over the roar. "I saw a big crab—" A sight in front of her made her stop short. A huge fin rose out of the water no more than three feet away.

Toni shouted, "Cal! It's a shark!" She looked up to see an empty diving board and the rippled water where Cal had dived in.

A few seconds later, Cal's head bobbed above water ten feet from the diving board.

Toni waved and pointed. "It's a shark!" she yelled. But Cal couldn't hear her above the noise of the boat.

Then Toni froze. The shark had been attracted by the splashing. It had turned and was now swimming toward Cal. Toni ran to the diving board. She screamed and waved as she ran. Out of the corner of her eye she could see a fin moving toward Cal.

Cal was puzzled by Toni's antics. Then, as she raced closer, he looked where Toni was pointing. Finally, he saw the huge shape.

The shark was only a dozen yards away. The same length lay between Cal and the diving-board ladder. He couldn't make it in time. The shark would head him off. There was only one other chance, and Cal took it.

It was high tide, and the diving board was only three feet above the water. Cal quickly swam beneath it. He ducked under the water and kicked as hard as he could. He pushed himself straight up out of the water. Then Cal reached for the end of the board with both hands and lifted his legs up out of the water. He grabbed the board just as the shark glided past below.

Toni was at the side of the diving board. She picked up stones and threw them at the shark. She couldn't distract it, so she called for help. "Mr. Hatch! Help!"

All this time Art and Tim had been working on their boat engine. Now Art looked over at the beach.

"Oh, no!" he cried. He jumped into the little dinghy at the back of the boat and began rowing toward the cousins. When Art was halfway across the harbor, he lost an oar. He could see that Cal was still hanging onto the diving board. "Hang on!" Art called.

Then he hit upon an idea. He picked up the other oar and beat the water with it to get the shark's attention. The shark swam around under Cal for a few moments, but then it broke away and headed for the dinghy.

When the shark reached the little boat, Art yelled to Cal, "Let go and get to the ladder, fast. The shark is over here with me!"

Fear made Cal act quickly. A few seconds later, he pulled himself up the ladder.

The dinghy drifted close to the bigger boat. Tim Carter threw Art a line and towed him along. The men and the two cousins were on opposite sides of the harbor. For a long while, they all just stared at the water.

Checking Comprehension and Skills

1. How does the reader learn on page 359 that Cal and Toni may swim where a shark is swimming? (359)
2. What sentences on page 360 hint that the shark is in the water? (360)
3. Why didn't Cal hear Toni when she first tried to warn him about the shark? (361)
4. How was Art Hatch quickthinking? (363)
•5. Do you think this story was fiction or nonfiction? Why do you think so?
•6. Tell why you think "The Story of Yakutat Barry" was fiction or nonfiction.

Choose the words that you think have the same meaning as each underlined idiom.
○7. Then he hit upon an idea.
    thought of   pounded
○8. The shark would head him off.
    push with its head   get in front of him

• Fiction and Nonfiction
○ Context: Idioms

Reading
Bonus

from The Shark in the Window

by Keo Felker Lazarus

In this humorous story, Shelly Todd's pet is a baby shark that hatched from an egg case he found on the beach. Now the shark is living and growing in Shelly's fish tank.

The baby shark began to move about the fish tank. A few days later it started swimming to the surface to grab some ground beef from Shelly's fingers. He could see its rows of tiny teeth. It was growing too. In a week it had grown to six inches.

Then one day when Shelly went to feed it, the shark was nowhere to be found in the tank. Shelly slammed into his brother Irving's room. "All right, what did you do with it?"

Irving looked up from the guitar he was playing. "What did I do with what?"

"You know what! My shark!"

"Shel, I haven't touched it!" Irving dropped his guitar on the bed and followed Shelly back into his room.

The boys peeked into the tank and behind the rocks, but no shark. A faint noise rose from a pile of papers on the desk.

Irving lifted a sheet of paper. "Here's your silly shark!" The baby shark lay in a damp puddle on Shelly's homework.

Shelly picked it up and slipped it into the water. The shark sank to the bottom. "That was close!" Shelly said. "How do you suppose it got out of the tank?"

"Flopped out. How else?" Irving answered.

When Shelly woke up the next morning, the shark was missing again. Irving came into Shelly's room to help look for the shark. Sandra, the boys' younger sister, followed Irving. This time Sandra found the shark among the blankets on Shelly's bed.

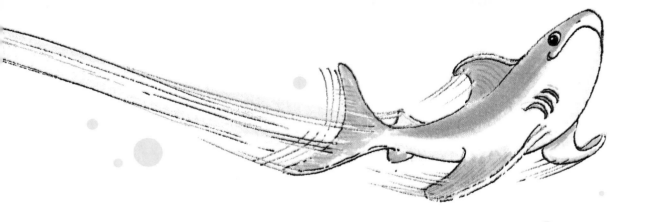

"How could it flop clear over there?" Shelly asked.

"Maybe it flew," Irving offered.

"Oh, sure, like a flying fish!"

Shelly slid his hands around the baby shark and headed for the fish tank. He could feel it wiggling as he opened his fingers to drop it into the water.

Instead of going into the water, however, the shark skimmed across the surface and rose into the air again. It flipped its tail a few times and drifted around the room as though the air were water!

The baby shark circled the room several times before it plopped on Shelly's bed again. Shelly reached down to pick it up, but the shark wiggled its tail and climbed into the air like a small plane taking off. "Quick! Close the door!" Shelly shouted. "Maybe it *is* a flying fish."

Irving shook his head. "It doesn't look like one. Flying fish have long front fins that open out. They use them to glide over the water. This little shark's fins aren't like that at all. They're short and fat. Look! It's swimming the way it was in the water!" The shark's tail swept slowly from side to side as it floated about the room.

"How can it breathe out of water?" Shelly asked.

"Maybe it's that vitamin E you've been feeding it. That's supposed to help the blood take in oxygen."

"Yes, I guess it wouldn't matter if the oxygen was in the water or in the air."

Sandra had climbed on Shelly's bed and was jumping up and down trying to catch the shark. "It's a balloon!" she shouted.

"Does it have a big bubble of air in it?" Shelly asked.

Irving scratched his ear. "I don't think it's air. Sharks haven't any air pockets like the ones in other fish. They have to keep swimming so that they can take oxygen out of anything that passes through their gill slits. When they quit moving, they sink to the bottom. It would have to be something lighter than air—maybe some sort of gas we don't know about."

"We'd better not tell Mom and Dad about the shark. They wouldn't let me keep it." Shelly sank down on the bed and watched the shark nose about the papers on his desk.

"If it won't stay in your fish tank, how are you going to keep it?" Irving asked. "Get a cage?"

"No. Mom and Dad would see that and ask questions. I'll keep it in a cardboard box in my closet, I guess."

"If you can catch it."

"Sure, I can catch it. See?" Shelly took the lid from a small jar with the ground beef-and-vitamin-E mix in it. He held up a bit of it in his fingers. "Here Sharky."

"That sounds silly!" Irving frowned. "Why don't you give it a really good name?"

"Like what?"

Shelly and Irving looked at the sleek shark circling Shelly's head. With several quick flips

of its tail, the shark darted in and grabbed the meat from Shelly's fingers.

"Ouch! It nipped me!" Shelly shouted.

"Then call it Nipper," Irving offered.

"I like Nippy better," Shelly said, holding up another piece of meat. As the shark took it, Shelly grabbed its wiggling body with his hand. "Okay, Nippy. You're going in the closet." He opened his closet door, slipped the little shark inside a large cardboard box, poked a few air holes in the box with a pencil, and slammed the door shut.

"Don't anybody tell Mom or Dad where Nippy is, see? And don't you tell Mom or Dad anything about the shark getting out of the tank and swimming around the room either."

Shelly was able to keep Nippy a secret for almost two weeks. The shark had grown over twelve inches when Sandra came in early one morning and left the door open a little. Shelly didn't notice, but Nippy did. Before Shelly saw that the shark had slipped out, he heard Mr. Todd roar loudly.

Shelly dashed down the hall. Nippy had drifted into the bathroom, where Mr. Todd was shaving, and had joined Shelly's father at the mirror. The shark bumped the glass gently as he stared at himself.

"What is *that?*" his father asked.

"Just my shark, Dad. I call him Nippy, but he won't hurt anyone."

"Your shark! A few weeks ago it was only four inches long!"

"I know. It's grown kind of fast."

"What's it doing out of the fish tank?"

"Well, you see, Dad, it's hard to explain. Nippy lives in the air instead of the water."

"That's impossible!"

"Watch him!" Shelly lifted Nippy and let him go. The shark swept his tail slowly from side to side, floated down the hall, and went into the kitchen. There was a loud shriek.

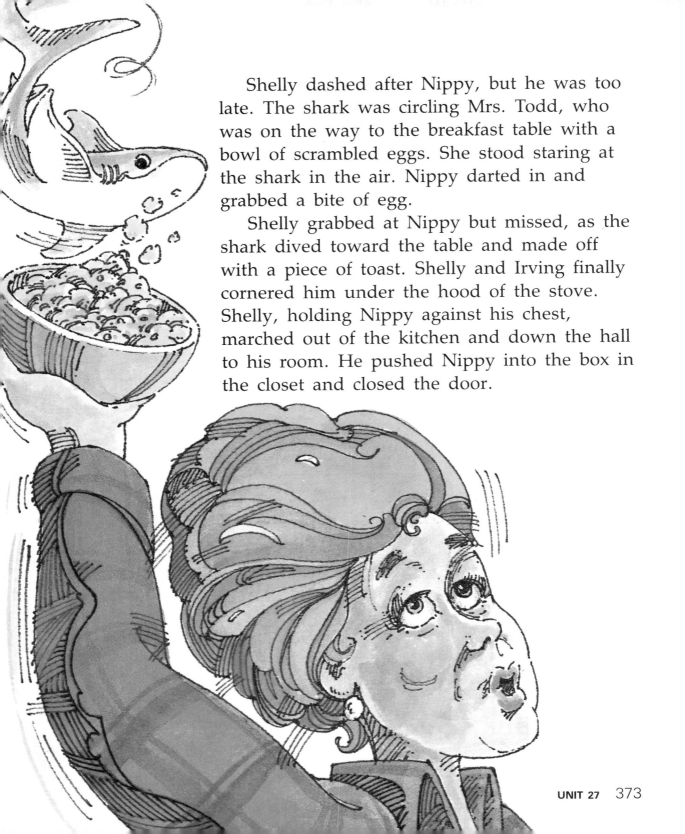

Shelly dashed after Nippy, but he was too late. The shark was circling Mrs. Todd, who was on the way to the breakfast table with a bowl of scrambled eggs. She stood staring at the shark in the air. Nippy darted in and grabbed a bite of egg.

Shelly grabbed at Nippy but missed, as the shark dived toward the table and made off with a piece of toast. Shelly and Irving finally cornered him under the hood of the stove. Shelly, holding Nippy against his chest, marched out of the kitchen and down the hall to his room. He pushed Nippy into the box in the closet and closed the door.

Shelly and Irving spent most of breakfast trying to explain about Nippy. Finally Mr. Todd said, "By the time I come home tonight, I want that shark out of this house!"

"But Dad! I can't turn him out on the street. Nippy would scare the neighbors. Besides, he's not hurting anyone here, and he's learning to do tricks like a dog. Please, Dad, can't I keep him? Please? I'll see that he doesn't bother you, and I'll teach him to stay with me and not grab things. He's pretty smart."

Mr. Todd chewed his toast grimly. "All right, Shelly. But see to it that no one, but no one, finds out about it." He shook his head. "A shark out of water, swimming in the air. . . . Who's going to believe us?"

Nippy grew bigger and bigger. Soon Shelly couldn't keep him hidden. Some neighbors saw Nippy and started asking questions. If you want to know what happened to Nippy, read the book The Shark in the Window.

Finding Facts on Charts and Graphs

Skill Bonus

Can you picture fishing for sharks with a rod and reel? It has been done. It's not easy to catch a shark. It's dangerous too. Sharks can fight hard. They can be strong and very heavy. How heavy? The biggest shark ever caught weighed about 2,600 pounds![1]

Sharpen Your Skills

Sometimes the same facts can be presented in several ways—in words, on a chart, or on a graph. Charts and graphs let you see all the

---

1. about 1,200 kilograms

facts at a glance. That's why it is sometimes easier to understand facts if you see them on a chart or a graph instead of in words. Charts and graphs help you compare facts too.

The chart below shows how many sharks several people caught in one year. The chart has two columns. The left column shows the names of the people who fished. The right column shows the number of sharks each person caught. Can you find the name of the person who caught the most sharks? Find Ernest's name in the left column. Run your finger from his name to the right column. How many sharks did Ernest catch? If you said eleven, you were right.

On the next page you'll see how the same information looks when it is shown on a graph.

Number of Sharks Caught in One Year

Name	Number of Sharks
Hiroko	
Joan	
Pablo	
Helen	
Ernest	

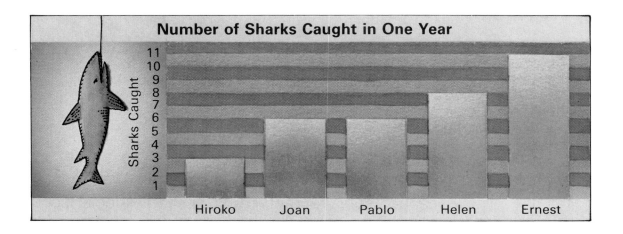

Number of Sharks Caught in One Year

Sharks Caught

Hiroko   Joan   Pablo   Helen   Ernest

The graph above is called a **bar graph** because it shows the facts with bars. Find the bar above Ernest's name. In one glance, you can see he caught more sharks than the others. Put your finger at the top of the bar for Ernest. Then run your finger across to the left side. That is where the number of sharks is shown. Your finger should be on the number 11. Use the chart on page 376 or the graph on this page to answer the following questions.

1. Who caught the fewest sharks? How many did that person catch?
2. Which two people caught the same number of sharks?
3. Did Pablo catch more or fewer sharks than Helen caught?

Remember that charts and graphs show facts at a glance. Use them to compare facts too.

Books to Read

From Anna by Jean Little. Harper.

Anna's older brothers and sisters have little patience with her. Then they learn that Anna cannot see well and must go to a special school. Read how Anna makes new friends at school and finds a new place for herself within the family.

Sharks and Whales by Burton Albert. Grosset & Dunlap.

Some tiger sharks eat their baby brothers and sisters. The humpback whale, on the other hand, is a gentle animal who sings beautiful deep, slow songs. Find out about these and other fascinating sea animals in this book.

Veronica Meets Her Match by Nancy K. Robinson. Scholastic.

Veronica was lonesome after her best friend moved away. The most popular girls in class made things worse with their Seven-Up Club and its secrets. When Crystal Webb moved into the apartment next door, Veronica's luck seemed too good to be true.

Beyond the Earth

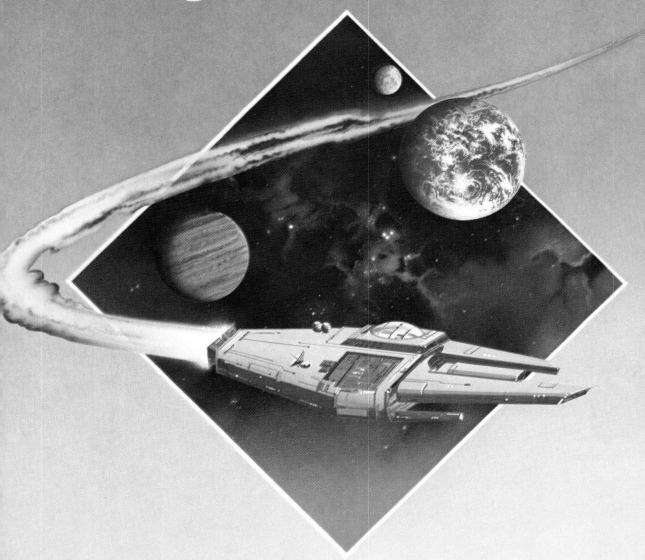

Farther Than Far

by
Margaret Hillert

I look into the sky and see
The leafy branches of a tree,
And higher still a bird in flight,
And higher still a cloud of white.
Beyond the cloud is lots more sky,
Farther than far, higher than high.
And where it ends, another place
Is filled with space and space and space.

WHAT IS SPACE?

Think about a beautiful sunny day. The sky is blue. There are a few soft clouds. Picture yourself leaving Earth and heading out into space. What would it be like? Would it be different from Earth?

One thing you would discover is that clouds form close to the earth. There are no clouds in space. There isn't any air. There isn't any wind either.

However, there is plenty of room. Space goes on and on and on. It is a very long way from one place to another in space. Venus is the closest planet to Earth. Yet the closest it comes to Earth is about twenty-six million miles.[1]

Venus and Earth are only two of the planets in space. Besides planets, there are moons, meteors, stars, and other things in space. There are also satellites that were made on Earth and sent into space.

_____

1. 42 million kilometers

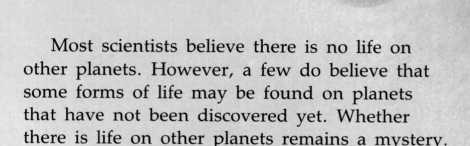

Most scientists believe there is no life on other planets. However, a few do believe that some forms of life may be found on planets that have not been discovered yet. Whether there is life on other planets remains a mystery.

Sharpen Your Skills

Sometimes the main idea of the article is not stated. You may have to figure it out by reading all the paragraphs and deciding what is the most important thing these paragraphs tell you about the topic of the article.
1. What is the topic of this article?
2. What is the main idea of this article?
   a. There are no clouds in space.
   b. Space is different from Earth in many ways.

As you read "The Space Shuttle *Columbia*" and "Space Stations," figure out the main idea of each article.

The Space Shuttle
COLUMBIA

by Marianne von Meerwall

Columbia is America's first space shuttle. A shuttle is something that goes back and forth between two places. That's what *Columbia* does. It goes out into space and lands back on the earth. A space shuttle is a spaceship that can be used again and again.

Columbia moves in three different ways. It leaves the earth. It journeys into space. Then it returns to Earth and lands safely. *Columbia* can do all three because it works in three different ways.

First, it's like a rocket. *Columbia* has three main engines. They work with two detachable engines, which drop off the ship after they have used all of their fuel. All these engines work together to lift the ship off the earth and move it into space. When *Columbia* is acting as a rocket, it uses engines to leave Earth and head into space.

Second, *Columbia* is like a spaceship. It journeys into space and circles the earth. It also carries cargo into space. Later it will be used to help the people who will build space stations. It will carry food, tools, and other things to them.

Third, *Columbia* is like an airplane. Instead of landing in water like other spaceships, it lands on the ground like an airplane.

When things come back to the earth from space, they move at very high speeds. Because they move quickly through air, heat builds up. The heat is so great that most things burn up before they reach Earth.

The chief reason *Columbia* does not burn up is because of its covering. *Columbia* is covered with more than thirty thousand tiles. Each tile has a certain shape. Each was tested over and over. Each was glued in place by hand. These tiles are able to stand the heat when *Columbia* returns to Earth.

The development of *Columbia* took ten years. Before it could be flown into space, people had to be sure it was dependable. Many tests had to be run to check it out.

Columbia
YOUNG · CRIPPEN

John Young

Robert Crippen

On April 12, 1981, *Columbia* was ready for its first test flight into space. It lifted off from the Kennedy Space Center in Florida.

The first flight lasted fifty-four hours and twenty-one minutes. In that time John Young and Robert Crippen tested the ship. One of the things they had to do was open and close the cargo doors. That was important if the ship was to carry cargo into space. The doors would have to open so cargo could be removed. *Columbia* passed all the tests.

Columbia landed on April 14 at Edwards Air Force Base in California. It glided quietly to the ground. *Columbia*'s wings glowed red hot with the heat as it passed through the air. But the tiles held up to the test. The team of John Young and Robert Crippen had returned safely.

That was the first in a round of test flights for *Columbia*. Most people are in agreement that the flight was successfully completed. The shuttle did the things it had to do. It left the earth, it journeyed into space, and it made it back home.

Space Stations

by Marianne Novak

A satellite is something that circles a planet or some other body in space. The moon is a satellite of Earth. It circles Earth once every month.

A space station is a kind of satellite built by people. A space station is made so that people can live and work in it. It can carry food, water, and air. It also has rooms in which people live while they are in space.

Uses for Space Stations

Because a space station moves in space, it can be used for several things. It can be used as a place for watching the earth or the stars. The air around the earth dims the view of stars and other things in space. This makes it harder to see them. However, there is no air in space to dim the view. So telescopes in the space station can show scientists more about space than can telescopes on Earth.

A space station can also serve as a gas station in space. A spaceship uses up most of

The United States' first space station.

its fuel just getting into space. To make a longer trip into space, it needs more fuel. If a space station were circling the earth, a spaceship could stop at it to get more fuel.

Workable Space Stations

Skylab was the first workable space station built by the United States. It was sent up to circle around the earth in 1973. *Skylab* was to have stayed in space until the space shuttle *Columbia* could journey to it. But *Skylab* stopped working and fell to Earth before *Columbia*'s first shuttle flight in 1981.

Space stations will be very important in the years to come. We can use them to build other satellites and even cities in space. We can also use them to learn more about planets, stars, and other things in space.

The drawing above shows how a giant platform could be built on top of a space station. The drawing below shows what living quarters might be like on a space station.

Checking Comprehension and Skills

1. How is *Columbia* like a rocket, a spaceship, and an airplane? (384 and 385)

•2. Tell which of these expresses the main idea of "The Space Shuttle *Columbia*" and explain your answer. a. John Young and Robert Crippen tested the *Columbia* in 1981.
b. *Columbia* is a successful space shuttle.
c. When things come back to Earth from space they move at very high speeds.

3. How does a satellite differ from a space shuttle?

•4. Which of these expresses the main idea of "Space Stations"? a. Space stations are satellites that have many uses. b. *Skylab* stopped working and fell to Earth. c. A space station can serve as a gas station.

5. Would you like to spend some time on a space station? If so, what would you do there?

Make a word from the word and word parts in order to complete the sentence below.

    –tion   –ment   work   –able   –ed

○6. *Skylab* was the first _____ space station built by the United States.

• Main Idea and Supporting Details
○ Structure: Suffixes *(-able, -ment)*

Learning About Space

One of the ways we learn about space is through space travel. Astronauts are trained to fly into space. They spend many hours on Earth learning about space and about the tools they will use when they fly into space.

In order to prepare for the astronauts' space flights, scientists must test new ideas and new tools to be used in space. Some of their discoveries lead to new space products that also change the way we live on Earth.

Getting the Main Idea and Supporting Details

Some people take a long time to tell a story. Others may want to say, "Get to the point!" This is a way of saying, "What is the main idea?"

Sharpen Your Skills

Most articles you read have a main idea. Here is how to find the main idea and details that support it.

1. Ask yourself, "What is the topic of the article?" The **topic** is what an article is about. You can state it in a word or two.
2. Decide what is the most important idea given about the topic. That's the **main idea**.
3. **Details** are small pieces of information in the article. Look for details that **support**, or tell more about, the main idea. Other details may be interesting, but they might not support the main idea.

Use the steps above to find the main idea and supporting details of the following article.

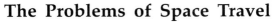

The Problems of Space Travel

To get to the moon, a spaceship has to go more than 200,000 miles.[1] The hardest parts of the trip are leaving earth and getting back.

The hardest part of getting a ship into space is pushing it away from the giant tug that pulls things back to earth. That tug is gravity. A spaceship has to get a push that is stronger than this pull. Rockets give this push.

Another problem in space travel is getting a ship to slow down when it returns. The ship may be going more than 25,000 miles an hour.[2] Several things slow it down. One is the earth's atmosphere. Another is rockets fired to act as brakes. Parachutes also slow down the ship.

1. What is the topic of the article?
2. Which of the following is the main idea?
   a. The biggest problems of space travel are taking off and getting back.
   b. Rockets help on take-off and return.
3. Which detail below supports the main idea?
   a. The moon is over 200,000 miles away.
   b. A spaceship must slow down to land safely.

Look for the topic, main idea, and supporting details in the next article.

---

1. 321,800 kilometers   2. 40,233 km per hour

Dr. Mary Cleave: ASTRONAUT in Training

by Barbara Johnson

Some people study the stars and planets. Others enjoy just looking at them. Dr. Mary Cleave wants to fly to them. She is an astronaut.

Dr. Cleave was chosen for membership in the astronaut group in 1980. Before that she went to college and studied to be a scientist. Math and engineering were some subjects she studied.

In 1980 the astronauts' group needed scientists to discover ways to live and work in space. Because of her training, Dr. Cleave was a good choice.

Unlike Dr. Cleave, the first astronauts selected in 1959 were not scientists. They were pilots. Most of them had some training in engineering too. However, their training as pilots was more important at the time. Those early astronauts helped us learn how to get to space and how to return safely to Earth.

When Dr. Cleave first joined the astronauts' group, she spent one year in training at the Johnson Space Center in Houston, Texas. During the first six months, she spent eight hours a day in classrooms. She trained very studiously. Dr. Cleave and the other new astronauts learned about computers and tools that are used in space. They also learned more about engineering.

When Dr. Cleave and the other new astronauts finished their classroom training, they began learning about space and spaceships in other ways. They flew in airplanes that had been built for astronaut training. When the astronauts rode in these special airplanes, they felt like they were floating. It was as if they had no weight. They felt just as they would in space, where there is less gravity than on Earth. In the training airplanes, the astronauts learned how to eat and drink in space. They also worked with tools they will use in space.

Astronaut Mary Cleave training in parachute/survival school.

Once astronauts are signed up for a certain space flight, they train more and more in simulators. These are test rooms like the spaceships in which the astronauts will fly into space. The cabin of a simulator looks just like the cabin of a real spaceship. Almost everything inside is the same. There is even a close relationship between what astronauts see outside the simulator windows and what they will see in space.

Flying is another part of the astronauts' training. Even though Dr. Cleave is not a pilot, she still must fly often. All astronauts must spend at least fifteen hours every month flying in airplanes.

All astronauts must be healthy and strong. Dr. Cleave swims every day during the hot summer months. She runs four miles a day during cooler weather. Other astronauts lift weights. Some play tennis.

Dr. Cleave even trains while she watches television. She plays with a stiff spring that fits nicely in her hand. Squeezing the spring makes her fingers stronger. This is important because other astronauts who have gone into space reported that their hands became weak during space flights. So playing with the spring is one way Dr. Cleave trains for her job.

Learning to be an astronaut is hard work. Dr. Cleave and the other astronauts in training may be called upon to work at any time, day or night, for many hours at a time. However, they accept this as part of an astronaut's life. After all, when their training is completed, they may have a chance to fly into space.

Astronaut Mary Cleave training in water survival school.

Space Spinoffs

by Mary Srutek

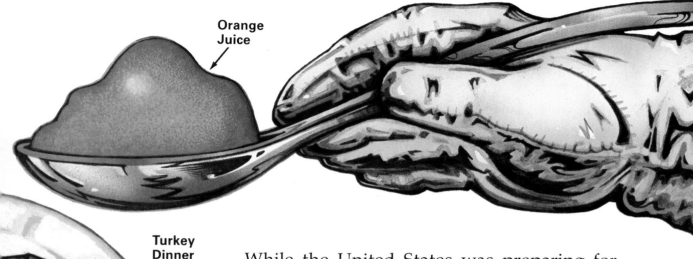

Orange Juice

Turkey Dinner

While the United States was preparing for its first space flights, it developed many products that would make life in space easier. New foods, new tools, and new clothes came about because of these marvelous discoveries. Some of these new items can be used on Earth as well as in space. They are called *space spinoffs*.

Space spinoffs have changed some foods we eat. Astronauts need food that will not spoil quickly, can be stored easily, and can be prepared without much trouble. Freeze-dried foods and orange juice that can be made from a powder were developed to serve these needs. People on Earth have found these foods useful too. Freeze-dried foods are light to carry on camping trips and simple to prepare.

Other space spinoffs have made the world a safer place. People in space must carry air tanks. Before work in space began, there were no small air-tanks. Now there are. These tanks hold more air than the larger ones did.

Even though small air-tanks were made for space flights, they are now being used by firefighters on Earth. In the past, firefighters had to carry large, heavy tanks. Moving around inside a burning building was dangerous. Small air-tanks have made fighting fires a little easier and safer.

Air Tank

Firefighters' clothes are also safer now. It can be very hot in certain places in space. It can also get very hot inside a spaceship. That is why clothes were made to protect astronauts from high heat. Firefighters need to be protected from heat too. So now they wear clothes like those worn by the astronauts.

Even though it can be very hot in space, it can also be very cold. To protect astronauts from the cold, new gloves and boots were made. Now people who enjoy the outdoors can buy gloves and boots like those worn in space.

Space spinoffs are very valuable. They help people overcome the hardships of space. They also improve life on Earth.

Checking Comprehension and Skills

1. How did Dr. Cleave's first six months of training differ from her later training? (395)

•2. Which of the following would you say is the main idea of the article about Dr. Cleave?
   a. The first astronauts were pilots.
   b. Astronauts train in planes, where they feel as if they are floating.
   c. Dr. Cleave is training to be an astronaut.

3. Describe three of the spinoffs you learned about in "Space Spinoffs."

•4. Which sentence expresses the main idea of "Space Spinoffs"? a. Orange juice made from powder is one space spinoff.
   b. Clothing that protects against cold is a space spinoff. c. Some items developed for space can be used on Earth.

5. Do you think astronauts are brave? Why?

6. If you were an astronaut, where in space would you like to go? Why?

Make a word from these words and word parts in order to complete each sentence below.
   marvel   hard   –ness   –ous   –ships

○7. New tools came about because of these ____ discoveries.

○8. They help people overcome the ____ of space.

• Main Idea and Supporting Details
○ Structure: Suffixes (-ous, -ship)

Saucer Landings

Here is a game you might enjoy playing. It is called *Saucer Landings:*

Mark a circle on the floor with a jump rope. Tell each player to stand ten feet away from the circle. Use paper plates for saucers. Have each player, in turn, throw a paper-plate saucer into the circle. The winner is the player who lands a saucer in the circle first.

Space Tomorrow

One hundred years ago people wondered what life would be like today. People today want to know what life will be like one hundred years from now. Nobody knows for sure, but it is fun to guess.

Lost in Space—Almost

Marcy lived in a space village. She worked in the day-care center for small children.

The children played happily in a brightly painted room. Outdoors was a playground where they could learn to walk, run, and bounce—without the help of gravity.

One Monday during lunch, Marcy helped the children with their food sticks and pink space juice. Then she put the children in cots that hung down from the ceiling like swings. Gently she pushed the cots back and forth and rocked the children to sleep.

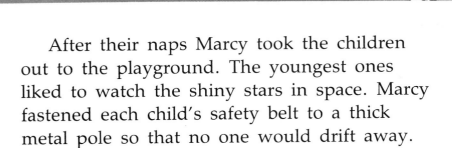

After their naps Marcy took the children out to the playground. The youngest ones liked to watch the shiny stars in space. Marcy fastened each child's safety belt to a thick metal pole so that no one would drift away.

Suddenly one boy's belt slipped off the pole. He began to float away. Quickly Marcy held up her arm. She was wearing a wide bracelet that gleamed with bright purple and blue stones. When the boy reached for the sparkling bracelet, Marcy grabbed his boot and pulled him back.

"You may fly into space some day," she said, "but stay here until you grow up."

Sharpen Your Skills

Writers often add special details about the people, places, and things in a story. The details help the reader picture and understand what is happening. Answer these questions about the details in "Lost in Space—Almost."
1. What was the space day-care center like?
2. What did Marcy's bracelet look like?

Use the details in "Aunt Elvira's Zoo" to picture what is happening.

Aunt Elvira's ZOO

by Pamela Sargent

The time is the future. Many people are leaving Earth and making their homes on other planets. Earth itself has become so overcrowded that every piece of land must be used for housing or farming. Julie's Aunt Elvira owns the last jungle on Earth. The animals living there are the last of their kinds. Soon the government will clear Aunt Elvira's land and build more houses. Julie and her aunt have only a short time to find a new home for themselves and the animals.

Julie's teacher-robot, Gerard, placed a history book in front of her. She began to leaf through it. There were pictures of old satellites in the book. Julie remembered that there were a lot of old things still circling Earth. There were even some space stations that no one used anymore.

She suddenly had an idea. "Maybe we can keep the animals in one of the space stations until they have a place to go," said Julie.

"Maybe," Aunt Elvira said. "We can't keep them there for long, though. They wouldn't have enough room."

"Let's put them in deep-sleep," said Gerard. "Then we can figure out what to do." Gerard knew that passengers on long space flights were put into deep-sleep so that time seemed to pass more quickly.

Aunt Elvira rubbed her hands. "I have a better idea! I'll buy a used space station. Our robots can fix it up. They can put in a star-drive engine. We'll turn the space station into a star ship. Then we can go somewhere else. I'll offer a free trip to another world to anybody who's willing to help us."

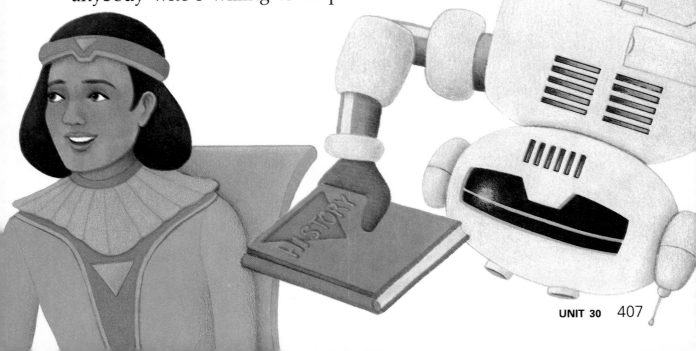

Aunt Elvira bought a space station that was still fairly new. Every day Julie and Gerard took a shuttle up to the space station. They went there to help the robots with the work.

The space station was very large. It looked like a giant wheel with spokes connecting the engine room in the middle to the rest of the station. It was a beautiful sight as it whirled in the black sky overhead.

There were other children working on the space station too. They and their parents were helping Aunt Elvira in return for a free trip to another world. While working, Julie made some new friends. She liked Mayli Soong, a cheerful girl, best.

When the space station was almost ready, Julie and the other children went into Aunt Elvira's jungle with the robots. They set traps in the undergrowth and trees and caught the birds. Later they put the birds in deep-sleep and took them to the space station in shuttles.

However, some of the large animals, like the elephants, wouldn't fit into the shuttles. Aunt Elvira called a meeting aboard the space station to decide what to do.

First the group talked about where they should go. They chose a planet called New Africa. This planet did not have any animals of its own. There were no people there either.

Finally, Aunt Elvira spoke. "Some of the big animals won't fit on the shuttles," she said. "We only have a week to get them out of the jungle and aboard the space station. Soon the machines will tear down the trees and start building. The animals will get frightened and run everywhere."

A woman stood up. "If we all put our money together," she said, "I think we can get two larger shuttles. We'll make shuttle trips back and forth between Earth and the space station until all the animals are aboard."

No one in the room disagreed with this idea. Everyone offered to help.

Julie was waiting near one of the large shuttles for her aunt. This was the last day they had to get the animals to the space station. All except the elephants had been caught.

It had been easy to herd the other animals into the oversized shuttles. Some of the most dangerous ones had been shot with small tranquilizer darts. Once the animals were asleep, it was safe to carry them aboard. However, the elephants were too heavy to be carried.

"Aunt Elvira!" Julie shouted as her aunt came out of the house. "I have an idea! We can herd the elephants into the large shuttles. We'll shoot them with the darts when they're inside. There are racks near the ceilings of the shuttles. Kids are small enough to lie up there and hit the elephants when they're inside."

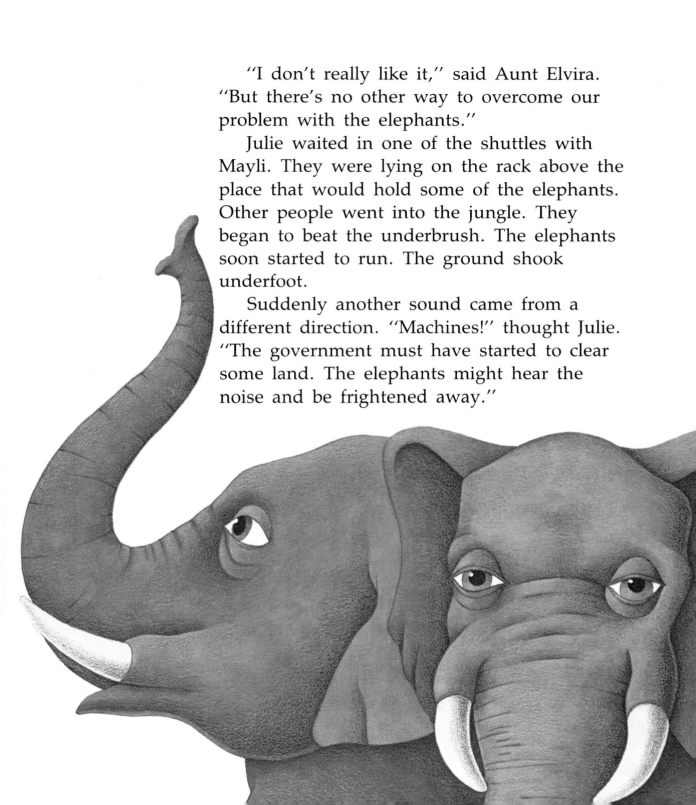

"I don't really like it," said Aunt Elvira. "But there's no other way to overcome our problem with the elephants."

Julie waited in one of the shuttles with Mayli. They were lying on the rack above the place that would hold some of the elephants. Other people went into the jungle. They began to beat the underbrush. The elephants soon started to run. The ground shook underfoot.

Suddenly another sound came from a different direction. "Machines!" thought Julie. "The government must have started to clear some land. The elephants might hear the noise and be frightened away."

Julie looked out a small window near her head. She saw the elephants. The machines were growing louder, and the elephants seemed to be slowing down. They kept coming, though. As the first one came into the shuttle, Julie aimed her dart gun. She hit the elephant in the side. She and Mayli took turns shooting the darts until there were six elephants lying asleep on the floor below them.

Julie and Mayli jumped down. The two friends walked over the elephants to the front of the shuttle. They got into their seats just as Aunt Elvira came inside.

Soon they were taking off. As they passed over the jungle, Julie could see the machines tearing down the trees below.

When the shuttle reached the space station, Julie could see other families arriving there in the other shuttle. The space station would be home to them for the next few months. However, the people as well as the animals would be in deep-sleep most of the time.

Julie looked out her window at the earth below. She knew she would be happier on New Africa. The robots would help everyone build new homes. There would be plenty of room too. Julie turned to Aunt Elvira and said, "I'm really glad we're going."

Checking Comprehension and Skills

- 1. What are three things about "Aunt Elvira's Zoo" that let you know the story takes place in the future?
  2. Why were Julie and her aunt being forced to leave their home? (406)
  3. Julie has an idea in the beginning of the story that leads to a solution of Aunt Elvira's problem. What was Julie's idea? (407)
  4. How did Aunt Elvira add to Julie's idea and move closer to a final solution? (407)
  5. Which is Aunt Elvira's space station most like—*Skylab* or *Columbia?*
  6. Why did Aunt Elvira and her friends buy two new shuttles? (409)
- 7. Julie developed a plan for getting the elephants on the new shuttles. What were the two parts to Julie's plan? (410)
  8. How would you feel about leaving Earth for a distant planet? Explain your answer.

Make a word from these words and word parts in order to complete each sentence below.

| size | brush | foot | −ed | over− | under− |

- ○ 9. It had been easy to herd the other animals into the ____ shuttles.
- ○10. People began to beat the ____.

- • Details
- ○ Structure: Prefixes (under-, over-)

Which Meaning Fits?

The moon is a body in space.

You might see a sentence like the one above in a science book or another textbook. Which of the pictures at left fits the sentence? The key to the meaning of the sentence is the word *body*. It can mean *the physical part of a person*, but it can also mean *a planet or other heavenly object*. The second meaning fits the sentence above. Did you pick picture 2?

Suppose you read a word like *body*, a word that has more than one meaning. How do you keep from getting mixed up?

1. Read the whole sentence the word is in.
2. Figure out a meaning that makes sense.
3. Check yourself by looking up the word in a dictionary or glossary. Read all the meanings given. Then pick the one that fits your sentence.

Don't be stopped by a word that has more than one meaning when you read textbooks. You can figure out which meaning fits!

TAKE COVER

When do the earth's most powerful winds blow?   416–425
Where would you go if the earth shook?   426–439
What great storms blow in from the sea?   440–456

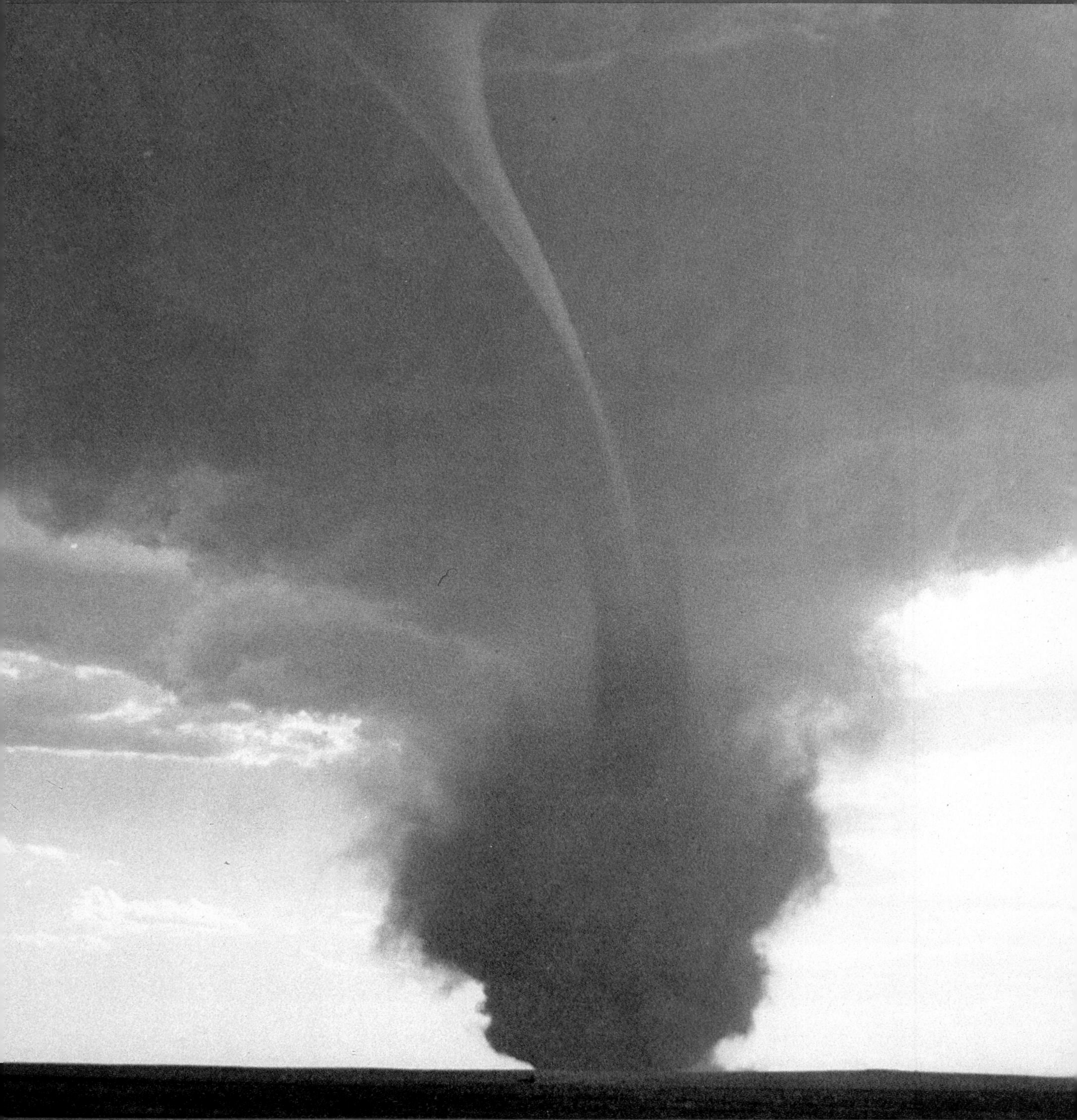

Tornadoes

The picture shows a tornado. A tornado is one of nature's most dangerous storms. A tornado's whirling winds are more powerful than those of any other storm.

Tornadoes strike in all parts of the world, but they hit most often in the United States. Tornadoes are seen in almost all of the states. Kansas, Iowa, Texas, Oklahoma, Arkansas, and Missouri are the states where they appear most often. Spring is the time of year when tornadoes strike.

Chasing Dust Devils

by Grant Alan Idso

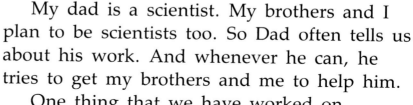

Grant and his brother walk toward a dust devil.

My dad is a scientist. My brothers and I plan to be scientists too. So Dad often tells us about his work. And whenever he can, he tries to get my brothers and me to help him.

One thing that we have worked on together for several years is dust deviling. We go to the desert to find and learn about the whirling columns of dust that are called dust devils. These act like tiny tornadoes. In fact, that is why we study them. They give us a safe and easy way to learn something about tornadoes, their larger and more dangerous cousins.

What have we learned? For one thing, we have found that, for its size, a dust devil can be as powerful as some tornadoes. One of my brothers says that he was lifted off the ground by a dust devil. (Some of us believe it was just his imagination that took flight.)

Dust devils and tornadoes are alike in other ways. Both are shaped like funnels. And both seem to have "mini-funnels" that move around their main funnels. These smaller ones are generally even more powerful than the main one.

Dust devils and tornadoes are also alike when they weaken and die. Often they become stretched thin. My brothers and I have charged into dust devils at this stage and destroyed them. This gives my younger brothers a feeling of power. They always return showing off and shouting like Tarzan.

Dust deviling for us is a great family adventure. When summer rolls around, we get out our face masks. Then we give Dad a hint about what's on our minds by polishing up our favorite sign to hang over our garage door.

Gone Dust Devilin'

The boys will let the balloons go inside a dust devil. They will photograph what happens to the balloons.

Sharpen Your Skills

When you find likenesses and differences, you are making comparisons. Writers often tell you how things mentioned in an article are alike or different from each other.

1. How do tornadoes and dust devils look alike?
2. How are dust devils different from tornadoes?

As you read "The Mystery of Tornadoes," note the comparisons that the writer uses.

The Mystery of Tornadoes

by Sandra Henneberger

Picture a giant whirling cloud. It is shaped like a long black funnel. It glows like a dim lantern. This cloud can tear steel buildings apart in seconds. But it can be gentle too. A tornado has been known to take feathers off chickens without harming the birds.

The Power of Tornadoes

Tornadoes are made up of the most powerful winds on earth. One tornado tore apart a building that had been built to stand winds of 375 miles an hour.[1] Scientists think that many tornadoes have winds of 500 to 600 miles an hour.[2] Sometimes wind speeds appear to reach 800 miles an hour.[3]

One of the worst tornadoes on record moved forward at a speed of 60 miles an hour.[4] It destroyed trees and buildings along a

By the Way
It was in Oklahoma in the 1950s that a tornado warning was first given over radio and TV. Before the 1950s, people knew a tornado was coming only when they saw it themselves.

1. about 600 kilometers (km)   2. about 800 to 965 km
3. almost 1300 km   4. almost 100 km

These pictures show a tornado near Osnabrock, North Dakota. The first photo shows the tornado soon after it touched the ground. The second photo shows the tornado a few minutes later. The last photo shows the tornado after it has lost much of its power.

path three-fourths of a mile wide.[1] The path crossed Missouri, Indiana, and Illinois. It hit in 1925. It killed 689 people. Today, people are warned of coming storms through radio and TV. This helps keep the number of deaths down.

All tornadoes are dangerous. Fortunately, they do not often last more than ten to thirty minutes. They seldom carve a path longer than fifteen miles.[2]

Very strange things can happen inside this path. Buildings blow apart. Windows burst before they are hit. A wheat straw can be driven like a nail into wood. Tornadoes often destroy what they hit. On the other hand, animals, people, or whole houses can be lifted into the winds, carried several feet or miles, and let down again without harm.

---

1. more than 1 km   2. about 24 km

Why Tornadoes Act As They Do

Where does the tornado's power come from? People who study the weather have long known something about the way tornadoes begin. A huge amount of dry, cold air pushes against a huge amount of wet, warm air. The warm air rises and begins to whirl. The rising, whirling air forms the tornado.

The rising air inside a tornado acts something like a huge vacuum cleaner. It sucks up everything it touches. However, the power of these rising winds changes from moment to moment. Imagine a vacuum cleaner turning on and off very suddenly. That is how a tornado can lift things in strange ways.

Why do buildings burst? The winds inside the tornado are whirling so fast that there is almost no air at its center. This means that the air inside the tornado is much lighter than the air inside the building. As the storm moves toward a building, the air in the building pushes out. The inside air breaks windows or walls as it rushes outward.

Observing Tornadoes

Some children in Nebraska once had a chance to look inside a tornado. They were

Facts and Figures

•Tornado winds once drove a large piece of wood through the side of a railroad car.

•A tornado once lifted sixteen schoolchildren from their chairs and put them down 450 feet away. The children were not harmed.

A tornado left this wreckage behind.

having a picnic in a park. The weather had been hot and sticky for three days. Suddenly someone shouted, "Tornado!" A huge, finger-shaped cloud spilled down from gray-green thunderclouds. Before the children could run, the funnel was hanging directly over their heads. They looked up into it. Inside, it was black. However, lightning was flashing every second in the funnel. This let the children see the whirling, black clouds inside. There was a noise like "ten thousand freight trains." Then the funnel moved off. Several miles away it touched ground, destroying trees and buildings.

From reports like this, we know that lightning inside a tornado causes its strange glow. This is why one may look like a lantern.

Their powerful winds and short lives make it hard to learn more about tornadoes. Balloons and planes are not able to carry recording tools inside these storms. Without knowing more about tornadoes, people can only guess about where, when, or why one will start.

Tornadoes are still a puzzle. The more we learn about them, the more we discover there is to learn.

Weather experts cannot predict tornadoes. They can, however, predict the kind of storms that often produce tornadoes. Photos taken from space, such as the ones shown here, help weather experts predict such storms.

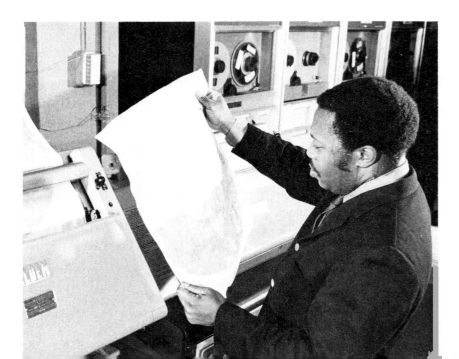

Checking Comprehension and Skills

- 1. How is a tornado like a funnel? (420)
  2. How fast do winds blow in the most powerful tornadoes? (420)
  3. About how long do most tornadoes last? (421)
- 4. In what way does a tornado act like a vacuum cleaner? (422)
  5. Why might it be a good idea to open your windows when a tornado threatens? (422)
  6. What causes tornadoes to glow like dim lanterns? (424)
- 7. Would you expect a tornado to be noisy or quiet? Explain your answer. (423)
  8. Almost everyone fears tornadoes. Tell how you or someone else in your family (even a pet) reacts when a thunderstorm hits.

   Divide each of the following words into syllables.
- 9. fortunately
- 10. driven

- Comparisons
- Structure: Syllables

Earthquakes

Earthquakes
Earthquakes

When something quakes, it shakes. So the word *earthquake* means a shaking of the earth. In some earthquakes, the earth shakes only a tiny bit. These earthquakes cause very little damage. If a strong earthquake happens where people live, it can cause much damage. The school in this picture was destroyed during the Alaskan earthquake of 1964.

Earthquakes happen in all parts of the world. In the United States, they happen most often in states near the Pacific Ocean.

Breaking Words into Syllables

Help! It's a quake—a wordquake! Can you read the long words in the top picture? If you need help, look at the bottom picture. A quake has broken each word into its parts. Put the parts together again and read the words.

Sharpen Your Skills

Here is a way to figure out long words like the words on page 428.

- First see if there is a prefix, suffix, or ending you can take off. Then try to read the root word. (See the word in the margin at left.)
- Next, if you need to, break the root word into syllables. Try to say the syllables. Then put the word together again.

disappear
dis appear

dis ap pear
disappear

Look again at the words in the bottom picture on page 428. See if you can explain how each word was broken into parts. Now use the tips on this page to read the underlined words below.

1. One day I heard an <u>announcement</u> on TV that made me sit up and listen.
2. It was <u>probable</u> that our town could have an earthquake someday.
3. This news surprised me because it was so <u>unexpected</u>.
4. A woman on TV explained the <u>precautions</u> we should take to stay safe.

As you read more about earthquakes, use the tips on this page to help you read long words.

Can Animals Predict Earthquakes?

by James R. Newton

When frogs swim in circles and croak at noon, watch out! An earthquake may be coming.

All through history there have been stories of animals doing odd things just before earthquakes. Mice have been seen rushing out of their homes in the ground. Flocks of sea birds have flown far inland. In zoos, lions and tigers and other great beasts have quit eating. Pandas have made strange screaming sounds.

People everywhere are beginning to pay more attention to animals when they start acting strangely. In China, in 1975, animals let people know that an earthquake was coming. Nearly a million people left their homes a few hours before it hit. The quake destroyed their city, but they were safe.

What did the Chinese see the animals do? Dogs howled for hours. Geese and ducks flew about wildly. Rats appeared as if from nowhere. Hibernating snakes crawled out of their holes.

Scientists want to find out what animals are sensing before an earthquake. When people know this, they might be able to build machines that sense the same things. In the meantime, scientists are watching animals closely.

We can't be sure that animals can tell us the exact times and places of earthquakes. But watching them may help save many lives.

Sharpen Your Skills

Often you may notice how things in your reading are alike or different from what you already know. You make comparisons.

1. How did sea birds act before an earthquake compared to how you think they normally act?
2. How did snakes act before the Chinese earthquake compared to the way you think they normally act?

Compare the information in "What to Do If an Earthquake Hits" with what the family in "Earthquake!" does.

What to Do If an Earthquake Hits

by Seymour Simon

Does the thought of being in an earthquake make you shake? Earthquakes do not happen very often. Most do little or no damage. But if you do feel the earth begin to shake one day, here are some rules to follow.

During the Earthquake

If you are indoors, stay away from windows, mirrors, and other kinds of glass. Watch out for high bookcases, shelves, or other furniture that may fall over or slide. To help protect yourself, get under a table, desk, or doorway.

If you are outdoors, move away from power poles, buildings, or anything else that might fall over. If possible, move to an open place.

If you are in a high-rise building on a high floor, do not dash down the stairs. They may be broken or jammed with people. Do not use the elevator, as the power may fail. Modern, high-rise buildings are most often built to stand earthquakes.

Did You Know?

Some part of the earth shakes every thirty seconds. That means there are about a million earthquakes each year.

Very light earthquakes can be felt only by special tools. Most earthquakes are of this type.

If you are in a school, follow your teacher's directions. If you are in a store or other crowded place, do not rush for a door. People are often hurt in crowds that jam exits. If you must leave the building, choose your way out carefully.

After the Earthquake

After the earthquake is over, you must still act carefully. If you are home, do not use matches or light an open flame until you are sure there is no gas leak. Do not switch on lights or appliances. Switches give off sparks that can set fire to gas from broken lines.

Don't walk around in stockings or bare feet. There may be broken glass on the floor.

Don't eat or drink anything that has not been covered. The food, also, may have glass in or on it.

Check for fires and report any that you find. Do not touch a fallen power line or anything touching a power line. Use your telephone only for reporting emergencies. If you have a portable radio, switch it on in a safe place to listen for news and directions.

Don't think that the danger is past just because the shaking is over. Sometimes **aftershocks** can cause more damage. If you live near the sea or another large body of water, move to high ground as quickly as possible. There may be danger from very high waves or flooding.

aftershocks, periods of shaking that follow the main earthquake.

Following the Alaskan earthquake of 1964.

EARTHQUAKE

by Tay Thomas

In 1964 an earthquake hit Alaska. It turned out to be the most powerful earthquake ever to hit North America. In this story, Tay Thomas tells what she and her young children, Anne and David, saw and felt during that quake.

About five o'clock in the afternoon I went upstairs with the children to watch TV. It was a little after five-thirty when I heard a rumble. I leaped off the bed, yelling, "Earthquake!" I grabbed Anne and called to David. They both moved with lightning speed. We had reached the front hall when the house began to shake.

We were about ten feet past the front door when it suddenly seemed the world was coming to an end. We were thrown to the ground, which was shaking up and down with the sharpest jarring I've ever felt. It seemed an eternity that we lay there in the snow.

In a few seconds the whole house started to fall apart. It split right at the hall we had just come through. We heard the noise of breaking glass, then the horrible sound of wood being broken apart. The trees were crashing all about us, adding to the terrible noise.

Next the earth began breaking up all around us. A great crack started to open in the snow between Anne and me. I quickly pulled her across it toward me.

Now the earth seemed to be rising just ahead of us. I had the strange feeling that we were riding backward on a Ferris wheel, going down. I also had the brief thought that we were falling down into the sea.

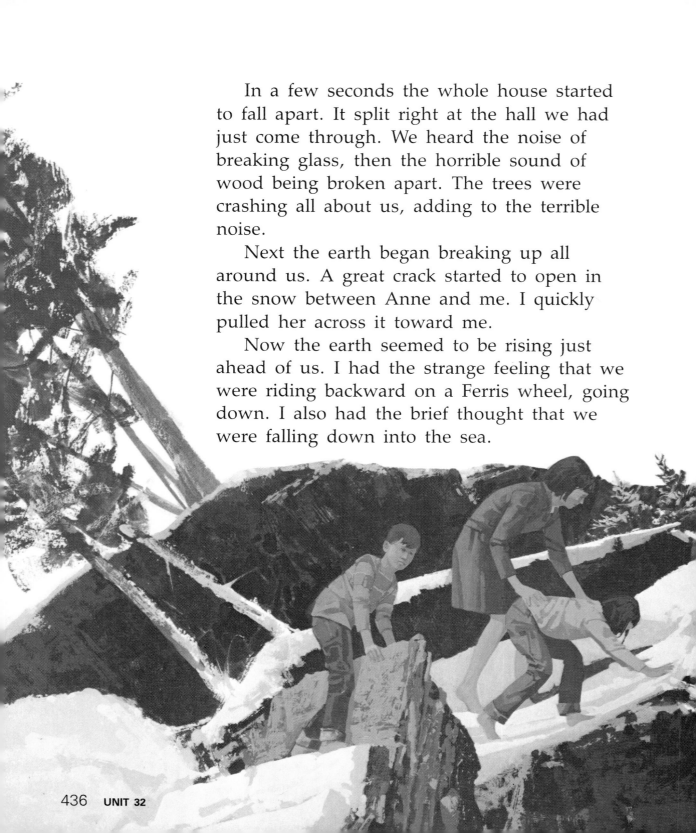

When the worst of the rocking stopped, I looked around. I saw that we, our house, and our yard had all fallen down to sea level. Before the earthquake our house had stood on a high bluff overlooking the sea.

The quake had left a steep cliff above us. All I could think of was that the water would probably rise and we would be trapped.

The children were both crying and saying over and over, "What will we do?" I knew we'd have to move carefully but fast. I had to find a way up that cliff.

The next fifteen or twenty minutes were one great nightmare. We climbed toward the cliff, up and down the great slabs of earth and snow.

I saw that many houses had been flattened. Electric wires lay across the rocks and snow. This alarmed me, and I warned the children not to touch the wires.

People soon helped the Thomases up the cliff. One of the helpers gave the Thomases a ride to his home. That evening, the radio warned of huge waves from the sea. To be safe, everyone moved farther away from the water. The Thomases slept safely that night. But they would never forget the earthquake of '64.

Checking Comprehension and Skills

1. According to Seymour Simon, what are three things to stay away from if you are inside a house during an earthquake? (432)

•2. Did Tay Thomas, the author of "Earthquake!" know about the flooding Seymour Simon warned of? Support your answer. (437)

•3. Did the Thomases have to avoid falling or fallen objects outdoors, as Simon warned? Give evidence to support your answer.

4. What is the most interesting thing you learned about earthquakes? Tell why.

Choose the word that fits each sentence. Show where you divided the word into syllables.
   overlooking   flattened   confusing

○5. Many houses had been ___.

○6. Before the earthquake, our house had stood on a bluff ___ the sea.

• Comparisons   ○ Structure: Syllables

Fruity Quake Shake

Earthquakes are no fun. But shaking up ice cream, milk, and fruit can be both fun and delicious. Follow the recipe below and find out for yourself.

Combine the ingredients below in a tall glass or pitcher. Then stir or shake until smooth.

1. one cup chilled, fresh milk
2. one-half to one cup vanilla ice cream
3. any of the following: fresh strawberries, mashed banana, crushed pineapple, orange juice, crushed raspberries

HURRICANES

Hurricanes are wind- and rainstorms that form over the oceans. Most often, hurricanes hit the United States in its far southeast corner.

Hurricanes are much larger storms than tornadoes. They may cover an area several hundred miles wide. The speed of a hurricane's winds is not as great as a tornado's winds, however. Sometimes, hurricane winds blow two hundred miles an hour.[1] Most often, they blow about one hundred miles an hour.[2] The center of a hurricane is called its *eye.* The eye is calm. The hurricane's winds whirl around the eye.

---

1. about 320 kilometers (km)
2. about 160 km

Stocking Up

Mom had been in a hurricane before. She knew what to do. After the man on the radio said that the storm would be on us by midnight, she began to move quickly. She sent me to the grocery store and told me to hurry. The last time she was in a hurricane, she said, the stores ran out of some things.

Pulling a wagon behind me, I made my way through the wind and the light rain.

---

1. Do you think the store will be crowded? Why or why not?

By the time I got to the store, it was already packed. There were no more shopping carts, so the wagon came in handy. I wormed my way up the aisles, grabbing food that didn't need a refrigerator or a stove—like Mom said.

---

2. What kinds of goods do you expect the boy to buy? Why do you think so?

"Canned fruit? That sounds good," I thought. "A box of cereal? But that needs milk. Oh! I can get powdered milk. Bread? They're out. Crackers will do. The canned fruit juice looks good. Raisins, peanut butter, tuna fish . . . ." I began to think this wouldn't be so bad after all.

I waited a long time to pay for the food. The line went halfway through the store. When I got home, Mom was filling big jugs of water to use in case the water lines broke.

"Might as well do your homework, kids. There is nothing to do but wait," Mom said.

Homework? Mary and I sat in front of our books and tapped our pencils. Mom turned on the news. It would be a long night.

Sharpen Your Skills

As you read, stop to predict what you think will happen next. Base your predictions on what has already happened and on things you already know.

3. Were your answers to the questions correct? If not, what clues might have helped you?

As you read "Hurricane!" try to predict what may happen next.

Hurricane!

by Percelle Leidy Coryell

"What's the latest report on the storm, Dad?" asked Sarah Hulse as she squinted up at the dull, gray sky.

Her father answered as he hammered the last board over the front window. "It looks like the first heavy winds will hit the coast in about six hours."

"What should we do now?" Sarah asked.

"We're pretty well prepared. Windows are all boarded up, and we have emergency food and water ready in case we lose electricity and water service."

Sarah's younger brother, Timothy, charged around the side of the house. "Willy-willy's coming! Willy-willy's coming!" he chanted.

Mr. Hulse smiled at Timothy. "Ever since he learned they call hurricanes 'willy-willies' in Australia, he can't stop saying it."

Timothy raced toward his father. "Did you know that all the families who live near the water have to go to shelters in town?"

"High tides could flood the whole beach area," said Mr. Hulse. "The families will probably stay at the high school."

"What about their pets?" asked Timothy, looking suddenly worried.

"Tim, there just isn't room to care for animals at the school," explained Mr. Hulse.

"But that isn't fair!" cried Timothy.

"You know, Dad, I have an idea," said Sarah. "Why can't we bring the pets up here? That big room over the garage is dry and safe."

"That's a great idea!" cried Timothy. "Please, Dad, let us do it."

Mr. Hulse hesitated for a long time. Finally, he said, "Go ahead, but be back here in three hours."

The children ran to get Timothy's big red wagon out of the garage. "Let's start at the north end of Beach Road," called Sarah.

They hurried to the beach. But before they could even see the water, it showered their faces with a salty spray. Swirls of sand stung their eyes.

They pulled the wagon up in front of Mr. Armbruster's white wooden fence. Timothy went inside, while Sarah crossed the street.

By the time the children had reached the end of the second block, the wagon was full. Their passengers numbered four dogs, three cats, two birds, and a monkey.

"It looks like we have our own zoo," laughed Sarah as they returned to the garage. Once there, they settled the animals inside. By now, gusts of wind were angrily snapping the branches of a big tree against the garage window.

As the children headed outside again, Sarah was wishing they could stay inside. By the time they reached the beach, it looked deserted except for a patrolling Coast Guard helicopter.

They checked the houses and found them empty. Sarah's voice sounded relieved as she called out to Timothy. "Guess our job is done. Let's get out of here fast."

"What about Mrs. Topping's cat, Tom?" asked Timothy as he looked toward a small offshore island.

"Oh, Mrs. Topping's probably gone to her daughter's house and taken the cat with her," answered Sarah. But as she turned to leave, she thought she saw a light flickering in one of the small windows.

"Our three hours aren't up yet," said Timothy. "Come on, Sarah. Let's have a look."

Sarah watched as Timothy ran to the dock and stepped into a small boat. The sky was darkening quickly.

"Well, I don't want to let old Tom drown," Sarah said. "But let's make this a fast trip."

A steady rain began falling during the ride to the island. The children anchored the boat to the island dock and hurried to the house.

Timothy bounded across the porch and tried the door. "It's open," he said.

Surprise and fear clutched at Sarah as she entered the cottage and saw the sight before her. "Mrs. Topping!"

The woman lay on the floor. "Oh, Sarah! Timothy!" she called. "I just knew someone would find me. Imagine! I hurried around so much to get away from the hurricane that I tripped and sprained my ankle."

Sarah licked her dry lips. The sound of her own voice seemed strange as she told Mrs. Topping that they would get her off the island. But she wasn't at all sure they could do it.

"Get the door open, Tim, and grab the cat," she ordered quietly. "We've got to move fast."

Timothy didn't make it to the door. The house began to tremble. Then it shook to its very foundation. Sarah ran to the window and saw that water was creeping toward the cottage. When she looked toward shore, Sarah could see nothing but a blinding wall of rain.

"Sarah, I'm scared!" called Timothy in a hollow voice.

Sarah had to steady her voice in order to speak. "We can't get off the island now. Let's do the best we can to ride the storm out here. Tim, open the back windows a few inches. That will change the air pressure inside the building and keep the glass from blowing out." Sarah hurried into the kitchen to find a flashlight and something with which to board up the front windows. Finally, she and

Timothy moved Mrs. Topping into a chair in the center of the living room. Then all three huddled together as the wind grew louder.

The old cottage groaned. The wind tore shingles from the roof, and rain drove down into the room. Sarah and Tim had to shout to be heard over the shrieking of the storm.

Suddenly blackness closed in. The power had gone off. Sarah's hand shook as she lit an oil lamp. Then glass shattered in one of the side rooms as a flying board crashed through a window. Sarah didn't know where they got the strength, but she and Timothy pushed a bookcase over the open window.

Sarah had no idea what time it was. She just knew that they were fighting a losing battle. She brushed the back of her hand across her mouth in frustration. Then her eyes widened in fear. Her hand tasted salty. She knew then that sea water had flooded the island.

There was nothing she could do. Water inched its way up the walls as the building shook helplessly. Then, something strange happened.

"It's stopped. The wind has stopped!" Sarah shouted. She ran to the window.

"It's over!" cried Timothy, jumping up and down in the water.

Sarah couldn't share Timothy's relief. "No, the storm isn't over. This is just the eye of the hurricane. It may be calm like this for five minutes or even half an hour. Then the second half of the storm will roar in." Thoughts were whirling around in Sarah's head. She had been warned never to go out in the eye of a hurricane. But she knew the old cottage wouldn't hold up much longer. And the water was still rising.

"Come on," said Sarah. "We're leaving the island. I don't think we'll make it if we wait."

She and Timothy helped Mrs. Topping to her feet. They moved slowly outside and toward the boat. Mrs. Topping, clutching her cat, was helped into the boat. Timothy climbed in too as Sarah pushed off.

Sarah started to row. There was no wind at all, but Sarah knew the calm wouldn't last. She strained every muscle as she pulled on the oars.

The boat was more than halfway across when a big wave hit. It slammed into the small boat so fast and hard that the left oar was ripped from Sarah's hand and lost in the water. Sarah's throat grew tight as the wind started up again.

Grabbing the remaining oar, Sarah paddled hard—first on one side, then the other. The waves tossed the boat up, then down. But Sarah could just about see the shore.

Sarah was using every last bit of energy in the effort to move her precious cargo. But sheets of rain threatened to swamp the boat, even if the waves didn't.

The wind screamed in again, and Sarah's heart sank. But, then, the wind started blowing the boat toward shore. Sarah couldn't believe it. She paddled as fast as she could. She could see the shoreline getting bigger.

When a great wave lifted the boat, Sarah thought they were done for. But then she saw that they were riding the wave! It carried their boat like a surfboard.

"Hang on!" Sarah screamed. And suddenly they were in the shallow water.

"We made it!" Sarah cried as the boat slid up on the sandy shore. Mr. Hulse and a number of other men splashed toward them.

The wind almost whipped Mr. Hulse's words away as he shouted, "We were going to send a helicopter after you. But it would never have made it in that wind!"

Someone put a dry blanket around Mrs. Topping's shoulders. "We did it on our own," she cried. "Or rather, Sarah did it!"

"Yeah!" Timothy shouted. "We can beat a willy-willy any old day!"

"Oh, no! Don't start that again," groaned Sarah happily.

Checking Comprehension and Skills

1. What sort of storm were the Hulses getting ready for? (445)
2. Why did Sarah and Timothy want to go to the houses in the beach area? (445)
3. Why, in the middle of the story, did Timothy and Sarah head for an island? (447)
•4. When the children left for the island, did you expect them to get back before the storm hit? Why or why not?
•5. In the last paragraph on page 450, Sarah realizes that the island has flooded. Things that were said or that happened earlier in the story provided clues to the fact that the island might flood. The first was on page 445. What was that clue? (445)
6. Do you think Sarah was wise to leave the island when she did? Why or why not?

Which of the words below fits each sentence? Show how you broke the chosen words into syllables.

frustration   foundation   damage

○7. The house shook to its very ___.
○8. Sarah brushed her hand across her mouth in ___.

• Predicting Outcomes
○ Structure: Syllables

It's Not a Story!

Would you prepare in the same way for a tornado, an earthquake, and a hurricane? No, of course not! These emergencies are alike in some ways, but different in other ways. You would handle each one differently.

When you read a textbook, you do it in a way that is different from reading a story. This is because textbooks are different from stories in some ways.

Suppose you are reading a social studies book. What can you do that is different from reading a story? Here are some tips:

- Look for headings. They tell you what each part of the book will be about.
- Use the charts, maps, and graphs. They help you compare facts at a glance.
- Be sure you understand the meaning of any special vocabulary words.
- You may need to read a textbook more slowly than a story, rereading parts of it to help remember the facts and ideas.

Use these tips as you read the part of a social studies book on page 456.

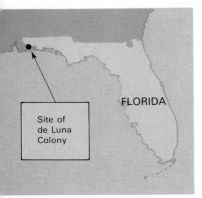

Site of
de Luna
Colony

FLORIDA

climate, the kind of weather a place has.

Florida's Climate

The **climate** of a place is the kind of weather it has. The climate in Florida is warm and moist. Most parts of Florida get plenty of rain. Florida also gets bad storms called hurricanes from time to time. Sometimes hurricanes have changed history!

A Famous Hurricane

In 1559 Tristán de Luna[1] brought 1,600 men, women, and children from Mexico to Florida. They were going to start the first permanent colony in Florida. A hurricane wrecked all their ships except three. Most of their supplies were destroyed. The settlers had to give up and return home.

What do the headings tell you about each paragraph above? How does the map help you understand the page? What special vocabulary word did you find?

Remember that you read stories and textbooks in different ways.

---

1. Tristán de Luna (trēs tän' dā lü'nä)

The Ends of the Earth

What places are the highest, coldest, and driest? 458–469
What's it like to walk where it's high or dry? 470–482
When doesn't a fire give warmth? 483–492

The Highest, Coldest, and Driest

The Highest

The highest places on earth are mountains. They are found on every continent. Africa and Australia do not have many mountains. But all the other continents have great mountain ranges. The highest mountain is Mount Everest in Asia.

The Coldest

The coldest places on earth are far from almost everyone. They are near the North and South Poles. The North Pole is sometimes called the "top of the world." The South Pole is sometimes called the "bottom of the world."

The Driest

The driest places on earth are deserts. Like mountains, they are found on every continent. To visit the largest and one of the driest deserts, you would have to go to Africa. Africa's great desert is called the Sahara.

Mountains Young and Old

To most people, mountains stand for everything that is solid. If we could watch the earth for millions of years, though, we would see that mountains are changing.

Most young mountains are big and rough. They are formed by powerful forces deep inside the earth that push land up toward the sky.

As young mountains grow older, they wear down. Wind and rain both help wear mountains down. Scientists think that high mountains may become low hills after many millions of years.

The Appalachians are very old mountains. They are in the eastern United States. Mount Mitchell, the tallest of the Appalachians, is small for a mountain. You can see that on the graph on page 461.

The graph shows the highest mountain in each of five mountain ranges around the world. The Appalachians are the oldest mountains shown on the graph.

How would our graph look if it were made a few million years from now? Some mountains would be higher. The Andes, for example, are still growing.

Others would be lower because they will wear down. If we look far enough into the future, the Rockies could be as low as today's Appalachians.

Does this mean the mountains will all be gone one day? Not at all. Old mountains do wear down. But new mountains are always being formed.

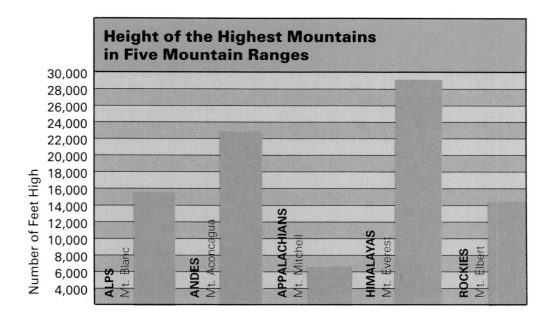

Height of the Highest Mountains in Five Mountain Ranges

Number of Feet High

- 30,000
- 28,000
- 26,000
- 24,000
- 22,000
- 20,000
- 18,000
- 16,000
- 14,000
- 12,000
- 10,000
- 8,000
- 6,000
- 4,000

ALPS — Mt. Blanc
ANDES — Mt. Aconcagua
APPALACHIANS — Mt. Mitchell
HIMALAYAS — Mt. Everest
ROCKIES — Mt. Elbert

Sharpen Your Skills

To read a bar graph, run your finger up to the top of one bar. Next, run your finger left to the number that is even with the top of the bar. If you do this on the Alps bar, you'll see that the highest mountain in the Alps is a little more than 15,000 feet high.[1]

1. What information is compared on the graph?
2. Which ranges have higher mountains than the Rockies?

The graphs in the next two selections will give you information about the coldest and one of the driest places on earth.

---

1. more than 4,572 meters

The Exploration of Antarctica

by Kathy Kain

Antarctica, continent around the South Pole. Antarctica is almost totally covered by ice and snow.

The continent that is farthest south is **Antarctica**. It is larger than the United States. Yet, until the 1800s nobody had ever seen it.

Early Explorers

On January 27, 1820, a Russian sea captain sighted a stretch of ice-covered hills. For several weeks his ship sailed along the edge of the ice. Finally, the captain realized that he had found an "icy continent."

In the next hundred years, people from many countries sailed to Antarctica. Some went to hunt seals and whales. Others went to find out about the life and the land of the coldest place on earth. The following words, written by a sailor, show what the cold was like: "I raised my head to look round and found I couldn't move it back. My clothing had frozen solid as I stood." The graph on page 463 shows how cold Antarctica can be.

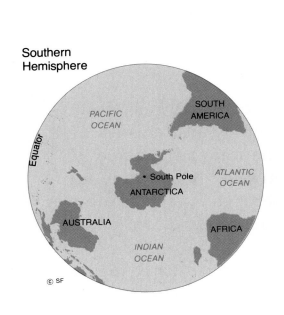

Southern Hemisphere

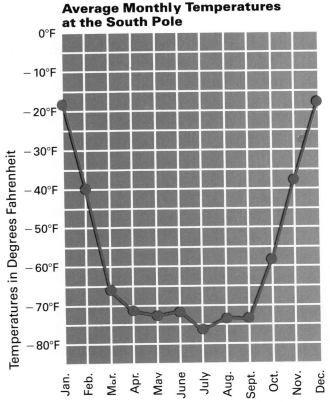

Average Monthly Temperatures at the South Pole

In l898 sailors from Belgium were the first people to spend a winter along Antarctica's coast. During an Antarctic winter the sun disappears for about seventy days. The Belgian ship's log tells how the darkness affected the men: "One seaman had fits . . . . Another went mad with fear . . . . Another died of heart trouble . . . ."

The Race to the South Pole

Thirteen years later, men from Norway led by Roald Amundsen[1] and men from England led by Robert Scott built bases on Antarctica's coast. Both groups planned to be first to reach the **South Pole**.

During this race to the South Pole, Scott and his men battled high winds, crossed dangerous cracks in the ice, and endured "snow like heavy wet sleet." One of the men wrote: "We are wet through; our tents are wet through . . . . Everything round, on, and about us is wet."

On January 17, 1912, Scott's party reached the South Pole. But the Norwegians had reached the Pole earlier—on December 14, 1911. Look at the graph on page 463 to find out why these explorers chose to travel in January and December.

Scott and his men died on the trip back to their base. Before Scott died, he wrote: ". . . feet frozen, no fuel, and a long way from food . . . . We are very near the end, but have not and will not lose our good cheer."

Some good may have come from the deaths of these men. Their brave spirit impressed others who went to Antarctica after them.

---

1. Roald Amundsen (rō′äl ä′mend sən)

South Pole, the point on earth farthest south.

Robert Scott

Desert Plants

by Kathy Duffy

Deserts are places on earth that average less than ten inches of rain or snow each year. This is much less than the twenty to sixty inches that fall where most people live.

The graph below shows average monthly rain in one desert. The facts on the graph may fool you. To get the facts on the graph, amounts of rain or snow were added up over thirty years and then divided by thirty. During some years, no rain or snow fell. During other years, rains flooded the desert.

A flowering cactus.

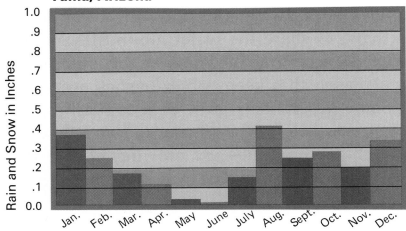

Average Monthly Precipitation Yuma, Arizona

Rain and Snow in Inches

Jan. Feb. Mar. Apr. May June July Aug. Sept. Oct. Nov. Dec.

cholla (a cactus)

barrel cactus

creosote bush

Most plants cannot live in deserts. Rain comes too seldom or the amount is too small. Plants that do grow in deserts have special ways of living with little water.

Some plants live as seeds during the long, dry spells. When heavy rains fall, the seeds grow into plants. The plants bloom into colorful flowers. The flowers soon die, but they leave behind more seeds. These seeds have hard coats that protect them from heat. The graph on page 465 shows the months in which rain is most likely.

Other kinds of desert plants keep growing during dry spells. These plants have special ways of getting the water they need.

Some cactuses have roots that lie near the surface of the ground. The roots spread out in all directions. When rain falls, the roots take in water from a very large area.

One type of bush keeps other plants from growing close by. In this way, the bush does not have to share the water around it. Some people believe that the roots of this bush give off a poison that keeps other bushes away.

Some desert trees grow next to washes, or dry stream beds. When it rains, water flows through these washes. By growing next to the washes, the trees get the water they need.

After desert plants take in water, they keep it in several ways. Cactuses store water in their stems. During dry spells, deep folds appear in the stems as the cactus uses water stored there. When rain falls, the stems fill with water again, and the folds disappear.

Some desert plants are covered with needles. The needles cast shadows that cool the plants' skin. The coolness helps keep the plants from drying out. Other desert plants are covered with wax or hairs. The wax and the hairs also help keep water inside.

Some desert plants look as if they die during long dry spells. But below ground, thick roots or large bulbs go on living. The plants store water in the roots and bulbs.

Desert plants seem to use every possible way to find and save water. In this way, they live where other plants cannot.

Checking Comprehension and Skills

1. What direction is Antarctica from the United States? (462)
- 2. What is Antarctica's average temperature in June? (462)
3. What are two reasons that people have gone to Antarctica? (462)
4. In what sense was there a race to the South Pole in 1911? (464)
5. What would be hardest for you to live with—Antarctica's cold or its winter darkness? Explain your answer.
6. What are two special ways desert plants get water? (466)
7. What are two ways desert plants keep water? (467)
- 8. Which month is usually the driest in Yuma, Arizona? (465)
9. Do you think the authors of these two articles had the same purpose in mind? What do you think their purpose was?

Which word fits each sentence?
cactuses   coolness   seldom
○10. ___ store water in their stems.
○11. Rain comes too ___ for most plants to grow.

- Graphic Aids: Graphs   ○ Word Study Strategies

from
The Desert Is Theirs

by Byrd Baylor

This is no place
for anyone
who wants
soft hills
and meadows
and everything
green
green
green . . .

This is for hawks
that like only
the loneliest canyons
and lizards
that run
in the hottest sand
and
coyotes
that choose
the rockiest trails.

It's for them.

And for birds
that nest
in cactus
and sing out over
a thousand thorns
because
they're where
they want to be.

It's for them.

And for
hard skinny plants
that do without water
for months
at a time.

Walking Where It's High or Dry

Walking on a mountain or in a desert can be difficult. In each case, the air can cause special problems. Mountain air is sometimes described as thin. That means it has less oxygen in it than air at lower levels. Less oxygen makes breathing more difficult. Desert air is very dry. Walking in a desert would make you thirsty faster than walking in other places.

Using What You Know

You know that if you walk very far in a desert, you might get lost. Sometimes you might get "lost" when you read too. There are times when you can figure out how to say words but still not know what they mean.

Sharpen Your Skills

Here are several ways you've learned to get the meaning of words when you are confused.

- **Words with more than one meaning**
  Sometimes a word may have another meaning than the one you know about. Try rereading the sentence that confuses you. For the problem word, figure out a meaning that makes sense. You can check yourself by looking up the word in a dictionary or glossary.

  Which meaning of *brush* makes sense below?
    The only thing growing along the desert road was the green <u>brush</u>.
    a. tool for painting
    b. bushes; small trees
    c. tool for fixing hair

- **Idioms** A sentence may have an idiom in it. An **idiom** is a group of words with a meaning that is different from the usual meaning of the words by themselves. To figure out the meaning of an idiom, look for clues in the words or sentences around it. Which meaning makes sense for the underlined idiom below?

If you think I like the desert, you're <u>all</u> <u>wet</u>. I don't like hot, dry weather.

a. all wrong   b. soaked with water

- **New words** Some words may be new to you. Use the **context,** the words and sentences around the new word, to get the meaning. What does *parched* mean below?

After walking in the desert, I was <u>parched</u>. I needed to drink water and cool off.

Use the tips on these pages to figure out the meanings of the underlined words below.

Our camp was <u>nestled</u> between two protecting hills. I didn't tell the others I was going for a walk. I didn't want them to <u>get wind of it</u>. By the desert I heard a howl. I was <u>paralyzed</u> with fear. When I could move again, I saw that it was only a <u>lean</u>, lost puppy. It just needed fattening up—and love.

Use what you know to figure out words as you read "The Shortcut."

The Ride from Vail to Frisco

"Can you see the bike path?" asked Lisa.

I squinted to see the narrow path that zigzagged up the side of the mountain.

Lisa and I were standing next to our bikes in Vail, Colorado, looking east. We were in the heart of the Colorado Rockies.

Once before, Lisa had ridden the twenty-six-mile[1] bike path from Vail to Frisco, Colorado. The path is shown on the map at right. Now, twenty-six miles is an easy ride on flat land. On this bike path, though, there's a 2,100-foot[2] climb. Vail Pass is the path's highest point.

When we reached the path, I began to ride very slowly. But even that didn't make the climb easy. By the end of the first mile my heart was pounding and I was gasping for air.

The next few miles were nothing but misery. Then a strange thing happened. I saw how blue the sky was. I noticed the white, purple, and red flowers against the deep green of the grass. I even began to forget my pain.

---

1. almost 42 kilometers   2. 640 meters

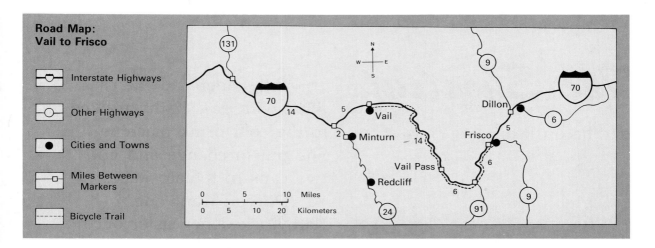

Road Map:
Vail to Frisco

Interstate Highways

Other Highways

Cities and Towns

Miles Between Markers

Bicycle Trail

As we neared Vail Pass, the sky turned black. Thunder roared and lightning crackled around us. Then a building appeared ahead. It was the Vail Pass rest stop! We took cover.

Within half an hour, the sun came out. As we started downhill toward Frisco, I was already looking forward to next year's ride.

Sharpen Your Skills

Road maps show you how to get from one place to another. The **scale of miles** shows how far one place is from another. The **map key** shows symbols that stand for things such as towns.

1. What kind of road runs near the bike path?
2. How far is Vail Pass from Frisco?

The map in "The Shortcut" will help you see where the girls in the story get lost.

The Shortcut

by Sharon Fear

While Janet had the car filled with gas, Kathy walked to the cold drink machine. She put in change and got two cans of tomato juice.

"Do you want one?" Kathy asked her sister once they were ready to leave.

"Maybe later," said Janet. "Look," she went on, pointing to a road map. "If we leave Highway 60 and take Route 9, we can save some time."

"OK," said Kathy. "You're the driver."

Even though they were tired, they were glad to be moving again. The little bit of breeze felt good. It was almost noon, and it was already over one hundred degrees.

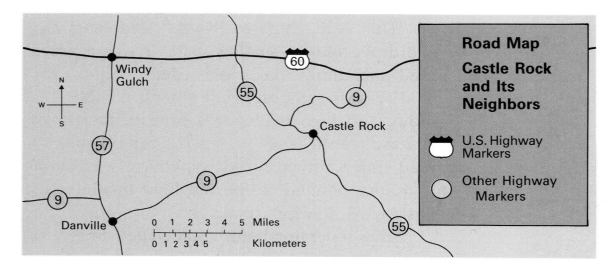

The girls had expected the desert to be hot, but they hadn't expected all this color. Clumps of pale green and yellow, pink, white, and purple flowers were everywhere. Even some of the cactuses had blossoms on them.

"I hope it looks like this where Gary and Anita live," said Kathy.

Their cousins Gary and Anita had moved from Colorado to Danville, Arizona, two years ago. The four cousins hadn't seen each other since. So, when Kathy's parents asked Kathy what she wanted for her birthday, she had said, "a trip to see Gary and Anita."

The girls' parents couldn't go, but they let the girls go alone.

"Janet is eighteen and a good driver," their mother had said. "She can handle it."

Their father had finally agreed.

"This is the turn we want," said Janet as she drove onto a smaller road. It was a gravel road and didn't look much used.

The girls sang along to a song on the radio, and then made up a song of their own. It wasn't until Janet pulled the car off the road that Kathy realized something was wrong.

Kathy pointed to the red light on the dashboard. "What's that?"

"The generator light," said Janet. She turned off the motor to let the car rest. When she tried to start it again, the engine groaned but didn't start. By the third turn of the key, the engine made no sound at all.

They waited for thirty minutes, but no cars came by. At last they got out the road map.

"We should be about here." Janet pointed to a spot on the map. "The town of Castle Rock is about five miles up the road. That's a two hour walk. But if we cut across the desert, it'll be less than half as far."

"We might get lost," said Kathy.

"Not if we're careful," said Janet. "And we won't be frying in this sun for as long."

From their suitcases they got hats to protect them from the sun. Janet changed her sandals for running shoes. Kathy grabbed the full can of juice as well as a water jug, and off they went into the desert.

Walking was easy where the ground was hard. But in many places the ground turned soft and sandy and seemed to suck at their feet. The sun was boiling hot.

"I read that it gets to 120 degrees in the desert," said Kathy. "But even in the hot summer it gets really cold at night."

"You're full of good news," said Janet as she looked around. The car and the road were now out of sight.

"I'm so hungry, I could almost eat that lizard," said Janet as a tan lizard ran from behind a bush.

"Some cactuses have fruit that's good to eat," said Kathy. "And some have water inside. You have to mash up the insides, but it makes juice. I saw it on television."

Janet laughed and put her arm around Kathy's shoulder. "Kathy, I'm surprised at the things you know."

The sun beat down. The girls were hot, thirsty, and exhausted. And there was no town in sight. Janet shook her head. "We should have seen that little town by now."

To make matters worse, the girls faced hills that they were going to have to climb.

"We might be able to see the road or the town from up there," said Kathy, pointing to the hill nearest them.

Slowly, the two girls climbed. But from the top they saw nothing but more hills.

Then Janet cried, "Look!" About a mile away was a cloud of dust. "It's a pickup! There must be a dirt road down there. Hey! Hey!" she shouted as she waved her arms.

The truck showed no sign of stopping.

"He can't hear us!" said Janet.

Suddenly Kathy grabbed the juice can. With its shiny bottom, she flashed sunlight onto the truck's windshield. She moved the can back and forth, flashing again and again.

The truck slowed, and Kathy flashed the can again. At last the truck stopped. A man got out and looked in their direction.

"Hey! Hello!" cried Kathy and Janet, waving their arms above their heads. The man waved back and started toward them at the same time they climbed down the hill.

As he drove into Castle Rock, the man told the girls how far off course they'd been. Castle Rock was nestled between hills almost four miles west of the hill they had climbed. "You're very lucky girls," he said.

"We know that now," said Janet. "We can't thank you enough." Then she turned to Kathy. "How did you know to signal like that? You read it, I suppose, or saw it on TV?"

"No," said Kathy. "I saw it in a movie."

Checking Comprehension and Skills

1. Describe the area in which Janet and Kathy were driving. (477)

• 2. Why did Janet think it would save time to leave Highway 60 and take Route 9? Give evidence from the map to support your answer. (477)

3. Why did the girls leave their car and begin to walk? (478)

4. Why did Janet think that she and Kathy would save time by walking away from the road? (478)

5. In which direction did the girls walk? (477)

• 6. In which direction should they have walked? (477)

7. What do you think caused Janet and Kathy to walk in the wrong direction?

8. Who was better able to solve the major problem the girls faced—Janet or Kathy? (481)

9. Do you think the decision to leave the road would have been wise under any conditions? Why or why not?

Choose the word that fits each sentence.
sandal   exhausted   pickup

○10. Janet saw a ___ moving along a road.

○11. The girls were hot and ___.

• Graphic Aids: Maps   ○ Word Study Strategies

Reading Bonus

The Fire on the Mountain

by Harold Courlander and Wolf Leslau

People say that in the old days in a faraway city, there was a young man by the name of Arha.[1] He had come to the city as a boy. He became the servant of a rich merchant, Haptom Hasei.[2]

Haptom Hasei was so rich that he owned everything that money could buy. Often he was very bored. He had tired of everything he knew, and there was nothing new for him to do.

---

1. Arha (är'hä)   2. Hasei (hä sā')

One cold night, when a damp wind was blowing, Haptom called to Arha to bring wood for the fire. When Arha was finished, Haptom began to talk.

"How much cold can a man stand?" he said, speaking at first to himself. "I wonder if it would be possible for a man to stand on the highest peak, where the coldest winds blow, through an entire night without blankets or warm clothing and yet not die?"

"I don't know," Arha said. "But wouldn't it be a foolish thing?"

"Perhaps, if he had nothing to gain by it, it would be a foolish thing to spend the night that way," Haptom said. "But I would be willing to bet that a man couldn't do it."

"I am sure a courageous man could stand without blankets or warm clothing throughout an entire night and not die of it," Arha said. "But as for me, it isn't my affair since I've nothing to bet."

"Well, I'll tell you what," Haptom said. "Since you are so sure it can be done, I'll make a bet with you anyway. Stand among the rocks on Mount Sululta[1] for an entire night without food, water, warm clothing, blankets, or fire. If you do not die of it, I will give you ten acres of good farmland for your own, with a house and cattle."

Arha could hardly believe what he had heard.

"Do you really mean this?" he asked.

"I am a man of my word," Haptom replied.

"Then tomorrow night I will do it," Arha said. "Afterwards, for all the years to come, I shall have my own farm."

---

1. Sululta (sú lŭl'tä)

But Arha was very worried, because the wind swept bitterly across that peak. So in the morning Arha went to a wise old man from his tribe. Arha told him of the bet he had made. The old man listened quietly and thoughtfully. When Arha had finished, he said:

"I will help you. Across the valley from Sululta is a high rock. It can be seen in the daytime. Tomorrow night as the sun goes down, I shall build a fire there, so that it can be seen from where you stand on the peak. All night long you must watch the light of my fire. Do not close your eyes or let the darkness creep upon you. As you watch my fire, think of its warmth, and think of me, your friend, sitting there tending it for you. If you do this, you will survive, no matter how bitter the night wind."

Arha thanked the old man warmly and went back to Haptom's house with a light heart. He told Haptom he was ready. In the afternoon Haptom sent Arha, under the watchful eyes of other servants, to the top of Mount Sululta. There, as night fell, Arha removed his robe. He stood in the damp, cold wind that swept across the mountain. Across the valley, several miles away, Arha saw the light of his friend's fire, which shone like a star in the blackness.

The wind turned colder. It seemed to pass through Arha's flesh and chill his bones. The rock on which Arha stood felt like ice. Each hour the cold numbed him more, until he thought he would never be warm again. But he kept his eyes upon the twinkling light across the valley. He remembered that his old friend sat there tending a fire for him. Sometimes wisps of fog blotted out the light. Then Arha strained to see until the fog passed. He sneezed and coughed and shivered and began to feel ill. Yet all night through he stood there. Only when the dawn came did he put on his robe and go down the mountain, back to the city.

Haptom was very surprised to see Arha. He questioned his servants thoroughly.

"Did Arha stay all night without food or drink or blankets or warm clothing?"

"Yes," the servants said. "He did all of these things."

"Well, you are a strong fellow," Haptom said to Arha. "How were you able to do it?"

"I simply watched the light of a fire on a distant hill," Arha said.

"What! You watched a fire? Then you lose the bet. You are still my servant and you own no land!"

"But this fire was not close enough to warm me. It was far across the valley!"

"I won't give you the land," Haptom said. "You didn't do as you promised. It was only the fire that saved you."

Arha was very sad. He went again to his old friend and told him what had happened.

"Take the matter to the judge," the old man advised him.

Arha went to the judge and told his story, and the judge sent for Haptom. When Haptom told his story again, and the servants said once more that Arha had watched a distant fire across the valley, the judge spoke:

"No, you have lost, for Haptom Hasei's rule was that you must be without fire."

Once more Arha went to his old friend with the sad news that he was doomed to the life of a servant. It was as though he had not spent the night on the mountain peak.

"Don't give up hope," the old man said. "More wisdom grows wild in the hills than in any city judge."

The old man got up from where he sat and went to find a man named Hailu,[1] in whose house he had been a servant when he was young. The old man explained to Hailu about the bet between Haptom and Arha. Then the old man asked if something couldn't be done.

"Don't worry about it," Hailu said after thinking for a while. "I will take care of it for you."

Some days later Hailu sent invitations to many people in the city to come to a feast at

---

1. Hailu (hā'lü)

his house. Haptom was among them, and so was the judge who had ruled that Arha had lost the bet.

When the day of the feast arrived, the guests came riding on mules with fine trappings. Their servants walked behind them on foot. Haptom came with twenty servants, one of whom held a silk umbrella to shade Haptom from the sun. Four drummers played music that let everyone know that great Haptom was here.

The guests sat on soft rugs and talked. From the kitchen came the smell of roast goat, roast corn, pancakes, and many wonderful sauces. The smell of the food only made the guests hungrier. Time passed. The food

should have been served, but the guests didn't see it. Only the tempting smells drifted in from the kitchen. The evening came, and still no food was served. The guests began to whisper among themselves. It was very strange that Hailu had not had the food brought out. Still the smells came from the kitchen. At last, one of the guests spoke out for all the others:

"Hailu, why do you do this to us? Why do you invite us to a feast and then serve us nothing?"

"Why, can't you smell the food?" Hailu asked with surprise.

"Indeed, we can, but smelling is not eating. There is no nourishment in it!"

"And is there warmth in a fire so distant that it can hardly be seen?" Hailu asked. "If Arha was warmed by the fire he watched while standing on Mount Sululta, then you have been fed by the smells coming from my kitchen."

The people agreed with him. The judge now saw his mistake, and Haptom was shamed. He thanked Hailu for his advice. He announced that Arha was then and there the owner of the land, the house, and the cattle.

Then Hailu ordered the food brought in, and the feast began.

Books to Read

Moog-Moog, Space Barber by Mark Teague. Scholastic.

Elmo Freem gets a terrible haircut just as school is about to start. Space monsters take him to the planet Moogie to get it fixed by Moog-Moog, the finest barber in the universe.

Silver by Gloria Whelan. Random House.

What would it be like to live in Alaska? Rachel lives there, near snow-covered Mount McKinley (Denali), the highest peak in North America. Her father raises sled dogs, and Rachel hopes to train her puppy, Silver, to become a great racer. Then suddenly Silver disappears.

Tornado Alert by Franklyn M. Branley. Harper.

A big tornado can wipe out everything in its path. Learn how to tell when a tornado is coming and what you can do to keep safe if one strikes.

Glossary

How to Use the Pronunciation Key

After each entry word in this glossary, there is a special spelling, called the **pronunciation.** It shows how to say the word. The word is broken into syllables and then spelled with letters and signs. You can look up these letters and signs in the **pronunciation key** to see what sounds they stand for.

This dark mark (′) is called the **primary accent.** It follows the syllable you say with the most force. This lighter mark (′) is the **secondary accent.** Say the syllable it follows with medium force. Syllables without marks are said with least force.

Full Pronunciation Key

a	hat, cap	**i**	it, pin	**p**	paper, cup	**ə**	represents:
ā	age, face	**ī**	ice, five	**r**	run, try		a in about
ä	father, far			**s**	say, yes		e in taken
		j	jam, enjoy	**sh**	she, rush		i in pencil
b	bad, rob	**k**	kind, seek	**t**	tell, it		o in lemon
ch	child, much	**l**	land, coal	**th**	thin, both		u in circus
d	did, red	**m**	me, am	**ŦH**	then, smooth		
		n	no, in				
e	let, best	**ng**	long, bring	**u**	cup, butter		
ē	equal, be			**u̇**	full, put		
ėr	her, learn	**o**	hot, rock	**ü**	rule, move		
		ō	open, go				
f	fat, if	**ô**	order, all	**v**	very, save		
g	go, bag	**oi**	oil, toy	**w**	will, woman		
h	he, how	**ou**	house, out	**y**	young, yet		
				z	zoo, breeze		
				zh	measure, seizure		

The contents of the Glossary entries in this book have been adapted from *Scott, Foresman Beginning Dictionary,* Copyright © 1983 Scott, Foresman and Company; *Scott, Foresman Intermediate Dictionary,* Copyright © 1983 Scott, Foresman and Company; and *Scott, Foresman Advanced Dictionary,* Copyright © 1983 Scott, Foresman and Company.

A a

a·cre (ā′kər), a unit of area equal to 43,560 square feet. Land is measured in acres: *The farmer owned 160 acres of land. noun.*

a hat	**i** it	**oi** oil	**ch** child	a in about
ā age	**ī** ice	**ou** out	**ng** long	e in taken
ä far	**o** hot	**u** cup	**sh** she	ə = i in pencil
e let	**ō** open	**u̇** put	**th** thin	o in lemon
ē equal	**ô** order	**ü** rule	**ŦH** then	u in circus
ėr term			**zh** measure	

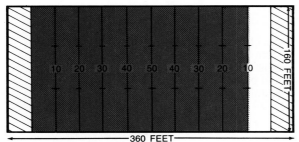

acre—An acre is smaller than a football field. The green part of this football field is an acre.

air·port (er′pôrt′ *or* ar′pôrt′), area used by aircraft to land and take off. An airport has buildings for passengers and for keeping and repairing aircraft. *noun.*

airport

aisle (īl), **1** passage between rows of seats in a theater, church, or school. **2** any long, narrow passage: *The aisles in a supermarket are often too narrow. noun.*

am·bu·lance (am′byə ləns), automobile, boat, or aircraft used to carry sick, injured, or wounded persons, usually to a hospital. *noun.*

an·ces·tor (an′ses′tər), person from whom one is directly descended. Your grandfathers, your grandmothers, and so on back, are your ancestors. *noun.*

an·chor (ang′kər), **1** a heavy piece of iron or steel fastened to a chain or rope and dropped from a ship to the bottom of the water to hold the ship in place: *The anchor kept the boat from drifting.* **2** hold in place with an anchor: *Can you anchor the boat in this storm?* **1** *noun,* **2** *verb.*

anchor

an·cient (ān′shənt), **1** of times long past. **2** of great age; very old. *adjective.*

an·tics (an′tiks), funny movements or actions: *The antics of the clown amused us. noun plural.*

ape (āp), a large, tailless monkey with long arms. Apes can stand almost erect and walk on two feet. Chimpanzees, gorillas, orangutans, and gibbons are apes. *noun.*

ap·pli·ance (ə plī′əns), thing like a tool or small machine used in doing something. A can opener is an appliance for opening tin cans. Vacuum cleaners, washing machines, and refrigerators are household appliances. *noun.*

ar·range (ə rānj′), put in the correct order or the proper position: *Please arrange the books on the library shelf.* verb, **ar·ranged, ar·rang·ing.**

ash·es (ash′iz), what remains of a thing after it has burned: *I removed the ashes from the fireplace. noun plural.*

ath·lete (ath′lēt′), person trained by exercise and practice to be strong, fast, and skillful. Baseball players and swimmers are athletes. *noun.*

ath·let·ic (ath let′ik), **1** of or like an athlete. **2** strong and active: *She is an athletic girl.* *adjective.*

at·mo·sphere (at′mə sfir), **1** air that surrounds the earth. **2** mass of gases that surrounds any heavenly body: *The atmosphere of Venus is cloudy. noun.*

at·tack (ə tak′), use force against; set upon to hurt; begin fighting: *The dog attacked the cat. The enemy attacked at dawn. verb.*

at·tract (ə trakt′), draw to itself or oneself: *The magnet attracted the iron filings. Honey attracts flies. verb.*

B b

ba·con (bā′kən), salted and smoked meat from the back and sides of a pig or hog. *noun.*

badge (baj), something worn to show that a person belongs to a certain job, group, school, class, or club: *The police officer wore a silver badge. noun.*

bald (bôld), **1** wholly or partly without hair on the head. **2** without its natural covering: *A mountain with no trees or grass is bald. adjective.*

beam (bēm), a large, long piece of timber, iron, or steel, ready for use or already used in building: *Our ceiling has heavy beams for support. noun.*

bean·stalk (bēn′stôk′), stem of a bean plant. *noun.*

be·hav·ior (bi hā′vyər), way of acting; conduct; actions: *Her behavior showed that she was angry. noun.*

bis·cuit (bis′kit), **1** soft bread dough baked in small shapes. **2** a thin, flat, dry bread; cracker. *noun, plural* **bis·cuits** *or* **bis·cuit.**

blur (blėr), **1** make less clear in form or outline: *Mist blurred the hills.* **2** become dim: *My eyes blurred with tears. verb,* **blurred, blur·ring.**

book·case (bùk′kās′), piece of furniture with shelves for holding books. *noun.*

burst (bėrst), **1** fly apart suddenly with force; explode: *If you stick a pin into a balloon, it will burst.* **2** be about to give way to a show of emotion such as laughter or tears. *verb,* **burst, burst·ing.**

C c

cac·tus (kak′təs), plant with a thick, fleshy stem that usually has spines but no leaves. Most cactuses grow in very hot, dry regions and often have brightly colored flowers. *noun, plural* **cac·tus·es, cac·ti** (kak′tī).

cactus

cane (kān), **1** a slender stick used as an aid in walking. **2** a long, jointed stem, such as that of the bamboo, often used in making furniture. **3** plant having such stems: *sugar cane. noun.*

ca·noe (kə nü′), a light boat pointed at both ends and moved with a paddle. *noun.*

canoe

car·go (kär′gō), load of goods carried by a ship or plane: *The freighter had docked to unload a cargo of wheat. noun, plural* **car·goes** or **car·gos.**

car·riage (kar′ij), **1** vehicle that moves on wheels. Some carriages are pulled by horses and are used to carry people. **2** a moving part of a machine that supports another part: *a typewriter carriage.* **3** manner of holding the head and body: *She has a queenly carriage. noun.*

cer·e·mo·ny (ser′ə mō′nē), a special act or set of acts to be done on religious or public occasions such as weddings, funerals, graduations, or holidays: *One of the ceremonies at the Olympic Games is the awarding of medals. noun, plural* **cer·e·mo·nies.**

chal·lenge (chal′ənj), **1** invitation to a game or contest. **2** invite to a game or contest; dare: *They challenged our swimming team.* **3** anything that demands or requires effort: *We face challenges every day.* **4** demand or require effort: *Explorers challenge the unknown.* 1, 3 *noun,* 2, 4 *verb,* **chal·lenged, chal·leng·ing.**

change (chānj), **1** make different; become different: *The wind changed from east to west.* **2** money returned to you when you have given a larger amount than the price of what you buy: *I handed the clerk a quarter for the candy bar, and he gave me five cents in change.* **3** small coins: *He always carries a pocketful of change.* 1 *verb,* **changed, chang·ing;** 2, 3 *noun.*

chap·ter (chap′tər), a main division of a book, dealing with a particular part of the story or of the subject. *noun.*

check·up (chek′up′), **1** careful examination. **2** physical examination: *I went to the doctor for a checkup. noun.*

chore (chôr), **1** odd job; small task: *Feeding my pets is my daily chore.* **2** a hard or unpleasant thing one must do: *My homework was a chore because I was tired. noun.*

clay (klā), a sticky kind of earth that can be easily shaped when wet and hardens when it is dried or baked. Bricks and dishes are made from various kinds of clay. *noun.*

col·lar (kol′ər), **1** the part of a coat, a dress, or a shirt that makes a band around the neck. **2** a leather or metal band for the neck of a dog or other pet animal. *noun.*

a hat	**i** it	**oi** oil	**ch** child	a in about
ā age	**ī** ice	**ou** out	**ng** long	e in taken
ä far	**o** hot	**u** cup	**sh** she	ə = { i in pencil
e let	**ō** open	**u̇** put	**th** thin	o in lemon
ē equal	**ô** order	**ü** rule	**ŦH** then	u in circus
ėr term			**zh** measure	

com·plete (kəm plēt′), finish: *She completed her homework early in the evening. verb,* **com·plet·ed, com·plet·ing.**

con·nect (kə nekt′), join one thing to another; fasten together: *connect a hose to a faucet. verb.*

con·tain·er (kən tā′nər), box, can, jar, or carton used to hold something. A pitcher is a container. *noun.*

con·ti·nent (kon′tə nənt), one of the seven great masses of land on the earth. The continents are North America, South America, Europe, Africa, Asia, Australia, and Antarctica. *noun.*

coun·try·side (kun′trē sīd′), the land outside cities and towns; the country: *I saw many cows in the countryside. noun.*

court (kôrt), **1** place set aside for a certain purpose: *a tennis court, a basketball court.* **2** place where a king, queen, or other ruler lives; royal palace. *noun.*

coy·o·te (kī ō′tē *or* kī′ōt), a small wolflike animal living on the prairies of western North America. *noun, plural* **coy·o·tes** or **coy·o·te.**

coyote

crab (krab), a shellfish with eight legs, two claws, and a broad, flat shell covering. Many kinds of crabs are good to eat. *noun.*

crab—shell about 4 inches (10 centimeters) wide

crate (krāt), a large frame, box, or basket made of strips of wood, for shipping glass, china, fruit, household goods, or furniture. *noun.*

crate

crunch (krunch), **1** crush noisily with the teeth: *She crunched a carrot.* **2** make such a sound: *The hard snow crunched under our feet. verb.*

cu·ra·tor (kyù rā′tər), person in charge of all or part of a museum, library, art gallery or zoo. *noun.*

cur·rent (kėr′ənt), a flow of air or water; a running stream. Running water or moving air makes a current: *The current swept the stick down the river. noun.*

D d

dam·age (dam′ij), **1** harm or injury that lessens the worth or usefulness of something: *The accident did some damage to the car.* **2** harm or hurt something so as to lessen its usefulness: *I damaged my radio when I fell.* **1** *noun,* **2** *verb,* **dam·aged, dam·ag·ing.**

dart (därt), a slender, pointed weapon thrown by hand or shot from a gun. *noun.*

dart gun, a tube through which a dart may be shot. The dart often carries drugs used to tranquilize animals.

dash·board (dash′bôrd′), panel with instruments and gauges in front of the driver in an automobile or aircraft. *noun.*

dead·ly (ded′lē), causing death; likely to cause death or serious injury: *a deadly disease. adjective,* **dead·li·er, dead·li·est.**

deal (dēl), **1** bargain: *He got a good deal on a television set.* **2** an understanding; a plan: *I have a deal to trade some old books with her. noun.*

de·ci·sion (di sizh′ən), the act of making up one's mind: *I have not yet come to a decision about going to the beach. noun.*

deck (dek), one of the floors of a ship. The upper, main, middle, and lower decks of a ship are like the stories or levels of a house. Often the upper deck has no roof over it. *noun.*

deed (dēd), **1** something done; an act; an action: *To feed the hungry is a good deed.* **2** a written or printed proof of ownership. The buyer of land receives a deed from the former owner of the land. *noun.*

de·gree (di grē′), unit for measuring temperature: *The freezing point of water is 32 degrees (32°) Fahrenheit. noun.*

de·pos·it (di poz′it), **1** put in a place to be kept safe: *Deposit your money in the bank.* **2** something put in a certain place to be kept safe: *Money put in the bank is a deposit.* **1** *verb,* **2** *noun.*

de·scribe (di skrīb′), tell in words how a person looks, feels, or acts, or how a place, a thing, or an event looks; tell or write about: *The reporter described the accident. verb,* **de·scribed, de·scrib·ing.**

de·ter·mine (di tėr′mən), make up one's mind very firmly: *He determined to become the best scout in his troop. verb,* **de·ter·mined, de·ter·min·ing.**

de·vel·op (di vel′əp), **1** come into being; grow: *Plants develop from seeds.* **2** bring into being: *Scientists have developed many new drugs to fight disease. verb.*

din·ghy (ding′ē), a small rowboat used for carrying people and supplies to and from a larger boat. *noun, plural* **din·ghies.**

dis·guise (dis gīz′), **1** hide what one is by looking like something else: *On Halloween I disguised myself as a ghost.* **2** clothes or other things used to hide or deceive: *Glasses and a wig formed the spy's disguise.* **1** *verb,* **dis·guised, dis·guis·ing; 2** *noun.*

dive (dīv), **1** plunge headfirst into water. **2** act of diving: *We applauded his graceful dive.* **3** plunge downward at a steep angle: *The hawk dived* *straight at the field mouse.* **4** A downward plunge at a steep angle: *The submarine made a dive toward the bottom.* 1, 3 *verb*, **dived** or **dove, dived, div·ing;** 2, 4 *noun.*

dive

drag (drag), **1** pull or move along heavily or slowly: *I dragged along on crutches.* **2** pull or draw along the ground: *A team of horses dragged the big log out of the forest. verb,* **dragged, drag·ging.**

E e

earth·quake (ėrth′kwāk′), a shaking or sliding of the ground, caused by the sudden movement of rock far beneath the earth's surface. *noun.*

e·lec·tric·i·ty (i lek′tris′ə tē), **1** form of energy which can produce light, heat, and motion: *Electricity makes light bulbs shine, radios and televisions play, cars start, and subways run.* **2** electric current: *Most refrigerators are run by electricity. noun.*

el·e·va·tor (el′ə vā′tər), **1** something which raises or lifts up. **2** a moving platform or cage to carry people and things up and down in a building or mine. *noun.*

a hat	i it	oi oil	ch child	(a in about
ā age	ī ice	ou out	ng long	e in taken
ä far	o hot	u cup	sh she	ə = { i in pencil
e let	ō open	u̇ put	th thin	o in lemon
ē equal	ô order	ü rule	ŦH then	(u in circus
ėr term			zh measure	

en·dure (en du̇r′ *or* en dyu̇r′), put up with; bear; stand: *The pioneers endured many hardships. verb,* **en·dured, en·dur·ing.**

en·er·gy (en′ər jē), **1** active strength or force: *I was so full of energy that I could not keep still.* **2** power to work or act: *All my energy was used to keep the fire from spreading. noun, plural* **en·er·gies.**

earthquake—houses damaged by the San Francisco earthquake in 1906

en·gi·neer (en′jə nir′), **1** person who takes care of or runs engines. **2** person who is an expert in engineering. *noun.*

elevator

en·gi·neer·ing (en′jə nir′ing), science of planning and building engines, machines, roads, bridges, canals, and the like. *noun.*

e·quip·ment (i kwip′mənt), supplies; things that are needed: *We keep our camping equipment in order. noun.*

ex·ag·ge·ra·tion (eg zaj′ə rā′shən), statement that goes beyond the truth: *It is an exaggeration to say that you would rather die than touch a snake. noun.*

ex·cuse (ek skyüz′ *for* 1, 3; ek skyüs′ *for* 2), **1** offer a reason for; try to remove the blame of: *She excused her lateness by blaming traffic.* **2** reason, real or pretended, that is given; explanation: *He had many excuses for coming late.* **3** pardon; forgive: *Excuse me; I have to go now.* 1, 3 *verb,* **ex·cused, ex·cus·ing;** 2 *noun.*

ex·ist (eg zist′), **1** be: *The world has existed a long time.* **2** be real: *Some people believe that ghosts exist. verb.*

ex·per·i·ment (ek sper′ə ment *for* 1; ek sper′ə mənt *for* 2), **1** try in order to find out something; make trials or tests. **2** a trial or test to find out something: *Scientists test ideas or theories by experiment.* 1 *verb,* 2 *noun.*

F f

fac·tor·y (fak′tər ē), building or group of buildings where things are made with machines, or by hand. *noun, plural* **fac·tor·ies.**

factory

fail (fāl), **1** be of no use when needed: *When I needed their help, they failed me.* **2** be missing; be not enough: *The power failed so the motor would not run. verb.*

false (fôls), not true; not correct; wrong: *false statements. adjective.*

fas·ten (fas′n), tie, lock, or make hold together in any way: *fasten a door, fasten a seat belt. verb.*

fern (fėrn), kind of plant that has roots, stems, and feathery leaves, but no flowers. Tiny seeds grow on the backs of the leaves. *noun.*

fern

fid·dle (fid′l), **1** a violin. **2** play on a violin. **3** make aimless movements; toy with: *The shy child fiddled with crayons and paid no attention to the guests.* 1 *noun,* 2, 3 *verb,* **fid·dled, fid·dling.**

fire·place (fīr′plās′), place built to hold a fire. An indoor fireplace is usually made of brick or stone, with a chimney leading up from it through the roof. *noun.*

fog·horn (fog′hôrn′), horn that warns ships in foggy weather. *noun.*

for·ward (fôr′wərd), **1** onward; ahead: *Forward, march!* **2** to the front: *to come forward.* **3** player in basketball, soccer, and some other games who plays in the front line. 1, 2 *adverb,* 3 *noun.*

freight (frāt), goods that a train, truck, ship, or aircraft carries. *noun.*

frown (froun), **1** wrinkling of the forehead to show anger, dislike for, or confusion. **2** wrinkle the forehead to show confusion or anger; look displeased or angry: *My teacher frowned when I came in late.* 1 *noun,* 2 *verb.*

fur·ni·ture (fėr′nə chər), movable articles placed in a room or house. Beds, chairs, tables, and desks are furniture. *noun.*

G g

ge·og·ra·phy (jē og′rə fē), study of the earth's surface, climate, continents, countries, peoples, industries, and products. *noun.*

gen·er·al (jen′ər əl), a high officer in command of many soldiers in an army. *noun.*

gen·e·ra·tor (jen′ə rā′tər), a machine for producing electricity. The generator on an automobile charges the battery. *noun.*

ge·ol·o·gist (jē ol′ə jist), person who is an expert in geology. *noun.*

ge·ol·o·gy (jē ol′ə jē), science that deals with the earth's crust, the layers of which it is made up, and their history. *noun, plural* **ge·ol·o·gies.**

gill slit, one of the openings in the throat of a shark and certain fish, through which water flows to supply oxygen.

gog·gles (gog′əlz), large, close-fitting eyeglasses to protect the eyes from light, water, or dust. *noun plural.*

grain (grān), the seed of wheat, oats, corn, and other cereal grasses: *Our breakfast cereal is made from grain. noun.*

grav·i·ty (grav′ə tē), the natural force that causes objects to move or tend to move toward the center of the earth. *noun.*

grum·ble (grum′bəl), complain in a low, gloomy, or angry voice; find fault: *She grumbled about the weather all day. The students are always grumbling about the cafeteria's food. verb,* **grum·bled, grum·bling.**

guard (gärd), **1** watch over; take care of; keep safe: *The dog guarded the child day and night.* **2** person or group that protects or watches. A soldier or group of soldiers protecting a person or place is a guard. **1** *verb,* **2** *noun.*

guest (gest), person who is visiting at another's house; visitor: *She was our guest for dinner. noun.*

gust (gust), a sudden, violent rush of wind: *A gust upset the small sailboat. noun.*

H h

harm (härm), **1** something that causes pain or loss; injury; damage: *He slipped and fell down but suffered no harm.* **2** damage; injure; hurt: *Do not pick or harm the flowers in the park.* **1** *noun,* **2** *verb.*

a hat	i it	oi oil	ch child	a in about
ā age	ī ice	ou out	ng long	e in taken
ä far	o hot	u cup	sh she	i in pencil
e let	ō open	u̇ put	th thin	ə = o in lemon
ē equal	ô order	ü rule	∓H then	u in circus
ėr term			zh measure	

har·vest (här′vist), **1** the gathering in of grain and other food crops, usually in the late summer or early autumn. **2** gather in and bring home for use: *The farmer harvested the wheat.* **1** *noun,* **2** *verb.*

hatch (hach), **1** bring forth (young) from an egg or eggs: *A hen hatches chickens.* **2** come out from an egg: *Three of the chickens hatched today. verb.*

hatch

health (helth), **1** a being well or not sick; a being free from illness of any kind: *Rest, sleep, and exercise are important to your health.* **2** condition of the body: *be in excellent health. noun.*

heart (härt), **1** the part of the body that pumps the blood. **2** middle; center: *in the heart of the forest. noun.*

hel·i·cop·ter (hel′ə kop′tər), aircraft without wings that is lifted from the ground and kept in the air by propellers. *noun.*

helicopter

hi·ber·nate (hī′bər nāt), spend the winter in sleep, as bears, woodchucks, and some other wild animals do. *verb,* **hi·ber·nat·ed, hi·ber·nat·ing.**

high school, school attended after elementary school or junior high school. High school usually includes grades 9 through 12 or 10 through 12.

hint (hint), a slight sign or clue that suggests something without actually showing or telling it: *A small black cloud gave a hint of a coming storm. noun.*

his·tor·y (his′tər ē), **1** story or record of important past events that happened to a person or nation: *the history of the United States.* **2** story of what has happened: *baseball history. noun, plural* **his·tor·ies.**

hot-air balloon, an airtight bag filled with heated air that will rise and float high off the ground. Some balloons have a basket for carrying people.

hot-air balloon

hu·mor·ous (hyü′mər əs), funny; amusing: *We all laughed at the humorous story. adjective.*

hump (hump), **1** a rounded lump that sticks out. **2** mound or small rise: *a hump in the plowed field. noun.*

hur·ri·cane (hèr′ə kān), storm with violent wind and, usually, very heavy rain. The wind in a hurricane blows at more than 75 miles per hour. *noun.*

I i

i·mag·i·na·tion (i maj′ə nā′shən), the power or the ability to form pictures in the mind of things not actually present. A poet, artist, or inventor must have imagination to create new things or ideas. *noun.*

im·press (im pres′), have a strong effect on the mind or feelings of: *The movie about the pioneers impressed us because it showed us their courage. verb.*

in·gre·di·ent (in grē′dē ənt), one of the parts of a mixture: *The ingredients of a cake usually include eggs, sugar, flour, and flavoring. noun.*

in·sist (in sist′), keep firmly to some demand; take a stand and refuse to give in: *He insists that he had a right to use his brother's tools. She insisted that she had told the truth. verb.*

in·tend (in tend′), have in mind as a purpose; mean; plan: *We intend to go home soon. verb.*

in·tro·duce (in′trə düs′ *or* in′trə dyüs′), make known for the first time; make acquainted with: *Mrs. Brown, may I introduce Mr. Smith? The principal introduced the speaker to the students. I introduced my visiting cousin to all my friends. verb,* **in·tro·duced, in·tro·duc·ing.**

in·vent (in vent′), make or think out (something new): *Thomas Edison invented the lightbulb. verb.*

J j

judge (juj), **1** a public official whose duty it is to hear and decide cases in a court of law. **2** person chosen to decide who wins a race or contest. **3** person who can decide how good a thing is: *a judge of dogs in a dog show. noun.*

L l

lan·tern (lan′tərn), case to protect a light from wind or rain. A lantern has sides of glass, paper, or some other material through which light can shine. *noun.*

lantern

lean¹ (lēn), **1** stand slanting; bend: *The small tree leans over in the wind.* **2** rest sloping or slanting: *Lean against me. Lean the ladder against the wall.* **3** tend toward: *The judge leaned toward a different explanation of the accident. verb.*

lean² (lēn), **1** not fat; thin: *a lean and hungry stray dog.* **2** meat having little fat. **1** *adjective,* **2** *noun.*

li·brar·i·an (lī brer′ē ən), **1** person in charge of a library. **2** person trained for work in a library. *noun.*

li·brar·y (lī′brer′ē), **1** a collection of books: *I know two girls who have libraries of their own.* **2** room or building where a collection of books is kept: *He goes to the public library to borrow and return books every Saturday. noun, plural* **li·brar·ies.**

li·cense (lī′sns), paper, card, or plate showing ownership of something such as a car or a dog. *noun.*

light·ning (līt′ning), a flash of electricity in the sky. The sound that it makes is thunder. *noun.*

lightning rod, a metal rod placed on a building or ship to conduct lightning into the earth or water.

loan (lōn), **1** let another have and use for a short time: *She asked him to loan her his pen.* **2** anything that is loaned, especially money: *He asked his brother for a small loan.* **3** make a loan: *Her friend loaned her the money.* **1, 3** *verb,* **2** *noun.*

log (lôg), **1** length of wood just as it comes from the tree. **2** the daily record of a ship's voyage. *noun.*

loom (lüm), machine for weaving cloth. *noun.*

M m

man·hole (man′hōl′), hole, usually in the street, through which a person can enter a sewer or a tunnel in order to work underground. *noun.*

mar·a·thon (mar′ə thon), **1** a foot race of 26 miles, 385 yards (about 42 kilometers). **2** any long race or contest. *noun.*

a hat	**i** it	**oi** oil	**ch** child	a in about
ā age	**ī** ice	**ou** out	**ng** long	e in taken
ä far	**o** hot	**u** cup	**sh** she	ə = i in pencil
e let	**ō** open	**u̇** put	**th** thin	o in lemon
ē equal	**ô** order	**ü** rule	**ŦH** then	u in circus
ėr term			**zh** measure	

meas·ure (mezh′ər), **1** find the size or amount of (anything); find how long, wide, deep, large, or much (a thing) is: *We measured the room and found it was 20 feet long and 15 feet wide.* **2** mark off or out (in inches, feet, or some other unit): *Measure off 2 yards of this silk. verb,* **meas·ured, meas·ur·ing.**

mer·chant (mėr′chənt), **1** person who buys and sells: *Some merchants do most of their business with foreign countries.* **2** storekeeper. *noun.*

me·te·or (mē′tē ər), mass of stone or metal that comes toward the earth from outer space with great speed; shooting star. Meteors become so hot from rushing through the air that they glow and often burn up. *noun.*

mis·chief (mis′chif), **1** action that causes harm or trouble, often without meaning it: *Playing with matches is mischief that may cause a fire.* **2** something that annoys, often done just in fun. *noun.*

mis·er·y (miz′ər ē), **1** a very unhappy state of mind: *Think of the misery of having no home or friends.* **2** state or condition of being in trouble or of having serious difficulties. *noun, plural* **mis·er·ies.**

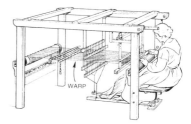
loom¹—To make cloth, the weaver passes the shuttle carrying the thread of the woof through the threads of the warp. Foot pedals raise and lower alternate warp threads.

WARP

mold (mōld), **1** a hollow shape in which anything is formed or cast, such as the mold into which melted metal is poured to harden into shape. **2** make or form into shape: *mold dough into loaves to be baked. Children mold figures out of clay.* **1** *noun,* **2** *verb.*

mon·u·ment (mon′yə mənt), **1** something, such as a building or statue, set up to keep a person or an event from being forgotten. **2** any area or place chosen and named by the government as having special historical meaning or natural beauty: *Statue of Liberty National Monument. noun.*

mut·ton (mut′n), meat from a sheep: *We had roast mutton for dinner. noun.*

N n

nip (nip), **1** catch hold of and squeeze quickly; pinch; bite: *The crab nipped my toe.* **2** a tight squeeze; pinch; sudden bite. 1 *verb,* **nipped, nip·ping;** 2 *noun.*

ni·tro·gen (nī′trə jən), a gas without color, taste, or odor which forms about four-fifths of the air. All animals and plants need nitrogen. *noun.*

notch (noch), **1** nick or cut shaped like a V, made in an edge or on a curving surface: *People used to cut notches on a stick to keep count of things or time.* **2** make an notch or notches in: *We notched the tent stakes so that we could fasten the ropes.* 1 *noun, plural* **notch·es;** 2 *verb.*

nour·ish (nėr′ish), make grow, or keep alive and well, with food: *Milk is all we need to nourish our small baby. verb.*

nour·ish·ment (nėr′ish mənt), **1** food. **2** things necessary to nourish the body. *noun.*

O o

oar (ôr), a long pole with a broad, flat end, used in rowing. Sometimes an oar is used to steer a boat. *noun.*

oars in a boat

old-fash·ioned (ōld′fash′ənd), out-of-date; of an old style or time: *old-fashioned clothing. adjective.*

o·pin·ion (ə pin′yən), what one thinks about something; a belief not so strong as knowledge: *I try to learn the facts and form my own opinions. noun.*

or·di·nar·y (ôrd′n er′ē), **1** usual; common; normal: *My ordinary lunch is soup, a sandwich, and milk.* **2** somewhat below the average or the usual: *The speaker was ordinary and tiresome. adjective.*

out·line (out′līn′), **1** line that shows the shape of an object: *We saw the outlines of the mountains against the evening sky.* **2** a brief plan that includes the main ideas: *Make an outline before trying to write a composition. The teacher gave a brief outline of the work planned for the term. noun.*

out·stand·ing (out stan′ding), standing out from others; unusually good: *an outstanding student, an outstanding painting. adjective.*

out·ward (out′wərd), **1** going toward the outside; turned toward the outside: *an outward motion.* **2** toward the outside; away: *A porch extends outward from the house.* 1 *adjective,* 2 *adverb.*

P p

pace (pās), **1** step: *He took three paces into the room.* **2** walk with regular steps: *The tiger paced back and forth in its cage.* 1 *noun,* 2 *verb,* **paced, pac·ing.**

old-fashioned—an old-fashioned valentine

par·a·chute (par′ə shüt), **1** device shaped something like an umbrella, made of nylon or silk, used in coming down safely through the air from a great height. **2** any device that serves to check or slow down a fall through the air. *noun.*

patch (pach), **1** piece put on to mend a hole or a tear. **2** piece of ground: *a patch of strawberries. noun, plural* **patch·es.**

peak (pēk), **1** the pointed top of a mountain or hill: *snowy peaks.* **2** mountain that stands alone: *Pikes Peak. noun.*

phys·i·cal (fiz′ə kəl), of or relating to the body: *physical exercise, physical strength. adjective.*

pick·up (pik′up′), **1** a picking up: *the daily pickup of mail.* **2** a small, light truck with an open back, used for light hauling. *noun.*

po·em (pō′əm), a form of writing using beautiful or colorful words which often rhyme. *noun.*

pot·ter·y (pot′ər ē), pots, dishes, or vases made from clay and hardened by heat. *noun.*

pow·er (pou′ər), **1** energy or force that can do work. **2** having its own motor; carrying force or energy: *a power drill, a power line.* **1** *noun,* **2** *adjective.*

pre·fer (pri fėr′), like better; choose one thing rather than another: *I will come later, if you prefer. She prefers swimming to fishing. verb,* **pre·ferred, pre·fer·ring.**

prin·ci·pal (prin′sə pəl), **1** main; chief; most important: *Chicago is the principal city of Illinois.* **2** head of a school. **1** *adjective,* **2** *noun.*

pro·duce (prə düs′ *or* prə dyüs′), make; create: *This factory produces stoves. He produced a work of art. verb,* **pro·duced, pro·duc·ing.**

Q q

quick·sand (kwik′sand′), soft wet sand, very deep, that will not hold up a person's weight.

a hat	**i** it	**oi** oil	**ch** child	a in about
ā age	**ī** ice	**ou** out	**ng** long	e in taken
ä far	**o** hot	**u** cup	**sh** she	ə = i in pencil
e let	**ō** open	**ù** put	**th** thin	o in lemon
ē equal	**ô** order	**ü** rule	**ŦH** then	u in circus
ėr term			**zh** measure	

Quicksand may swallow up people and animals. *noun.*

R r

rare (rer *or* rar), seldom seen or found: *a rare bird, a rare coin. adjective,* **rar·er, rar·est.**

rec·i·pe (res′ə pē), a set of directions for preparing something to eat: *Please give me your recipe for chocolate cake. noun.*

rel·ic (rel′ik), thing left from the past; an object interesting because of its age or its connection with the past. *noun.*

relic—These relics found in Israel are more than 3000 years old. At the top is a jar; the three pieces below are oil lamps.

re·move (ri müv′), move from one place or position to another; take off; take away; get rid of. *verb,* **re·moved, re·mov·ing.**

re·search (ri sėrch′ *or* rē′sėrch′), a careful hunting for facts or truth; a search for or a study of new ideas: *Medical research has done much to lessen disease.* noun, plural **re·search·es.**

re·tire (ri tīr′), give up an office or occupation: *Our teachers retire at 65.* verb, **re·tired, re·tir·ing.**

rid·dle (rid′l), **1** a puzzling question or problem with a surprise answer. EXAMPLE: When is a door not a door? ANSWER: When it is ajar. **2** person or thing that is hard to understand or explain. *noun.*

rip·ple (rip′əl), **1** a very little wave: *Throw a stone into still water and watch the ripples spread in rings.* **2** anything that seems like a tiny wave. **3** make little waves on: *A breeze rippled the water.* 1, 2 *noun,* 3 *verb,* **rip·pled, rip·pling.**

ripple—ripples in sand

robe (rōb), **1** a long, loose, outer garment: *The priests wore robes.* **2** covering or wrap: *a beach robe. noun.*

rock·et (rok′it), a tube, open at one end, filled with fuel. The burning fuel creates gases that force the tube and whatever is attached to it upward or forward. Rockets are used to send spacecraft beyond the earth's atmosphere. *noun.*

row·boat (rō′bōt′), boat moved by oars. *noun.*

S s

sanc·tu·ar·y (sangk′chü er′ē), **1** a holy or sacred place. A church is a sanctuary. **2** a place that provides shelter or protection: *a bird sanctuary. noun, plural* **sanc·tu·ar·ies.**

sar·dine (sär dēn′), one of several kinds of small fish preserved in oil and packed tightly in small cans. *noun, plural* **sar·dines** or **sar·dine.**

sat·el·lite (sat′l īt), **1** a heavenly body that revolves around a planet or other larger heavenly body. The moon is a satellite of the earth. **2** a man-made object shot by a rocket into an orbit around the earth. Such satellites are used to send weather reports, scientific information, and television programs back to earth. *noun.*

scent (sent), **1** smell: *The scent of roses filled the air.* **2** a particular odor or smell left in passing: *The dogs followed the fox by the scent. noun.*

score (skôr), **1** record of points made in a game, contest, or test: *The score was 9 to 2 in favor of our school.* **2** make points in a game, contest, or test: *score two runs in the second inning.* **3** make an addition to the score: *She scored five runs for our team.* 1 *noun,* 2, 3 *verb,* **scored, scor·ing.**

sea·man (sē′mən), **1** sailor. **2** sailor who is not an officer. *noun, plural* **sea·men.**

se·lect (si lekt′), choose; pick out: *Select the book you want. The contestants were selected because of their ability to speak in public. verb.*

serv·ant (sėr′vənt), **1** person employed in a household. Cooks and nursemaids are servants. **2** person employed by another. *noun.*

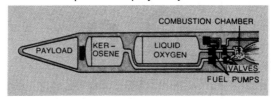

rocket which uses liquid fuel

shab·by (shab'ē), wearing old or much worn clothes: *She is always shabby. adjective,* **shab·bi·er, shab·bi·est.**

shat·ter (shat'ər), break into pieces: *A stone shattered the window. The vase shattered when I dropped it. verb.*

shin·gle (shing'gəl), **1** a thin piece of wood, used to cover roofs and walls. Shingles are laid in overlapping rows with the thicker ends showing. **2** cover with such pieces: *shingle a roof.* **1** *noun,* **2** *verb,* **shin·gled, shin·gling.**

shut·tle (shut'l), bus, train, airplane, etc., that runs back and forth regularly between two places. *noun.*

silt (silt), very fine bits of earth or sand carried by moving water and left behind as it settles to the bottom: *The harbor is being choked up with silt. noun.*

score—She tried to **score** a basket.

sil·ver (sil'vər), a shining white precious metal. Silver is used to make coins, jewelry, spoons, knives, and forks. *noun.*

a hat	**i** it	**oi** oil	**ch** child	a in about
ā age	**ī** ice	**ou** out	**ng** long	e in taken
ä far	**o** hot	**u** cup	**sh** she	ə = { i in pencil
e let	**ō** open	**ů** put	**th** thin	o in lemon
ē equal	**ô** order	**ü** rule	**ŦH** then	u in circus
ėr term			**zh** measure	

sim·u·late (sim'yə lāt), act like; look like; give the effect of: *Certain insects simulate flowers or leaves. verb,* **sim·u·lat·ed, sim·u·lat·ing.**

sim·u·la·tor (sim'yə lā'tər), a test room or a testing machine that simulates conditions which are likely to occur in actual operation. *noun.*

sin·gle (sing'gəl), one and no more; only one: *The spider hung by a single thread. Single* is often used for emphasis with words such as *every: every single day. adjective.*

sleeve (slēv), part of a piece of clothing that covers the arm. *noun.*

sleeve

smack (smak), a loud slap or crack; a sharp slap or blow: *She gave the volleyball a sharp smack. noun.*

sol·dier (sōl'jər), person who serves in an army. *noun.*

space·ship (spās'ship'), spacecraft; vehicle used for flight in outer space. *noun.*

space shuttle, a winged spacecraft that can be launched into orbit around the earth by a rocket, and can glide back to earth and land like an airplane. Space shuttles are reusable.

spar·kle (spär'kəl), **1** send out little sparks: *The fireworks sparkled.* **2** shine; glitter; flash: *The jewels in the crown sparkled. verb,* **spar·kled, spar·kling.**

spir·it (spir'it), **1** soul: *Some religions teach that at death the spirit leaves the body.* **2** a being that is above and beyond what is natural. Ghosts and fairies are spirits. **3 spirits,** state of

507

mind or feelings: *I am in good spirits.* **4** energy; liveliness: *A race horse must have spirit. noun.*

steel (stēl), **1** iron mixed with carbon so that it is very hard, strong, and tough. Most tools are made from steel. **2** made of steel: *a steel bridge, a steel hammer.* **1** *noun,* **2** *adjective.*

stee·ple (stē′pəl), a high tower on a church. Steeples usually come to a point called a spire. *noun.*

steeple

step·lad·der (step′lad′ər), a short ladder with flat steps: *She used the stepladder to reach the top shelves. noun.*

stew (stü *or* styü), **1** cook by slow boiling: *The cook stewed the chicken for a long time.* **2** food cooked by slow boiling: *beef stew,* **1** *verb,* **2** *noun.*

stiff (stif), **1** not easily bent: *New boots are usually stiff.* **2** hard to move: *The old hinges on the barn door are stiff.* **3** not able to move easily: *My neck is stiff. adjective.*

storm (stôrm), **1** a strong wind with rain, snow, hail, or thunder and lightning. In deserts there are storms of sand. **2** a heavy fall of rain, snow, or hail; violent outbreak of thunder and lightning. *noun.*

stump (stump), the lower end of a tree or plant that is left after the main part has been cut off: *We sat on top of a stump. noun.*

stump

suf·fer (suf′ər), **1** have pain: *He suffers from headaches.* **2** come to harm, loss, or defeat: *Our team suffered three defeats. verb.*

suit·case (süt′kās′), a flat case or bag for carrying clothes, etc. *noun.*

sur·vive (sər vīv′), **1** remain alive after: *Only ten of the crew survived the shipwreck.* **2** continue to live; remain alive; live on: *The wild animals survived through the long winter.* *verb,* **sur·vived, sur·viv·ing.**

sweat (swet), **1** moisture coming through the skin: *After mowing the lawn she wiped the sweat from her face.* **2** give out moisture through the pores of the skin: *We sweated because it was very hot.* **1** *noun,* **2** *verb,* **sweat·ed** or **sweat, sweat·ing.**

sweat·er (swet′ər), a knitted jacket, usually of wool or nylon, worn to keep the body warm. *noun.*

swim (swim), **1** move along on or in the water by using arms, legs, or fins: *Fish swim. Most girls and boys like to swim.* **2** act of swimming: *Her swim had tired her. She had had an hour's swim.* **1** *verb,* **swam, swum, swim·ming;** **2** *noun.*

T t

taught (tôt). See **teach.** *That teacher taught my mother. verb.*

teach (tēch), **1** help to learn; show how to do; make understand: *He is teaching his dog to shake hands.* **2** act as teacher: *She teaches for a living. verb,* **taught, teach·ing.**

team·work (tēm′wèrk′), the acting together of a number of people to make the work of a group successful: *In football teamwork is more important than the skill of any one member of the team. noun.*

text·book (tekst′bùk′), book for regular study by pupils. Most books used in schools are textbooks. *noun.*

ther·mom·e·ter (thər mom′ə tər), instrument for measuring the temperature of something. Most thermometers contain a liquid in a narrow tube that rises when the temperature goes up and falls when the temperature goes down. *noun.*

thermometer

a hat	i it	oi oil	ch child	a in about
ā age	ī ice	ou out	ng long	e in taken
ä far	o hot	u cup	sh she	ə = { i in pencil
e let	ō open	u̇ put	th thin	o in lemon
ē equal	ô order	ü rule	₮H then	u in circus
ėr term			zh measure	

tu·na (tü′nə), a large sea fish used for food. It sometimes grows to a length of ten feet or more. *noun, plural* **tu·nas** or **tu·na.**

tun·nel (tun′l), an underground passage: *The railroad passes under the mountain through a tunnel. The mole made a tunnel in the ground. noun.*

tunnel

U u

un·der·growth (un′dər grōth′), bushes, shrubs, and small trees growing under large trees in woods or forests. *noun.*

V v

val·ley (val′ē), low land between hills or mountains: *Most large valleys have rivers running through them. noun, plural* **val·leys.**

va·nil·la (və nil′ə), flavoring used in ice cream, candy, and other foods. It is made from the bean of a tropical plant. *noun.*

thun·der (thun′dər), the loud noise that often follows a flash of lightning. *noun.*

thun·der·cloud (thun′dər kloud′), a dark cloud that brings thunder and lightning. *noun.*

ton (tun), a unit of weight equal to 2000 pounds in the United States and Canada. A **metric ton** is 1000 kilograms. *noun.*

tor·na·do (tôr nā′dō), a very violent whirlwind. A tornado extends down from a mass of dark clouds as a twisting funnel and moves over the land in a narrow path. *noun, plural* **tor·na·does** or **tor·na·dos.**

tornado

tow (tō), pull by a rope or chain: *The tug is towing three barges. verb.*

tran·quil·iz·er (trang′kwə lī′zər), a drug that calms and quiets. It relaxes muscles and slows down bodily activity. *noun.*

tribe (trīb), group of people united by race and customs under the same leaders: *an American Indian tribe. noun.*

vic·tor·y (vik′tər ē), defeat of an enemy; success in a struggle; the winning of a contest: *The game ended in a victory for our school.* *noun, plural* **vic·tor·ies.**

vis·it (viz′it), make a call; stay with; make a stay; be a guest: *I visited my friend last week.* *verb.*

vis·i·tor (viz′ə tər), person who visits; person who is visiting; a guest: *This weekend we are having visitors from New York. noun.*

vi·ta·min (vī′tə mən), any of certain special substances necessary for the normal growth of the body. Vitamins are found especially in milk, butter, raw fruits and vegetables, and in wheat and other grains. Lack of vitamins may cause certain diseases. *noun.*

W w

war·ship (wôr′ship′), ship armed and ready for war. *noun.*

weave (wēv), **1** form (threads or strips) into something. People weave thread into cloth. **2** make out of thread or strips of the same material: *She is weaving a rug. verb,* **wove, wo·ven** or **wove, weav·ing.**

girl **weaving** a rug

whale (hwāl), animal shaped like a huge fish and living in the sea. Oil from whales used to be burned in lamps. *noun, plural* **whales** or **whale.**

whale
1. blue whale—about 90 feet (27 meters) long
2. humpback whale—about 45 feet (14 meters) long
3. Minke whale—about 28 feet (8 meters) long
4. sperm whale—about 50 feet (15 meters) long

whisk·er (hwis′kər), **1** one of the hairs growing on a man's face. **2 whiskers,** *plural,* the hair or part of a beard that grows on a man's cheeks. *noun.*

wind·shield (wind′shēld′), sheet of glass to keep off the wind. Automobiles have windshields. *noun.*

wipe (wīp), **1** rub in order to clean or dry: *We wipe our shoes on the mat. We wipe the dishes with a towel.* **2** take (away, off, or out) by rubbing: *Wipe away your tears. I wiped off the dust. verb,* **wiped, wip·ing.**

wound (wünd), **1** any hurt or injury to the body of a person or animal. **2** injure with a weapon; hurt: *The hunter wounded the deer.* **3** any hurt or injury to feelings: *Being fired from a job can be a wound to a person's pride.* **4** injure the feelings of: *Their unkind words wounded me.* **1, 3** *noun,* **2, 4** *verb.*

Pages 139–142: Adapted from "Boy of the Canyon Rim" by Anne Morris, *Boys' Life,* August 1982. Reprinted by permission of the author.
Pages 198–204: Adapted from *Harold Sets a Record* by Thomas Woldum. Copyright © 1977 by Creative Educational Society, Inc. Reprinted by permission.
Pages 207–208: From *Guinness Book of Young Recordbreakers* by Norris McWhirter & Ross McWhirter. Copyright © 1976 by Sterling Publishing Co., Inc. Reprinted by permission.
Pages 240–248: Adapted and reprinted by permission of Coward, McCann & Geoghegan, Inc. from *Nate the Great and the Missing Key.* Text Copyright © 1981 by Marjorie Weinman Sharmat.
Pages 270–276: Adapted excerpt from *Jacob and the Owl,* text copyright © 1981 by Ada and Frank Graham. Reprinted by permission of Coward, McCann & Geoghegan, Inc. and JCA Literary Agency, Inc.
Pages 300–307: From *Young World* magazine, copyright © 1978 by The Saturday Evening Post Company, Indianapolis, Indiana. Adapted by permission of the publisher.
Pages 324–325: From *More Two-Minute Mysteries* by Donald J. Sobol. Copyright © 1971 by Donald J. Sobol. Reprinted by permission of McIntosh and Otis, Inc., as agent for the author.
Pages 326–333: "Frightened Town" from *Wayfaring Stranger* by Burl Ives. Copyright 1948 by Burl Ives. Adapted by permission of the author.
Pages 338–339: From *Seven True Bear Stories* by Laura Geringer. Copyright © 1979 by Laura Geringer. Reprinted by permission of Hastings House, Publishers, Inc.
Pages 342–350: From *Seven True Bear Stories* by Laura Geringer. Copyright © 1979 by Laura Geringer. Reprinted by permission of Hastings House Publishers, Inc.
Page 352: "Bears" by Elizabeth Coatsworth. Reprinted by permission of the author.
Page 353: First eight lines from "Furry Bear" from *Now We Are Six* by A. A. Milne. Copyright 1927 by E. P. Dutton & Co., Inc., renewed 1955 by A. A. Milne. Reprinted by permission of E. P. Dutton, Inc., McClelland and Stewart Limited and Methuen Children's Books.
Pages 358–363: Adapted from "The Wolf From the Sea" by Mike Eagle, *Cricket* Magazine, July, 1977. Reprinted by permission of Dilys Evans, Agent.
Pages 365–374: From pages 32–49 of *The Shark in the Window* by Keo Felker Lazarus. Copyright © 1972 by Keo Felker Lazarus. Adapted by permission of William Morrow & Company.
Pages 380–381: "Farther Than Far" from *Farther Than Far* by Margaret Hillert. Copyright © 1969. Reprinted by permission of the author who controls all rights.
Page 401: From "Have a Creatures-From-Outer-Space Party" by Carolyn Ann Jones from *Jack and Jill* magazine, copyright © 1975 by The Saturday Evening Post Company, Indianapolis, Indiana. Adapted by permission of the publisher.
Pages 406–412: Adaptation of "Aunt Elvira's Zoo" by Pamela Sargent from *Night of the Sphinx and Other Stories.* Copyright © 1974 by Lerner Publications Company. Reprinted by permission of Lerner Publications Company, 241 First Avenue North, Minneapolis, Minnesota 55401.
Pages 418–419: "Chasing Dust Devils" by Grant Alan Idso, *Highlights for Children,* August/September 1982. Copyright © 1982 Highlights for Children, Inc., Columbus, Ohio. Reprinted by permission.
Pages 420–424: From *Child Life* magazine, copyright © 1982 by Benjamin Franklin Literary & Medical Society, Indianapolis, Indiana. Adapted by permission of the publisher.
Pages 430–431: "Earthquakes—Do Animals Know They're Coming?" by James R. Newton. Adapted from *Ranger Rick's Nature Magazine,* © May 1979, by permission of the publisher, the National Wildlife Federation.
Pages 432–434: From *Danger from Below* by Seymour Simon. Copyright © 1979 by Seymour Simon. Adapted by permission of Four Winds Press, a division of Scholastic Inc.
Pages 435–438: "Earthquake!" excerpted and adapted from *Only in Alaska* by Tay Thomas. Copyright © 1969 by Tay Thomas. Reprinted by permission of the author and Doubleday & Company, Inc.
Pages 444–453: From *Young World* magazine, copyright © 1973 by The Saturday Evening Post Company, Indianapolis, Indiana. Adapted by permission of the publisher.
Page 469: Byrd Baylor, "This is no place. . ." in *The Desert Is Theirs.* Copyright © 1975 Byrd Baylor. Reprinted with permission of Charles Scribner's Sons and Toni Strassman, Author's Representative.
Pages 483–492: Adaptation of "The Fire on the Mountain" from *The Fire on the Mountain* by Harold Courlander and Wolf Leslau. Copyright 1950 by Holt, Rinehart and Winston. Copyright © 1978 by Harold Courlander, Wolf Leslau and Robert W. Kane. Reprinted by permission of Harold Courlander.

Photographs

Page 16: © David Muench 1983; Page 30: Tom Bledsoe; Page 31: Stephen J. Krasemann/Photo Researchers; Page 38: Arthur Shay; Pages 66–67: Anneke Davis/KITE LINES, The Journal of Kiting; Page 74: Library of Congress; Page 76: Anneke Davis/KITE LINES, The Journal of Kiting; Page 77(l): Theodore L. Manekin; Page 77(m): Craig Aurness/West Light; Page 77(r): Theodore L. Manekin; Pages 132–133: © David Muench 1983; Page 141: Edward L. Lallo; Page 154: Al Abrams Photo/Graphics, Courtesy The Heard Museum, Phoenix, AZ; Pages 158, 161–163: New Mexico Tourism & Travel Div., Commerce & Industry Dept., Sante Fe, NM; Page 165: Peabody Museum, Harvard University. Photograph by Hillel Burger, 1977; Pages 170–171: Stewart M. Green/Tom Stack & Associates; Pages 175–176: Mount Everest Foundation; Page 186: UPI; Pages 188–189: Thai/Sygma; Page 191: Lynn Pelham/SPORTS ILLUSTRATED; Pages 194–195: T. Zimmerman/FPG; Page 228: By permission of the Master and Fellows, Magdalene College, Cambridge; Page 230: Pierre Perrin/Gamma Liaison; Page 231: Peter Jordan/Gamma Liaison; Page 354: Carl Roessler/FPG; Page 356: Marty Snyderman; Page 380: ANIMALS ANIMALS/Charles Palek; Page 381: Tom Stack/Tom Stack & Associates, Russ Kinne/Photo Researchers; Pages 384, 386–388, 390, 394, 396 and 397: NASA; Page 416: Sheila Beougher; Pages 418, 419: Sherwood B. Idso;

Page 421: Mrs. Edi Ann Otto;   Page 423: Shelly Katz/Black Star;   Page 424: NASA;   Page 426: Marshall Lockman/Black Star;   Page 434: Stan Wayman/LIFE Magazine © 1964, Time, Inc.;   Pages 440–441: Herman J. Kokojan/Black Star;   Pages 458–459: Stephen J. Krasemann/Peter Arnold, Inc.;   Page 464: Scott Polar Research Institute;   Page 465: W. H. Hodge/Peter Arnold, Inc.;   Pages 466, 467: C. Allan Morgan;   Page 470: Peter Arnold, Inc.

Glossary: Canoe—Walter Chandoha; Earthquake—Library of Congress; Old-fashioned valentine—from the collection of Lois Metcalf; Relic—from the collection of Rabbi Hillel Gamoran; Tornado—E.S.S.A.

Artists
Kim Behm, 209;   Leon Bishop, 174, 215, 216, 220, 382–383, 456, 475, 477;   Mark Braught, 224, 225;   Dick Brooks, 167, 168, 278;   Laura Camps, 312–313;   Ted Carr, 343;   Michael Carroll, 166, 357;   John Craig, 144–145;   Ralph Creasman, 99, 100–101, 102–103;   Jim Cummins, 326, 329, 331, 333;   David Cunningham, 44, 47, 49, 50, 147, 358–359, 360–361, 362–363, 435, 436–437;   Marla Frazee, 56–57, 118, 121, 123, 125, 126, 457;   Jackie Geyer, 406–407, 408–409, 410–411;   Michael Glascott, 398–399, 402–403;   Jean Hellmer, 33, 34–35, 36, 54, 342, 356, 469;   Pamela Ford Johnson, 131;   Polly Johnson, 55;   Laurie Jordan, 70–71, 206;   Carl Kock, 94, 184, 198, 200–201, 202–203, 204, 211;   Carol LaCourse, 87, 89;   Tom Leonard, 136, 222–223;   Diana Magnuson, 314, 317, 320;   Robert Masheris, 338–339;   Steve Miller, 324–325;   Paul Moch, 169;   Daryl Moore, 60, 62–63;   Mike Muir, 177, 179;   Nancy Munger, 196;   Steve Musgrave, 156;   Keith Neely, 149, 151, 152;   Anita Nelson, 344–345, 346–347, 348–349, 350, 430;   Mitch O'Connell, 404–405;   Stephen Osborn, 40, 414, 428, 472;   William Peterson, 366–367, 370–371, 373;   Marc Phelan, 322–323;   David Povilaitis, 105, 298–299;   Susan Randstrom, 310–311;   Phil Renaud, 20–21, 22–23, 24, 270–271, 272, 275;   Jane Rigie, 68, 258, 260–261, 263;   Cindy Rosenheim, 108, 253, 340;   Roger Roth, 483, 484, 487, 489, 491;   Linda Rothberg, 249, 392–393;   John Sanford, 18–19, 233, 235, 268, 294–295, 401;   Eliza Lee Schulte, 72;   Jerry Scott, 212–213, 375, 376, 377;   Slug Signorino, 91, 106–107, 285, 286, 293;   Elwood Smith, 337;   Ray Smith, 182;   Terri Smith, 280, 281;   Mark Stearney, 379;   Robert Steel, 256, 476, 479, 480;   Rick Thrun, 289, 290, 300–301, 302, 304–305, 307, 352, 353;   R. Valicenti Design, 75, 76–77, 79, 127, 136, 138, 139, 141, 158, 161, 162, 163, 194–195, 226–227, 228–232, 238–239, 309, 426–427, 433, 440–441, 461, 463, 465, 470–471;   Jack Wallen, 207, 208;   Don Wilson, 15, 172, 296;   Chuck Wimmer, 26, 93;   Judith Witschonke, 52;   Leslie Wolf, 240, 241, 242, 244–245, 246–247;   John Youssi, 110, 112, 115

Cover Artist
Tom Bookwalter

Freelance Photographs
William Burlingham, 34–35, 80–81, 127, 254–255, 291, 307, 335, 439, 442, 444, 446–451, 453